SLAY BELLS

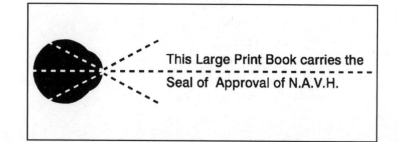

This Large Print Book carries the
Seal of Approval of N.A.V.H.

A ST. ROSE QUILTING BEE MYSTERY

SLAY BELLS

ANNETTE MAHON

WHEELER PUBLISHING
A part of Gale, Cengage Learning

GALE
CENGAGE Learning·

Farmington Hills, Mich • San Francisco • New York • Waterville, Maine
Meriden, Conn • Mason, Ohio • Chicago

LIBRARY OF CONGRESS CATALOGING-IN-PUBLICATION DATA

Names: Mahon, Annette, author.
Title: Slay bells : a St. Rose quilting bee mystery / by Annette Mahon.
Description: Large print edition. | Waterville, Maine : Wheeler Publishing, 2016. |
  Series: Wheeler Publishing large print cozy mystery
Identifiers: LCCN 2016022477 | ISBN 9781410493644 (softcover) | ISBN 1410493644
  (softcover)
Subjects: LCSH: Quiltmakers—Fiction. | Large type books. | GSAFD: Mystery fiction.
Classification: LCC PS3563.A3595 S58 2016b | DDC 813/.54—dc23
LC record available at https://lccn.loc.gov/2016022477

Published in 2016 by arrangement with Annette Mahon

Printed in the United States of America
1 2 3 4 5 6 7 20 19 18 17 16

SLAY BELLS

CHAPTER 1

Thursday, December 3rd; 22 days before Christmas.

"Did you hear about Kathleen Romelli?" Clare Patterson asked the moment she walked in the door.

As the St. Rose Quilting Bee members gathered on that cool December morning, the hot topic of conversation was not Christmas shopping or the lovely Phoenix weather, but an incident they had all heard reported on the previous evening's news.

"It's just terrible," Anna Howard said, tears in her eyes.

"What an awful time of year for it to happen," Theresa Squires said.

"There's never a good time of year for something like this." Maggie Browne placed her jacket in the closet and took her place at the quilt frame. "No matter when it happens, it's a dreadful thing."

The evening news had been full of the

grisly story, the reporters standing in the street where strobing red and blue lights made a stark contrast to the tasteful white icicle lights lining the eaves of the house. Inside, a woman's body had been found, dead of a gunshot wound. Lying on the back patio, the body of her twelve-year-old son, also shot. The police had been called by a neighbor who could see the boy lying on the cold concrete and knew something had to be wrong. The story was personal to the Quilting Bee women because Kathleen Romelli's mother, Bridget Murphy, was a charter member of the St. Rose Senior Guild and very well liked. The guild members gathered every morning in rooms at the church campus in old Scottsdale, where they made handcrafted items to sell at their annual All Hallow's Eve Bazaar. The bazaar was the main fund-raiser for the parish, and the Quilting Bee's contribution was an important one. Every year they hand-quilted twelve to twenty quilts, which were auctioned off to a worldwide audience. In a good year, their quilts could bring in as much as all the rest of the bazaar profits. And since they all loved to quilt, it was no hardship for them to gather every day to work on their quilts.

As Clare removed her jacket, Victoria Farrington took her usual seat beside Maggie. "I feel so sorry for Bridget. I can't imagine how awful it must be to lose your child and grandchild that way."

"So senseless," Theresa agreed. "Do you suppose it was a burglary gone wrong?"

"Wouldn't be surprised," Edie Dulinski said. "One of those home invasions, more than likely. There's been a lot of them in the valley recently."

No one commented on Edie's pronouncement. She was always ready to look on the dark side, and increasing crime was a favorite rant of hers. There had indeed been some home invasions in the greater Phoenix area, and she had been telling them about it for weeks. However, Maggie had checked, and none had been in Scottsdale itself, or even in the vicinity of Scottsdale.

Clare sat down across from Maggie and Victoria and picked up a needle. The women were seated around a nine-patch quilt top with redwork, stitching a crosshatch pattern in the embroidered squares, and a sun in the nine-patch pieced squares. The bee had enlisted women from other senior guild groups to help with the embroidered blocks, which, despite the redwork name, had been stitched in a golden-brown thread. Regardless of the thread color, the technique was still termed "red" work because the original embroidered pieces were usually worked all in red. Red remained the color of choice for the embroidered blocks, but they had chosen the copper color to go with the desert scenes in the embroidery. The pieced blocks were done in several copper-brown prints that coordinated with the embroidery floss. Maggie and Victoria had found all of the western embroidery motifs that turned it into a beautiful southwestern quilt, making heavy use of specialized coloring books for pattern ideas. They hoped that cowboys everywhere would love it and bid highly for the privilege of ownership.

Clare spoke after inserting her needle and beginning her first line of stitches. "Kathy was such a lovely young woman. Always ready to help someone out. I can't imagine who would want to hurt her."

"They'll look at the ex-husband, of course." Edie was already at the end of a row of stitches, and traveling her needle to another spot so that she could continue stitching.

"Oh, no, Rusty could *never* hurt her," Clare protested.

"It's just routine to look at family members," Victoria reminded her. "Most murder victims know their killer."

"Kathy was getting remarried, you know." Clare pulled her needle a little too hard and managed to unthread it. With a sigh, she proceeded to rethread it, adjusting her glasses as she peered at the tiny eye.

"Was she?" Louise Lombard asked. "I hadn't heard. Here, at St. Rose?"

"No. Bridget was really disappointed," Clare told them, "but she said Kathy didn't want to wait for an annulment from the church. It can take years, you know. And Dylan Markham — that's the new fiancé — wasn't a Catholic. They were going to have a civil ceremony at the Desert Botanical Garden. Dear little Matthew, God rest his soul, was going to be best man."

"Oh! That's so sweet." Anna sighed. Then, realizing that "dear little Matthew" had just been murdered, she gulped. Her eyes filled with unshed tears.

"Dylan Markham." Anna's brows drew together, and her fingers paused with the needle halfway through the cloth. "He's some kind of developer, isn't he? I've heard his name."

Clare nodded, barely looking up from her stitching. "Yes. Bridget said he's really charming. She said that's how he got Kathy; he just charmed her socks off. She said it's also how he gets people to invest in his

11

properties."

"I've heard his name too." Louise pulled her thread through and set the needle for the next stitch. "I probably heard it from Vinnie. He keeps up with that kind of thing, and he'll often tell me about what he reads on the financial pages."

"Gerald and I have been friends with the Romellis for years, you know," Clare told them. "Don't you think the newscasters made it sound like Rusty may be responsible? But Rusty's just the nicest man — the whole family is wonderful. You should see Rusty around Samson. Samson just loves him." She released a sigh as she thought of how well Rusty interacted with her beloved Schnauzer. "He's active with Big Brothers too. He'd bring his little brother to family barbecues and such. He loves kids. I just can't imagine him shooting his own son. Or anyone's child, for that matter. It's inconceivable."

"Love can do odd things to people," Edie said. "Lots of men kill the women they claim to love." She reached for the spool of thread. "I stopped to talk to some people on the way in, and I heard that Rusty wanted to get back together with Kathleen. Also that Rusty called her new fiancé a jerk and a gold digger, and that he threatened to do whatever he could to stop them getting married."

"Why does it have to be the ex-husband when a woman is killed?" Clare heaved a heavy sigh.

"You want every case to be as complicated as an Agatha Christie novel," Louise said. "But, especially in real life, the answer usually is the most obvious one."

"Occam's razor," Victoria said with a nod. "The simplest explanation is usually the correct one."

"That's right," Maggie said. "And it's an unfortunate fact that men very often do kill their girlfriends, wives, or ex-wives."

"They had that beautiful house in Arcadia," Clare said. "I remember going over there with Bridget for a meeting, years ago. It was when Kathy was recruiting people to knit caps for the newborns at the hospital. It's the same house they showed on the news clip last night, so Kathy continued to live there after the divorce." Clare continued, elaborating on the home's features. "Beautiful hardwood floors and a large eat-in kitchen. There had been some renovations, of course, because it's an older house. You should see the walk-in closet in the master suite! You could live in it, it's so large." She smiled in remembrance of the gorgeous closet space. Not that she needed such an enormous closet herself, but, still, it was a lovely thing to see.

"I was surprised that she got the house. In most divorce cases, they have to sell the house and share the profits," Victoria said.

"She got to keep the house because it was her inheritance from her grandparents."

Maggie had to smile. Leave it to Clare to know about such things.

"Her family had a lot of money, and Kathy inherited that house when her grandparents, Bridget's parents, died in a plane crash."

"Oh, how terrible," Anna said.

"It sounds like a very tragic family," Theresa said.

"It was awful," Clare told them. "Her grandfather flew his own small plane, and they crashed in the Superstition Mountains. I remember, because Kathy and Rusty were supposed to go with them, but she changed her mind at the last minute. She and Rusty decided on a family weekend instead, and it turned out to be a good thing. They were a nice couple and a lovely family. I just don't know what went wrong."

"Didn't she accuse him of cheating on her?" Edie asked.

"She did," Clare said. "Though he's

always denied it. From what I know of him, I just don't believe it. He is a good Catholic too. He wouldn't cheat on his wedding vows."

"Well, he isn't that *strict* a Catholic," Edie objected. "After all, he was divorced."

"*She* got the divorce," Clare said.

"Surely he had to agree to it," Edie insisted.

"Did Kathy have grounds for an annulment?" Maggie asked, changing the subject to stop the bickering. Senior citizens could sometimes sound like squabbling children. "You don't get one just for asking; it's not like a no-fault divorce. You have to have a good reason for why the marriage broke up."

"Isn't adultery good enough?" Anna asked.

"Yes," Louise agreed, "she accused him of cheating, remember?"

"Which he always denied," Clare quickly repeated.

"But is an accusation a legitimate reason, or would she have to have some kind of solid evidence?" Theresa asked.

Clare frowned. "I don't know."

"I'll look it up online this evening," Edie said. "I've only known one person who had her marriage annulled through the church, and her husband was abusive. She had

15

medical reports to back her up."

"There was a time when just about anyone could get an annulment just by petitioning for it, but they cracked down," Louise said. "A friend of mine whose husband deserted her had a difficult time because she applied just as they tightened the rules."

"I still can't believe Rusty would cheat on Kathy," Clare said. "He's such a good guy, and he was really in love with Kathy. Still is. He never wanted the divorce, and he was really torn up about it. Especially the way it affected their son and Rusty's time with Matthew. It's always hard on the children when a marriage comes apart." Clare finished pulling her needle through the quilt sandwich before looking up at the others. "That's the thing that really tells me Rusty is innocent," she continued. "He would *never* harm Matthew, much less shoot him. He loved that boy."

"Matthew was Bridget's only grandchild," Anna said, her voice filled with sadness.

"Kathy was her only child," Clare said. "She's often said how much she wanted more children, but she was never able to conceive again."

There was a moment of silence as they all considered their friend, Bridget, who had just lost her only child and grandchild in a

16

most violent way. Who'd already lost her husband to a heart condition and her parents in a plane crash. Silent prayers winged toward the heavens as their needles pulled thread softly through the layers of the quilt. Orchestral strains of "Greensleeves" filtered through the partially open door, and the faint trickling of the fountain also helped bring a certain peace to the women.

"We should do something special for Bridget," Maggie said. "Some meals if her knitting group isn't already planning for that."

"Good idea," Louise said. "She certainly won't feel like cooking — or even eating, more than likely."

"If her friends come over with food, they might be able to convince her to have a little something," Maggie suggested.

"Why don't we go over to the break room and see who's there," Clare suggested, rising from her place at the quilting frame. "We can plan something together."

CHAPTER 2

Officially labeled the social hall, the Senior Guild break room was a large open space with a kitchen at one end. There were sliding doors that could divide the room into smaller ones, but for the Senior Guild mornings, it was best as one big room. A long, wide counter separated the kitchen area from the main room and eased serving. There were always a variety of drinks on Senior Guild mornings, and members tended to bring in snacks, usually homemade. Because it was December, there were several types of Christmas cookies, slices of pumpkin and cranberry breads, and a festive bowl of party mix composed of cereal, nuts, and colorful chocolate candies.

As usual when something happened to anyone in the parish, the room was full of gossiping guild members. The noise level was already high but rose even more when the Quilting Bee members arrived to a loud welcome. Everyone knew that the Quilting Bee women took an interest in local crime.

"Maggie, what do you think of this business with Bridget's daughter?" someone shouted. The noise level immediately dropped as everyone waited to hear Maggie's opinion. Maggie was a highly respected member of the guild, and she had credibility when it came to murder. Her son Michael was a Scottsdale police officer, and she and the Quilting Bee had been instrumental in helping to solve several past murders involving parish members.

"I don't have an opinion yet," Maggie informed them as she headed for the coffee urn. "I don't have enough facts to form one," she added.

"We were just talking about Kathy's ex-husband," Clare said. "Gerald and I have known the Romellis for years."

Everyone started talking again. The noise level continued to spiral, and Maggie briefly wondered what they thought they could learn from this group. But she filled her mug and sat down at a table where she saw some members of Bridget's knitting group. Clare quickly joined her.

"How are you all?" Maggie asked. "Have you heard from Bridget?"

Victoria joined them in time to hear this

last. "She must be devastated, the poor lamb."

"She is." This came from Yolanda Grant, who Maggie knew was Bridget's best friend. "I went over as soon as I heard last night, and she could barely talk, she was so upset. I stayed with her overnight, but she urged me to come to church this morning. I hope she'll be okay on her own. I doubt she got any sleep, but maybe she'll be able to nap this morning from sheer exhaustion."

And she wasn't the only one, Maggie thought, observing Yolanda's haggard face and the dark smudges visible beneath the lower edges of her glasses.

Victoria patted Yolanda's arm. "You're a good friend to her."

Yolanda sighed. "I wish I could do more for her, but what *can* you do? Her only child and only grandchild, both gone and in such a terrible manner."

"She's had so much tragedy. She lost her parents in that plane crash, remember?"

The comment came from a woman at the next table. Everyone at Maggie's table sighed.

"Kathy was a fine woman. Bridget was so proud of her. You know, she decided when she was just a child that she would become a nurse. Bridget and Sean tried to talk her into medical school — her grades were good, and they felt sure she would get in. But she stuck to her guns. She said nurses were the ones who really took care of the patients, and that's what she wanted to do." Yolanda shook her head. Her admiration of her friend's daughter was obvious to everyone at the table.

"And she worked in the emergency room," Norma Hyland, another of the knitters, said. "That has to be a difficult area. My daughter used to work there with her, but she got burnt out fairly quickly. It's such a fast pace, and some of the cases can tear your heart out."

As Maggie and Clare broached the subject of plans to take meals over to Bridget, Edie joined the group at an adjacent table. She'd spotted the Eckholds, who lived next door to Kathy, and managed to grab a seat at their table as someone rose to leave. Everyone wanted to hear from the Eckholds, who had been so close to all the activity the previous evening.

Edie listened for a while as Leo and Sharlene talked about the circus in front of their house.

"Police cars and flashing lights! And the neighbors were coming by to see if we knew anything — which we didn't. And it was still going on this morning," Sharlene complained. "We could barely make it out of our driveway with all the police vehicles and media trucks parked in the street."

"But didn't you hear anything?" a ruddy-cheeked man at the end of the table asked. "Gunshots are pretty loud. I'm surprised you didn't hear it."

"Maybe he used a silencer," a tiny woman suggested.

"It's not a silencer, it's called a suppressor," another man objected.

Edie could barely hold in a sigh. Everyone was an expert in these days of television shows filled with forensic detail. She just hoped he wasn't a vigilante type with a concealed-carry permit and a gun under his jacket. As much as she deplored the rising crime rate, Edie feared that vigilantes were just as dangerous as the criminals.

"You know, I wondered about that," Sharlene said. "When I heard they were shot — later on the news, you know. Leo was working until late, but I was home from three o'clock on, and I didn't hear a thing until the police showed up."

"It wasn't on the early news," Edie began.

"No," someone else interrupted. "It was breaking news around eight, eight thirty. They interrupted the program for the announcement and showed the house and the police cars and all. I recognized the house right away, even though they didn't say who lived there."

"I thought you might have been the neighbor who called it in," a lean man with thick gray hair added. "A reporter said the nine-one-one caller reported seeing a young boy lying on his patio, and he wasn't moving."

"That was the neighbor on the back," Sharlene said. "They have a two-story house, and when she went upstairs to change after work, she could see Matthew from her upstairs bedroom window. I talked to her last night — nice young woman. She was pretty upset, even though she said there wasn't any blood or anything that she could see. She just thought it wasn't natural, seeing him lying there not moving, and it so cold outside. The sun was pretty low in the sky by then, and you know how quickly the temperature can drop at this time of year."

"Last night's low was thirty-five degrees." Leave it to Edie to know that, Maggie thought.

"They didn't say *when* it happened," one of the men said.

"They probably don't know yet," Edie said. "That takes time and will probably have to wait for the medical examiner to determine."

"So who do you think did it?" The questioner was a thin woman with faintly pink hair.

"I can't imagine who would want to kill Kathy, let alone Matthew," Leo said, shaking his head. His eyes were sad, an incongruous look with his rosy Santaesque cheeks. A stout man with thick white hair and a full beard, Leo Eckhold played Santa at a local mall every afternoon during the Christmas season. His plump wife made a lovely Mrs. Santa, and they often hired out as a couple. The children loved them. "Such good people. Kathy was always ready to lend a helping hand. And Matt would come over if he saw one of us doing a big job. Helped me in the yard more times than I can remember."

"When I came in this morning, someone told me you'd heard Rusty threaten Kathy," Edie told Leo.

Leo looked startled at Edie's statement. His hand flew up to his beard. "Me? I never!"

Sharlene poked his arm. "I told you what you said could be taken the wrong way," she admonished him.

"Rusty didn't call Kathy's new fiancé a jerk and a gold digger and say he would do

24

anything to prevent the wedding?" Edie asked.

The woman seated beside Edie gasped as Sharlene sighed. "Well, obviously Rusty didn't like that she was engaged. Rusty did call Dylan a jerk, but his idea of preventing the wedding was to convince Kathy to come back to him. And, of course, Matthew was all for that. Like a lot of children of divorce, he wanted to see his parents together again. He was supposed to be the best man at Kathy and Dylan's wedding, but I know he didn't want them to marry."

"We don't really know Dylan," Leo said. "We'd see him with Kathy sometimes — out in the yard, you know. He was always polite, but he's not the outgoing type like Rusty. Keeps to himself."

Sharlene nodded. "Usually just a friendly wave, or a how-are-you. Our view is a bit biased, though, since we knew Matt didn't like him."

"But Rusty is a good guy," Leo went on. "He kept in touch after the divorce. He would stop in for coffee whenever he dropped Matt off, and he'd ask us how Kathy was doing. I guess she hadn't had much to say to him herself."

"That's right." Sharlene's forehead creased as something occurred to her. "In fact, I thought he might stop in yesterday because I knew it was Matt's afternoon with Rusty. I saw his car pull in and stop. I think he was there for a while — probably talking about Christmas for Matt." Sharlene and the pink-haired woman both sighed at the thought of the poor dead child.

"Did Rusty often spend time there when he brought Matt home?" After all that had been said about the ex-couple, Edie was surprised by this.

"Not usually," Leo replied. "But he's been trying to talk Kathy into marrying him again. He said he had to work harder at it, before she remarried and it was too late. So he may have been trying to persuade her to try counseling, or dating, or something."

"You have to give him credit for trying so hard to save his marriage and family," Theresa said.

"Rusty was so nice. He was always ready if we needed help with anything around our place," Sharlene agreed. "That's probably where Matt learned to be so helpful. Rusty still stops by periodically. You know how it is when you get older, there are some things you just can't manage on your own." She glanced at her husband. "Or some things you *shouldn't try to do* on your own." She turned back toward Edie after making her point to her husband, who smiled benignly back at her. "Rusty knows our son lives out of state, so he was always ready to lend a hand."

"Rusty is a good and gentle man," Leo repeated his earlier opinion. "He would never have killed Kathy, let alone Matt. He doted on that boy. And he was still in love with Kathy. Any idiot could see that."

"We heard he cheated on her," Theresa said.

Several of the others sitting at the table murmured that they had heard the same.

"Everyone heard that." Sharlene sighed again, running her finger down the side of her mug, tracing part of the large floral design.

"Rusty always denied it," Leo said, "and I believe him. He never found out who started the rumor that he was having an affair, or who convinced Kathy that it was true."

Sharlene continued, "Later, after the divorce, and when she got engaged so quick, he suspected it might be Dylan. But no one ever heard anyone but Kathy accuse him of cheating, so he couldn't *prove* anything when he was fighting the divorce."

Edie nodded. "It's very difficult to prove a negative."

"What?" the woman sitting beside Edie

asked, her face puzzled. "What do you mean, prove a negative?"

"Someone filing for divorce can usually prove that a spouse is having an affair, because they can find someone who saw the couple together, or get receipts from a motel. That kind of thing," Edie said. "But in Rusty's case, he wanted to prove that he was *not* having an affair, but how do you do that? You can get as many people as you want to say they'd never seen Rusty with another woman, but that doesn't prove that he didn't ever meet with another woman. You see what I mean?"

As understanding brought a knowing nod from the other woman, Edie turned back to Leo and Sharlene, who were both nodding their own agreement.

"The way our kitchen is situated," Sharlene said, "I have a good view of their driveway where it curves around to the back of the house and the garage. I'd always see Rusty coming in from work. I don't know when he was supposed to be seeing someone else, because he always seemed to be there for dinner. And I don't recall seeing the car leave after dinner when I was in there cleaning up."

"Really?" Theresa said. "I'd think a plumber might go out on emergency calls

28

in the evenings, at least sometimes."

"Sure," Leo said. "But you forget Rusty was in charge. He took over the business from his father, and while he still did plumbing work himself, he did a lot more delegating. He told me more than once that was the upside of having to do so much administrative work. He didn't have to go out at odd hours anymore, not unless he wanted to."

Edie pursed her lips, deep in thought. "I suppose someone like a plumber, who works for himself, could get away during the day for a romantic tryst. But in that case, someone at the office was sure to know about it, don't you think?"

People all around the table nodded.

"Unless he put it down as a service call," the man with the thick head of gray hair said. "But it would mean falsifying the books and accounting for the missing funds from the nonexistent calls. It would all be involved and complicated, not Rusty's style at all."

"I agree with you there," Leo said. "He might have enjoyed the evenings at home, but he hated the paperwork. He delegated as much as possible."

"It seems odd that Kathy wouldn't believe her own husband over something like that,"

Theresa said. "I didn't know her, but *I'd* certainly believe my husband over anyone else if he swore to me that he wasn't cheating."

Sharlene frowned. "I tried to discuss it with Kathy once, but she just refused to talk about it. To anyone. Even Rusty says she would never discuss it. He tried to get her to go to a marriage counselor. He got a recommendation on a counselor from the diocese office. But she wouldn't go."

"Rusty said that she'd only talk about Matt with him, nothing else," Leo said. "He told her one time that a light bulb was out at the front of the house. He noticed it when he was bringing Matt home. He offered to replace it right then, but she told him not to bother and just closed the door on him. But he thought she was softening up because she let him hang the icicle lights over Thanksgiving."

Other guild members spoke of Kathy and Rusty and what a lovely couple they had been. Both were active enough at the church that they were well-known in the parish. *Everyone* at St. Rose had been shocked when they learned that Kathy asked for a divorce.

"It didn't take her long to start seeing Dylan Markham," the woman with the pink hair said, disapproval rife in her voice.

By now the entire room was following the discussion at the Eckhold table. Maggie shared a quick glance with Victoria. Although with Rusty such a popular figure among the parishioners, anyone Kathy dated would probably have been looked at in a similar disapproving manner.

"Dylan Markham. That name sounds so familiar. Does he belong to St. Rose too?" The question came from a tiny wisp of a woman with thinning reddish hair. Small as she was, Maggie knew that she was one of the woodworkers, doing sanding and staining.

"Oh, no." A new voice broke in, this one from a man standing along the wall, coffee mug in hand. "You probably recognize his name because he's a big deal with commercial real estate. Over the years, there have been several articles in the paper about him."

"He does financial investments too," another man offered. "Gets groups together to invest in commercial projects, like remodeling an old strip mall."

Recognition hit Theresa's face. "Oh, yes! That's it! I knew his name was familiar. I think I met him once when some friends wanted us to attend one of his investment parties with them. Carl looked into it but thought it might be a little risky. It was just about the time the real estate market tanked. Even though the commercial properties were still supposed to be viable investments, Carl and I are conservative with our money."

"He's a real charming fellow," Leo said. His friendly Santa-like face was surprisingly neutral. Maggie thought that in itself was telling. Leo had met Dylan more than once, and it looked to her that he did not like the developer.

"Dylan belongs to that big Christian church north of here," a large red-faced man said. "I have a contractor friend who knows him. My friend is a member of that church, and he figures Dylan joined mainly for the business-networking opportunities with their large congregation."

"Interesting," Edie commented.

"Cynical," someone else said.

"It's the way of the world these days," someone else added. And many of those present nodded.

"I've met him a few times," said a handsome woman with salt-and-pepper hair pulled back into a neat bun. "So I wasn't at all surprised to hear Kathy had fallen for him. He's very good-looking and *so* charming. He always reminds me of James Bond, but without the accent."

One of the men said, "Markham. Dylan Markham," in a plummy voice, and the room erupted in laughter.

It was just what was needed, Maggie thought. After the laughter, everyone appeared much less worried.

Before they could return to the topic of the murders, a large man in a Cardinals sweatshirt stood. "We should all be getting back, don't you think? It's been a long coffee break."

No one objected to his curt manner. Everyone knew he was ex–career military and used to giving orders. And they *had* been gossiping for an extended period of time. Gossip was the not-so-secret guilty pleasure of the Senior Guild membership.

CHAPTER 3

As the Senior Guild members began rising to return to the craft rooms, Sharlene reached under the table, producing a leather strip of sleigh bells. Shaking them above her head to gain everyone's attention, she called out. "Don't forget the Secret Santa." Just before Thanksgiving, Sharlene had told everyone about her plan for a Secret Santa gift exchange for the Senior Guild members and collected the names of everyone interested. She wanted each participant to pull a name, then make a small gift for that person.

"Since we're all crafters, something handmade would be perfect," she told them. "Don't spend a lot of money, no more than ten dollars at the very most. Less if possible. That's not what this is all about."

The whole thing would culminate at a Senior Guild party on the last Saturday before Christmas. On that day, they would have a big potluck bash and exchange their little gifts. The response was good, and everyone thought it would be lots of fun.

"The names are in a bowl there by the door," Sharlene called out. "Be sure to take one on your way out."

As they filed through the door, the bee members dutifully pulled names from the punch bowl. Maggie pushed hers into her pocket without even looking, but Clare opened her slip and groaned.

"What is it?" Louise asked, coming to a halt a few steps from their door. She'd glanced quickly at her slip and folded it again.

"I've drawn Bridget's name." Clare groaned again. "What can I possibly get for someone whose entire family was just murdered?"

Maggie grimaced at the drama, but of course Clare was right. There was nothing that could cheer up someone in Bridget's place, not this close to the tragedy.

"Chances are she might not come to the party," Edie remarked, practical as ever.

"That's true," Victoria said. "But you can still make her a small quilt, Clare." Victoria took Clare by the arm and led her toward the quilt room. "I'm sure Bridget would like that, whether or not she comes to the party. Everyone likes a small quilt. They can be very comforting."

Clare brightened as they all entered their sewing room. "That's a good idea, Victoria. I'll do it. Something green," she mumbled to herself, her mind already paging through patterns.

Clare continued to mutter to herself as they settled back down to their stitching. But Louise had something else on her mind.

"Did you notice Julian Chasen in there?" Louise asked. "He's lost a *lot* of weight."

"I noticed that too," Maggie said. "Do you think he's been ill?"

"He's certainly gone downhill as far as his appearance goes," Edie said. "He was always so well dressed, but this morning he looks like he slept in his clothes. He won't be selling much stock looking like that."

"Do you think he has cancer?" Anna asked. "Losing a lot of weight and neglecting personal hygiene can go along with cancer treatment."

"And the depression that often goes with it," Louise added.

As they resumed stitching, they all looked to Clare. She was the people person, the one who kept up with everyone. Clare always seemed to know everyone's personal information. But Clare was still busy mentally planning a lap quilt for Bridget. After getting her attention, they had to repeat their observations about Julian.

"I haven't heard anything," Clare said with a frown. "I did hear he was having a hard time. Lots of those financial advisers are in trouble because of the bad economy."

"Well, he can't be too hard up," Edie commented. "He entered the parking lot behind me this morning. He was driving a big SUV. It was rather dirty, unusual for a car like that, I have to say. But it was definitely an expensive model."

"He could be having problems with his business but still have an expensive car that was purchased during better times."

Maggie and Louise nodded at Victoria's astute observation.

"I'll ask Hal what he knows this weekend," Maggie said. The others knew she'd see her oldest son on Sunday when the entire Browne clan met for brunch. "His company used to do business with Hal's firm, but I don't know if they still do."

"I guess a tax lawyer and a financial planner would be a natural fit," Clare said.

Maggie shrugged. "Hal has had some drop-off in his business too, since the economy went downhill. But he says things are picking up now and should continue to do so."

"Housing prices are certainly up," Edie said. "Do you know that house two doors down from me — the one where the owner was upside down and just walked away? It just sold for fifty-thousand dollars more than what the bank was asking. I heard there was a bidding war with three different buyers wanting it."

"I suppose they'll be selling Kathleen's house now." Clare sighed heavily.

Maggie thought there was altogether too much sighing going on this morning.

"Who do you suppose will get the house?" Louise asked. "Is Bridget her only remaining relative?"

"I think there's an aunt and a couple of cousins. On Sean's side," Clare added, mentioning the name of Bridget's late husband. "They never talked about them much, so there must have been a rift of some kind."

"It's so sad when that happens," Anna said. "Especially in a small family."

"Do they live here in town?" Theresa asked.

"In Prescott, I think," Clare replied. "I've heard Bridget mention her a time or two. It's Sean's sister, and she has two children, a boy and a girl. I think the rift came after Bridget's parents died in that plane crash and left all that money to Kathleen."

"But why would that cause a rift?" Edie asked. "It's not like Sean's sister was related to Bridget's parents. There shouldn't have been any expectations."

"I never figured that out, but the timing seems about right," Clare said. "I got the impression that the sister was always a little jealous of Sean and how successful he was. Maybe she thought if Bridget and Sean inherited, he would have shared their windfall with his only sister."

"Family dynamics are always interesting," Louise said. "Sometimes there's no clear reason for the things that spring up between siblings. It could go way back to childhood and the perception that Mom and Dad loved him better."

"And heaven knows, that's common enough between a brother and a sister," Theresa said. "So many parents prefer a son who can carry on the family name."

"Oh, Sean was definitely their golden boy, following his father into his law firm, then becoming a judge." Clare snipped off a thread. "I wonder if there's a way we could find out more about Sean's family."

"I'm sure they'll come for the funeral,"

Maggie said. "No one can resist a funeral of two murder victims. But I doubt they would be able to shed any light on Kathy's murder, not if the family has been estranged for years."

"What if Kathy never got around to updating her will after the divorce?" Edie speculated. "If they had wills made during their marriage, it's quite possible that Rusty is still her heir."

"Well, now, that would certainly be interesting," Louise commented.

"And definitely throw suspicion in Rusty's direction," Maggie said.

Clare groaned. "That would be awful. The police will think he has the best motive."

"Not necessarily," Maggie said. "There's still the problem of Matthew's death. The police may suspect jealousy and even greed, but everyone who knew him would disagree. And everyone *knows* he would never harm Matt."

There was a momentary silence while the women all considered this aspect of the case. Then Clare nodded. "I don't see how they could blame Rusty. There's just no way he could have harmed his son. He absolutely doted on him."

Clare seemed to relax after this pronouncement, and she began to talk about her ideas for a lap quilt for Bridget.

By the time they climbed into Victoria's car for the drive home, both Maggie and Victoria claimed to be thoroughly confused.

"I hope the police can settle this quickly," Victoria said. "Otherwise, Clare will drive us all crazy with her speculations every morning."

"I do understand how she feels," Maggie said. "Rusty's parents have been good friends of theirs for years. And I like a good puzzle as much as the next person. But I don't want our Christmas spoiled with this either." Maggie clicked her seat belt into place and turned the key. "And Edie will keep suggesting a home invasion. She'll probably try to tie in drug cartels and gang activity too."

Victoria grimaced. "December is usually such a pleasant month, with conversations about relatives, gift ideas, and holiday traditions."

"And don't forget recipes." Maggie smiled at the thought of a normal Quilting Bee session in December. "I've always enjoyed exchanging recipes and talking over gift suggestions for the grandchildren. Or the nieces and nephews," she added, nodding toward Victoria who, alone among the Quilting Bee

41

women, had never been married and had no grandchildren. "It would be a shame if the entire month is lost to speculation over the murders of Kathy and Matthew. So I agree," Maggie finished. "I hope they find the person responsible as soon as possible."

"Clare will want to solve this herself," Victoria said. "And she'll want us all to help."

"Oh, I know," Maggie replied with a sigh. "I know."

CHAPTER 4

Maggie put some leftover chili on to warm for her supper, then settled in front of the television to watch the early news. She was anxious to see if there was any new information about the Romelli murders. Like so many others in the Senior Guild, she had pleasant memories of Rusty bringing Matthew to the bazaar and of seeing father and son working together at the biannual Boy Scout pancake breakfasts. She and the other bee members were always touched by the love apparent between father and son. Maggie could not imagine Rusty Romelli killing his ex-wife. And she was convinced he would never do anything to harm his only son.

Before Maggie could pick up her sewing, Rosy leaped into her lap. With a light laugh, she chided the young dog. "You never want me to get any sewing done." But her voice was filled with love and affection as she rubbed the dog's head. That summer, her sons had surprised her with the young rescue pup, seen by her granddaughter, Megan, who was sure it was the perfect dog for Maggie. Her sons had envisioned a larger, scarier dog for her during a tense summer of explosive diversions cropping up around the city. They felt a dog would alert her if anyone tried to leave anything dangerous on her property. But Megan had seen little Rosy in an adoption area of the pet store and declared it the perfect match for her grandma. Megan had named her too, claiming the dog's fur was a rosy color, and Maggie hadn't the heart to disagree. Personally, she thought Rosy's fur was more on the beige side, but in certain light she could see the rosy tint, somewhat like the color of apricot poodles. Perhaps one of Rosy's ancestors was an apricot poodle. Her son Frank, the veterinarian, thought Rosy was part poodle and part Bichon or miniature Schnauzer.

Maggie ran her hand down Rosy's soft back, and the dog's large, warm brown eyes closed in pleasure.

"Megan was right, wasn't she, Rosy? You are the perfect pet for me, even though you keep me from my stitching and you're too small to romp along on my desert rides."

When Maggie indulged in horseback rides through the desert, Hal's golden Retriever, aptly named Goldie, was her intrepid canine companion.

Maggie sighed as she moved her hand to Rosy's ear and scratched lightly.

She looked up when she heard the intro to the news program. With the hand not occupied scratching puppy ears, she reached for the remote and pressed the button to increase the volume.

"We begin with the tragic deaths of Kathleen Romelli and her son, Matthew, in their Arcadia home yesterday. Police spokesperson John Solomon reports that they are in the initial stages of the investigation and are following up several leads. Anyone with information that might be helpful is asked to call the Scottsdale Police Department or Silent Witness." The reporter went on to say that all the information anyone needed could be found on their website.

With nothing substantially new to report, the anchors quickly moved to a reporter standing outside the Romelli house, where a vigil for Matt was in progress. The reporter stood to one side, speaking in a low voice, while the camera panned over the scene. There was a large crowd of mostly young people holding candles and standing in a wide arc before the makeshift memorial setup at the curb. Flowers, balloons, teddy bears, notes, and cards — even a basket of apples — comprised a large display to one side of the driveway. Behind the young mourners, a bagpiper in full regalia played "Amazing Grace." The house itself continued to look elegant and stately with its strings of white icicle lights and, in the front window, the multicolored lights on a large Christmas tree.

Maggie blinked back tears at the sight of the Christmas tree, realizing that it must be on a timer that no one had thought to disconnect. It was an incongruous element, a bit of hopeful Christmas cheer in the midst of a sorrowful tableau.

She was reaching for the remote to turn off the television when they suddenly switched over to Matthew's school. Another memorial was set up there, below the marquee with the school's name and the message "Rest in Peace, Matthew Romelli." More candles, more flowers, more balloons, more notes and teddy bears. And another basket of apples. Maggie wondered at the significance of the apples, but she hadn't long to wait. The reporter stood beside the girl who had left them.

"Matt loved apples," she said. "He always

brought a couple to school. For his lunch and for a snack. Sometimes he brought extra for his friends." Her voice trailed off as tears rolled down her cheeks, and the reporter thankfully left her to her sorrow.

She found other children to interview, though, most of them with tears streaming down their faces. Maggie wondered where their parents were. Surely the television station needed the parents' consent for that kind of thing.

"I get to go home tonight. I get to grow up and have a career. Matt doesn't get to have any of that," a young girl said, the television lights causing the tears on her cheeks to sparkle.

Maggie snapped the television off. How could they take advantage of those poor kids for a better rating? She supposed the other channels were airing similar interviews, and she sighed in resignation. Sensing her upset state, Rosy whined softly, then rose on her hind legs so that she could wash Maggie's chin with her tongue.

Laughing, Maggie pulled her down into her lap and stroked the soft fur. With a sigh, she turned the television back on. There might be something of interest mentioned, if they could just leave the friends and family alone and try to find some real news.

But she was lucky to have Rosy there to keep her grounded. And give her a warm body to hug.

Rosy was still in Maggie's lap, interfering with her stitching, when the phone rang. It was her son Michael, the Scottsdale police officer, and Maggie's main source of information when crimes affected the people around her.

Michael got down to business after a brief exchange of hellos and how-are-yous.

"I'm thinking the St. Rose grapevine is going strong on the Kathy Romelli story."

"Oh, yes," Maggie agreed. "That's all anyone wanted to talk about in the break room this morning. Except for the Secret Santa party. Sharlene Eckhold put that idea together before Thanksgiving and was reminding everyone to pull a name."

Maggie went on to explain the concept to Michael. "It's going to end with a big party on that final Saturday before Christmas. After this, the timing is bad, but it is nice that there's something to counteract all the tragedy."

"The Senior Guild takes off those two weeks around Christmas and New Year's, right?"

"Oh, yes. A lot of people don't come regularly during November and December anyway. The bazaar is just over, and the holidays are on top of us. Lots of people entertain relatives from out of town, or go out of town themselves. And of course, there's a lot going on at the church, with all the plans and preparations for the liturgies, music, and decorations for the Christmas masses. Sharlene is very excited about this idea of hers, but no one knows how well it will go over. Clare is already upset about it because she pulled Bridget Murphy's name."

"Kathy Romelli's mother, right?"

"Yes." Maggie sighed.

"I remember Mrs. Murphy. I went over there with Frank a few times, remember? Kathy would invite Frank over to help her with her science homework, and they would let me hang around. Mrs. M was always really nice. She made these wonderful chocolate-chip cookies for us afterward. Man, I haven't thought about those in years." Maggie heard what she could only call a blissful sigh carry across the phone line. "They were the absolute best — sorry, Ma. Not that your chocolate-chip cookies aren't great. But hers had oatmeal, and big chunks of both chocolate and nuts. Boy, were they good."

Maggie heard him sigh again in remembrance before returning to the reason for his call.

"So, did anyone at the church have any insights into who might have wanted to kill Kathy and her son? Detective Warner asked me to talk to you, by the way. He said so far everyone he's talked to claims to love her. Wonderful person, and so on. No one has any idea why someone would want her dead. I told him that was the Kathy I knew. If the crime scene didn't indicate otherwise, I would have said someone shot Matt, then shot Kathy when she came after him. But they seem pretty sure Kathy was shot first, then Matt."

"Clare said the reporter on the late news seemed to infer that the ex-husband was the main suspect. She was really upset because the Romellis are good friends of hers."

Michael didn't dispute it. "You know how that is. You always have to look at the husband, the ex-husband, or the boyfriend."

"That's what I told her."

"However, and this is absolutely not to go any further, Ma — in this case it makes a lot of sense. She was shot in her bedroom. That more than likely means she knew her killer. There may be some talk of a home invasion, but it's unlikely. It's sure to be someone she knew well who did this."

"I hadn't heard it referred to as a home invasion," Maggie said. "Well, except for Edie, and you have to take everything she says with a grain of salt."

"Some reporters are trying to tie it in with a couple of other incidents around the valley," he told her. "Personally, I doubt it."

"There was a lot of talk about Kathy's ex-husband this morning," Maggie told him. "He's also very well liked, a really nice guy. And no one can believe he'd ever harm his son. And I have to agree, Michael. You've seen Rusty and Matthew at the Boy Scout functions. He could never harm that boy. He must be devastated."

"The problem is that we couldn't find Rusty until very late that night. He says he was driving around, thinking about Kathy giving him another chance. His cell phone was off, and he can't give us names of anyone who saw him or anywhere that he stopped. It doesn't look good."

Maggie's eyes widened at this information. It did not sound good for Rusty.

"The thing that really complicates it is the death of the child." Michael sighed. Maggie knew that dead children were hard, even for experienced cops.

"Yes, why kill the boy?" Maggie mused.

"The theory is that he saw something, so the shooter had to kill him too."

Maggie was quick to see what that must mean. "You mean he was shot in the back?" Maggie shuddered just thinking of it, and her voice faltered. "Running away?"

"Yes. It was either a very lucky shot, or the killer was an expert. It went through his back and lodged in his heart. He must have died immediately."

"Shot in the back," Maggie murmured. "Oh, Michael."

"That supports the theory that he saw his mother being attacked and ran away."

"We heard about the neighbor who called nine-one-one," Maggie said. "She told another neighbor that there was no blood. She said she called because it was cold, and she could see him lying there on the concrete, not moving at all."

"Yeah, that was about it. All the bleeding must have been internal."

Maggie sighed deeply. "Well, at least having that poor boy lose his life made the discovery of Kathy's body happen sooner than it might have. If her killer had any plans to try to cover up, this will throw him off."

"Let's hope so," Michael said. "I have to go, Ma, but there have been numerous reports coming from parking lots around the church, and also around downtown Scottsdale. Items taken from cars, but with no indication of how the thieves are gaining access. It's the kind of thing that often happens at mall parking lots at this time of year, and that's why the sheriff's posse watches them. But this is different."

"I always lock my car, Michael." Maggie used her I-am-an-adult, I-am-your-parent voice.

"That's good," Michael said. "However, these are all reports of things taken from *locked* cars. Tell your friends at church. Don't leave anything in their cars."

"I will."

"Good. I have to go. Remember what I said about the Romelli murders, okay? The details go no further. But keep your ears open for anything that might help the investigation. You can mention that aspect of it. I'm sure that will excite Clare."

"No kidding." Maggie smiled. "You know how she loves to think she's helping the police. She'll be over the moon hearing that Detective Warner wants our help."

"Your *input,*" Michael corrected. "Your *input.*"

Maggie could hear the amusement in his voice as he repeated the phrase. "Semantics," she mumbled. "Are you afraid she'll come up with some crazy theory?"

"Sometimes those crazy ideas of Clare's have some merit," he said, much to Maggie's surprise. "You just never know. Good night, Ma."

CHAPTER 5

*Friday, December 4th; 21 days before
  Christmas.*

The lovely, soothing strains of an orchestral version of "O Little Town of Bethlehem" drifted through the open door of the Quilting Bee room on Friday morning when Clare rushed in, hair flying, face ashen. Both arms clutched her purse tightly to her chest, as though she was using it to protect herself.

"Call nine-one-one! Call nine-one-one!" Purse still pressed to her ample bosom, Clare gulped air into her lungs in rapid pants. Her hurried gait and obvious stress had rendered her breathless.

Rising quickly from their places at the quilt frame, her fellow bee members rushed forward. Maggie pushed a folding chair behind Clare, then guided her down into it. Louise opened a bottle of water and pressed it into Clare's hand. At the same time, she managed to ease her purse away, tucking it beneath her chair.

"What happened?" Theresa asked. She had her phone in her hand, but hesitated to press the final number until she had an idea of what she should say to the operator. Edie, also holding her phone, looked to Clare for an answer.

"I was carjacked!" Clare panted out the response, her voice strained.

"Here at church?" Anna's voice reflected her shock.

You should be able to feel safe at church, Maggie thought. Even in the parking lot. But they all knew that was not the case. The diocese repeatedly warned parishioners against leaving anything of value in their parked cars, or even in the pews during the communion service at mass.

"Well, at least they didn't get your purse," Maggie told her, though she wasn't sure Clare could hear any of them over her heavy breathing.

Louise, who had put her fingers against Clare's neck, clicked her tongue. "Your pulse is racing. Take a deep breath and try to hold it in for a while. You need to calm down before you start hyperventilating. Your blood pressure must be sky-high."

"What do I tell the nine-one-one operator?" Theresa asked, finger hovering over that final "1."

But Edie had already punched in all three numbers and was speaking to an operator, relaying what little Clare had told them.

"I stopped at the convenience store," Clare said. She tried to take deep breaths as instructed by Louise, but didn't seem capable of following through. Her breathing remained short and choppy.

"Is that where it happened?" Victoria's soft voice urged Clare to continue.

Maggie noticed that Victoria's soothing tones seemed to help Clare focus, and she was able to take in more air and even hold it in for a few seconds before exhaling.

"Yes. I stopped because we used the last of the bread for breakfast and I thought it would be easier to stop on the way over. It's on that side of the road, you know, and going home I'd have to cross over, and then it can be hard to get out."

"So, did you run all the way over here?" Louise asked. "No wonder your heart is racing!"

Clare looked at Louise, raising her eyebrows. "Why would I have walked? I drove."

Louise frowned at her. "You told us you were carjacked."

"But he didn't take my car!" Clare looked

around at her friends. She seemed surprised that they thought her car was gone — highlighting her frazzled state of mind. "I always keep the doors locked when I drive, and I had just pulled in. Before I even turned off the engine, this man came up and grabbed my door and tried to open it. He looked like a homeless guy, and I thought he was going to ask for money. But then I saw there was a gun in his waist-band!"

Color had come back into Clare's cheeks, but as she relayed this bit of information, every bit of new, healthy pink slipped from her countenance. Her coral lipstick, usually a flattering shade on her, suddenly appeared garish against the stark white of her face.

"I think he was saying something to me, but with the window up and the radio play-ing, I didn't hear what it was. And then I saw that gun, and I was so scared, I just put the car in reverse and rushed over here. I didn't even look to see if he tried to come after me, or if I was going to hit him with the car." Clare must have seen Anna's shocked expression. She blinked rapidly at them, then added, "But I know I didn't hit him because I would have heard that, or felt it. And he was beside the car," she added, justifying her actions to her own satisfaction. She clutched the water bottle to her chest and took a deep breath that shuddered from her lungs in a series of panting exhales.

Maggie stepped back close to Victoria and spoke softly to her friend. "Someone needs to call Gerald."

Victoria nodded and reached for her phone as they heard a siren nearing the church.

The women were distracted when Michael Browne walked in, announcing that the ambulance was right behind him. "I heard the church address on the call and headed right over. Luckily, I was only two blocks away." He turned toward Clare. "Are you all right? There have been some incidents in the area, but I don't know if the word has gotten out."

"In the area!" Edie's temper exploded. "Why on earth haven't we who live in the area been told!"

"It's been very recent — only in the last few days," Michael told her. "And I'm talking about thefts of goods left in vehicles, not carjacking. Carjacking is completely different."

"Michael called to tell me about the thefts, and I was supposed to warn everyone this morning," Maggie said. "Do you think this ties in with the stolen packages?"

she asked Michael.

Clare suddenly sat up straighter. "I have several packages on the backseat of my car right now. Things I was bringing in for the rummage sale next month. You don't suppose he thought it was new stuff I just bought?" Clare appeared agitated. "It's too early for shopping at the stores."

"Oh, I don't know," Louise said. "Places like Big-Mart are open around the clock at this time of year. Is your stuff in plastic bags from the stores or in reusable bags?"

"I use those nice shopping bags with the long handles from Ann Taylor and Nordstrom," Clare told them. "I always save them because they are so much easier to handle than those flimsy plastic bags from the grocery stores."

Michael frowned. "Those bags would probably look very desirable to a thief who thought you were out shopping early."

As Michael took Clare through her story, her breathing once again became short and stressed. Holding one hand over her heaving chest, she gasped.

"Oh, dear." Beseeching eyes sought Louise's. "Am I having a heart attack?"

Holding her fingers over Clare's wrist, Louise gestured to Michael. "I think she's probably having a panic attack, but I can't be sure it's *not* a heart attack."

As she spoke, the EMTs Michael had said were right behind him entered the room, and Louise heaved a sigh of relief.

"Thank goodness you're here," she told them. "Her pulse is much too rapid, and her blood pressure is sure to be very high."

Then she moved back and let the medics do their jobs.

CHAPTER 6

The Quilting Bee members were early to the break room, but they felt the need for sustenance after their experience with Clare. There was a reason those British mysteries included so much making and drinking of tea. To their surprise — though Maggie thought they shouldn't have been surprised — the large room was filled to capacity, but it became eerily quiet as the Quilting Bee women entered. Chairs were quickly vacated and offered to the quilters.

Yolanda didn't wait for them to get drinks and snacks, much less sit down. "How is Clare?"

It was the question everyone present wanted answered.

"She'll be fine," Maggie told them. "It wasn't a heart attack."

"A panic attack, I think," Louise added. "Probably just stress."

"What happened?" The question came

from several different members.

Victoria had moved past Maggie while she talked, and returned now with two mugs of tea. She put one into Maggie's hands, and Maggie offered her a grateful smile.

"Someone tried to carjack Clare," Edie said. "Over at the convenience store. She thought she'd make a quick stop on the way over," she added.

Yolanda nodded. "That makes sense. If she stopped on her way home, she would have a hard time making the left turn to get out again."

Maggie almost smiled. It was exactly what Clare had said in her uniquely rambling way.

"How did she get away?" someone asked.

"She always drives with her doors locked," Maggie said. "She'd just stopped, and a man tried to open her door. She saw that he had a gun tucked into his belt, and panicked. So she backed out and hightailed it over here."

"But why would someone pick on a nice woman like Clare? Does she drive a fancy car?"

The questions came from a tiny elderly woman whose name Maggie could not recall. Maggie thought it a ridiculous question, but rushed to answer it before Edie told her as much.

"She drives a nice looking car. I hate to say it, but older people make good targets. We're none of us as strong or as fast as we used to be, unfortunately."

"The crime rate is going up all the time." Edie, still standing, and with a mug of tea held in both hands, looked ready to expound on the topic. But Maggie breathed a sigh of relief when she stuck to the subject. "Officer Browne said there have been a lot of robberies around this area, and we all have to be extra careful."

Suddenly, there were shouts from all over the room, asking Maggie if this was true and what else did she know. Several people declared themselves recent victims of thieves.

"Michael had just spoken to me about these robberies, and asked me to pass the word along. I was going to tell everyone this morning at break time." She sighed. "Too late, as it turns out."

"Clare will be fine," Louise told them. "She was bringing in donations for the rummage sale, and her backseat was filled with a lot of bags from expensive stores. The thief must have thought she'd made an early trip to the mall."

Maggie nodded. She hoped they all remembered that Clare's health was the main issue here.

"Michael didn't say anything about car-jacking when he spoke to me yesterday," Maggie went on. "He told me to warn everyone not to leave anything in your cars. Not when you're shopping, or if you park outside your home, or if you stop at a friend's house. Not even locked in the trunk. There have been a lot of cases of things disappearing from parked cars. They can't figure out how it's being done either. The cars are locked and aren't damaged in any way; the packages are just missing. He said some people don't even realize things have been taken until days afterward."

There was a babble of voices as everyone began to talk. Maggie could hear at least one voice saying she knew someone who had had that happen. And a gruff male voice said it had happened to him. Finally, everyone quieted to listen to those with some experience in the matter.

"It happened to my neighbor," the first woman said. "She was shopping for Christmas gifts, and she left everything in the trunk of her car because she didn't want the family to see what she'd gotten. But when she went out to get everything the next morning — after her husband left for work, and the kids for school — the trunk was empty. The car was parked in the circular driveway right before her front door. She said it was a weird feeling; she even wondered if she'd dreamed the shopping trip. But she had the receipts in her purse, so she knew she *did* go."

The gentleman with the gruff voice recounted a similar experience. "I had gotten a small sculpture for my wife, a piece she'd been admiring for some time. I had it in the car, in the trunk, which should have been safe. But I stopped at my daughter's for a while. She had a dentist's appointment and asked if I'd watch her toddler. By the time she got back and I took her out to my car to show her the piece, it was gone. She lives just the other side of the high school, nice quiet neighborhood, and I was parked right in front of her house. I didn't see or hear a thing. Neither did any of her neighbors." He shook his head.

"That is what Michael described has been happening. You also have to be careful if you expect any packages delivered," Maggie said. "Apparently packages are disappearing from front doors. That is something that happens at this time of year, though, so I hope everyone does know to keep a watch."

"Oh!" The scream, for it could only be called that, came from Bella Duncan.

"What?" Edie asked, her face showing her impatience for this kind of dramatic response.

But Maggie knew that Bella lived near Kathy Romelli and the Eckholds, so she was more patient. Bella had been on the news the previous night, being interviewed because she happened to live next door to Kathy Romelli. Or was it across the street? In any case, she might have seen something important. "What is it, Bella?"

"I completely forgot until you mentioned that," Bella said. "And the police asked for any information like that too," she said with a great sigh.

"Well, don't keep us waiting," Edie said, suddenly more interested in what Bella had to say. "What did you remember?"

"I saw a delivery van in front of Kathy's house last Wednesday, in the early afternoon. The driver left three large boxes at her door. I remember thinking they must be Christmas gifts for Matt. I was thinking" — her voice broke — "how lucky he was, and how happy he would be." She began to cry softly, and the woman sitting beside her patted her back and handed her a tissue.

"Did you notice if Kathy took them inside?" Maggie asked.

Still crying, Bella wiped her eyes with the

tissue. She didn't speak, just shook her head.

"Well, now," Edie said. "Do you think someone stole them from her front door? Someone who might have seen or heard something important in the murder investigation?"

Maggie knew she would have to call Michael so that he could relay this information to Detective Warner right away. This might be important. Michael often said that the littlest thing could solve an important crime.

CHAPTER 7

When the quilters returned to their sewing room and the work on the redwork quilt, they returned to their speculations about the Romelli murders.

"This new information about the package delivery might be important," Louise said.

Maggie agreed. "Michael actually asked me to see if the people who knew Kathy could come up with any good input on the case." She sighed. "Clare would have been so excited, and I never even had a chance to tell her."

"There's still a *lot* of coverage on television, but they don't seem to have any new information," Anna said.

"I turned off the television, I was so disheartened by the reporter putting those grieving children on camera," Maggie said.

"I couldn't watch those poor children talk about losing their friend either. That young girl with the tears streaming down her face . . ." Victoria shook her head. "I don't know how the reporters can justify taking advantage that way."

"I don't understand why the parents allow their children to be interviewed," Louise said. "Surely they have to get the parents' permission to show their children on the air."

"The kids might want their fifteen minutes of fame," Edie said. "Look at the stuff they post on social media. It doesn't bother them at all to be on television; they probably love it."

"The reporter at the school said they had grief counselors there yesterday and that they would be available again today," Victoria said. "Let's hope Matthew's friends take advantage of that."

"Did you see Bella on the news last night?" Edie asked. "I didn't know she was a neighbor of Kathy's. That's an area of very expensive homes. Wasn't her husband a teacher?"

"I think so," Maggie said. "I think he became an administrator at the end of his career. But I'm pretty sure there's some family money. Bella was always a stay-at-home mother, and that's hard to manage on one teacher's salary."

"I don't think I know Bella," Theresa said.

"She was the one who saw the package delivery to Kathy's house," Edie told her. "Neighbors often have significant information. They might not even realize it. That's why I joined Leo and Sharlene at their table yesterday."

"And had they heard anything?" Maggie asked.

"No. And Sharlene was quite curious about it," Edie said. "She said she was home all afternoon and didn't hear a thing. Yet gunshots are quite loud."

"The houses there are all on one-acre lots." Louise tugged at a thread that had formed a knot, and the loop loosened and disappeared. "So the houses aren't close together, and they're well insulated against the heat. Also, I'll bet most people have their windows closed. If Sharlene heard it, there are any number of things she might have mistaken it for."

"You mean a car backfiring?" Edie harrumphed. "How often have you heard a car backfire?"

Maggie was quick to reply. "It does happen, even if it's not a common occurrence. By the time the sound traveled to the Eckholds' it probably registered as a bit of airplane or motorcycle noise. Even a plane or helicopter. All common enough sounds.

Their house is very well insulated. Don't you remember when they had the work done a few years ago? They told everyone about it, and how it cut their electric bills in half."

"Well, at least you have the information from Bella to pass along to Detective Warner." Louise tucked her knot neatly out of sight and looked up. "And won't Clare be excited when she hears he wants our input?"

Everyone agreed that was so. It would have to be enough for Maggie. But she did wish they were all reminiscing about Christmases past instead of debating the innocence of an old friend in his ex-wife's murder.

"Listen to that." Victoria cocked her head to one side. Bing Crosby had just begun crooning about palm trees in Beverly Hills, LA. The sound system in the courtyard was playing "White Christmas."

Thank you, Father Bob, Maggie thought, as Victoria reminded them about the year they had snow flurries in Scottsdale on Christmas Eve. Then Anna began a story about her last white Christmas back east. This was more like it, Maggie thought with a small smile.

CHAPTER 8

*Sunday, December 6th; 19 days before
  Christmas.*

The Browne family brunch was a Sunday tradition. Wherever they might attend mass on Sunday morning, they all gathered at the old homestead afterward. This was the site of the Browne family ranch where Maggie and Harry, her late husband, had raised their sons. Harry had raised cattle on the property, though it was already being phased out when the children were young. Over the years, much of the land had been sold off and developed, but Maggie's eldest son, Hal, lived in the old ranch house with his family. The horse set-up remained, and Maggie stabled her favorite old riding horse on the property. She enjoyed going for rides in the desert and often headed out when something troubled her or she needed to relax.

That Sunday, the adult members of the

family spent quite a bit of time discussing the Romelli murders. Hal had gone to school with Rusty, and Frank with Kathy, so there was a connection with their own family. Both men knew Rusty and joined Maggie's Senior Guild friends who praised him as a nice guy.

"I can't believe Rusty would do anything to Kathy," Hal told them. "He was crazy about her, always was. He couldn't believe how lucky he was when she agreed to marry him. A lot of people thought she was marrying beneath her because he's a plumber. But he has a college degree in business, which is the equivalent of her nursing degree."

"It is a shame that so many professional people think tradesmen are beneath them," Maggie said. "I've always had Rusty, and his father before him, do my plumbing, and they have both been excellent. I always recommend them to others."

"Rusty and his dad *are* professionals," Frank insisted. "They own the business after all, and it's a thriving one. They have at least a dozen men working for them."

"I called Rusty the other day, to see how he was doing," Hal said. "He's pretty depressed, not least because the police keep questioning him." He shot a look toward his brother, the Scottsdale police officer. "It turns out he was just driving around town the day she was killed, so he has no alibi."

"Hey, don't look at me!" Michael told him. "The detectives handle that kind of stuff. And most people *don't* have alibis; unless they're guilty and set up something special. I like Rusty too. I don't know him as well as you do, but I worked with him in Big Brothers and with some of the church youth group events. Nice guy."

"I haven't heard one person say anything else," Maggie said. "And his son was also killed. How can they believe he would kill his only son? He was so proud of that boy."

"I know," Michael said. "You're preaching to the choir here."

"What did he say about the murders?" Hal's wife, Sara, looked over to him for an answer.

"He's so torn up he couldn't talk about it. But he did say that he never trusted that man she was planning to marry. Rusty suspects he's the one who claimed Rusty was an adulterer," Hal said. "You know Rusty tried to make things up with Kathy."

Frank nodded. "Last time I saw Kathy, she said Rusty was a real nuisance, always calling and texting. I have to say, at that point she didn't seem interested in saving her marriage, even though she admitted that Matt was all for it. But I hadn't seen her since the beginning of the summer. She'd just gotten engaged then."

"You can't blame the guy for trying," Hal said. "He genuinely wanted to get their family back together again. He said it was really hard on Matthew, this back and forth in the shared custody."

"Why was it so difficult?" April, Frank's wife, asked. "That kind of thing is so common these days. There must have been other children at his school who were going through the same thing."

Hal frowned. "Rusty was probably causing the problem, because he was so upset himself. Maybe even just transferring his feelings onto his son."

Maggie nodded. "Bridget hasn't been to the Senior Guild since it happened, and she's always been there, every day."

"Why did they get divorced in the first place?" Merrie asked. Married to Hal's younger brother Bobby, she didn't know all of Hal's school friends.

Maggie replied. "People at church say they got divorced because Kathy accused him of cheating. But Rusty's friends say he claims he *never* played around, and he didn't know *who* accused him of it. Or how they convinced Kathy it was true."

"He's always said he never cheated," Hal agreed. "He tried to find out how that rumor got started, but he was never able to track it down. All he knows is that one day, out of the blue, Kathy started crying and accusing him of cheating. She told him to get out of the house the same day. Gave him twenty-four hours."

"Who did she think he was cheating with?" April asked.

"She never said. Just told him he knew."

"Wow, what a nightmare that had to be." Sara patted Hal on the arm. "I hope I'd never believe something like that without proof."

"She had plenty of money of her own," Michael said. "Maybe she hired a private detective."

"But why would she do that if he never gave her any reason to be suspicious?" Maggie asked. "It's not as if he had the kind of job where he was traveling all the time and had a lot of opportunities to cheat."

"Now that you mention it," Hal said, "he said it happened right after he'd been to some kind of convention or expo in Vegas. He'd gone to see the latest in new products, and they had workshops on new tools and techniques. I remember talking to him before he left. He got the plane ticket and the convention pass in the mail. It was some kind of special award thing he said, but he'd never heard of it beforehand. He figured it would be good for business to go, but later he really regretted it."

"And he didn't check it out?" Michael asked. "That sounds mighty suspicious to me."

Kimi Tanaka, Michael's girlfriend, patted his arm. "That's because you're a cop, so you're naturally suspicious."

"No, it sounds suspicious to me too," Frank said. "But that's one thing Kathy never mentioned, and I didn't like to ask. She never would talk about the split. I figured it was too painful."

"You have to admit that would be a good way to set Rusty up so someone could accuse him of cheating on his wife," Maggie said. "A trip to Vegas is a perfect time for the most faithful husband to stray. Lots of drinking, lots of girls."

"Rusty isn't much of a drinker," Hal said. "A beer or two, and that's about it."

"And so easy to slip a roofie into that one beer," Michael said with a grin. "Get him in a room, take his picture. Mail it to his wife."

"Mail it?" Kimi laughed. "You're really out of touch. They would have texted it, or e-mailed."

Hal shrugged. "Could happen, I suppose."

"That would be an awfully elaborate plan just to get him thrown out of his house," Kimi observed. "Someone must have really hated him."

"Or really wanted Kathy for himself. She was very pretty, and had a great personality." Frank frowned. "But there are dozens of other nice, pretty women out there."

"And rich," Bobby added. "Don't forget Kathy was rich."

Maggie frowned too. Looking at the Romellis' divorce with this new information cast a whole new light on things. "If someone was desperate enough to concoct such an elaborate scheme to win Kathy for himself, he would be more than willing to kill her if she decided to leave him, don't you think?"

"It does sound like it would have to be a narcissistic personality to do something like that," Sara agreed.

"That certainly wouldn't be Rusty," Maggie said, and Hal agreed. "We'll have to see what we can learn about Dylan, the new fiancé. From what little I've learned so far, he's a possibility. Big businessman, lots of charm, risky investment opportunities. And he joined a large Christian church for the networking possibilities."

There was silence for a time as the adults thought this over while watching the children play on the wide lawn. Rosy and Goldie ran about with them, Rosy barking from time to time as she romped happily among them. Maggie thought how lucky she was to have such a lovely family. There was nothing like grandchildren to let you see how bright the world could be. She thanked God for them every evening when she asked him to protect them all from harm. Had Kathy and Bridget done the same?

Pulling her thoughts away from the Romelli mess, Maggie turned to her oldest son. He looked so much like his father, it sometimes gave her heart a lurch when she caught sight of him unawares.

"Hal, have you seen Julian Chasen recently?"

"No. I heard he's been having a hard time these past few years. I guess he's trying to save money by not conferring with us about his accounts. After all, he can just advise his clients to call us if they need tax advice."

Maggie recounted the conversation they'd had at the Quilting Bee after seeing him in the break room.

"I suppose his business must be real slow if he's going to the Senior Guild," Hal said.

"Does he show up every day?"

"He's been coming for over a year, but I don't think he comes every day. Two or three days a week, maybe. He can do wonders with a jigsaw. He makes the most amazing wooden ornaments, long thin ones with birds and flowers in them. They look a little like bookmarks."

"Oh, my gosh, I *love* those!" Merrie said. "I got several at the bazaar, and I hope they'll have them again next year. Let him know if you see him. The birds are my favorite."

"I will," Maggie said to Merrie. "They are beautiful. I purchased one with a crane myself."

Then she turned back to Hal. "Julian has told everyone he's cutting back at work with a view toward retirement. But that doesn't explain why he's gotten so thin. And his color is bad. He looks ill."

"Isn't he one of that financial group being investigated for running a Ponzi type scheme?" Michael asked. "Chasen, Chasen, and Douglas, right?"

Hal nodded. "It was his father's firm, and Douglas was his partner. Then Julian joined them. I think Julian is the only partner left now. His son is still in college as far as I know. I think Julian kept the name for now, hoping Jude, the son, will join the firm eventually, and they'll be Chasen and Chasen again."

"There's a Bernie Madoff right here at St. Rose?" Merrie asked. "Wow."

"Oh, my, I wonder how Clare managed to miss hearing about that." Maggie stirred some milk into her refilled cup of coffee. "She's usually right on top of that kind of gossip."

"I think the Feds are trying to keep it low-key," Michael said. "You might want to keep it quiet for now. These financial scammers tend to flee the country when they hear they might be arrested."

"Or they're so sure of their expensive lawyers that they just try to play it innocent," Hal suggested.

"That might be why he's looking so ill," Sara suggested. "Stress can do that to a person. And the chance he might be going to jail has to be the worst kind of stress. Even just deciding what to do — you know, running, fighting the charges, hiding your assets." She grinned at the others.

Maggie had to smile. Sara was a registered nurse, though she'd only worked part time since the boys arrived. But as a working mother with two young boys, Maggie was sure she knew all about stress.

"She's got a point," Hal said. "I'll ask around and see if anyone has heard that he's ill."

Rosy jogged up to Maggie, her pink tongue hanging as she panted in exhaustion. She'd been running hard for the past half hour playing with the children, and while the temperature was in the seventies, the sun was bright and hot. Maggie picked her up and put her in her lap — where Rosy immediately tucked her head between Maggie's arm and torso and closed her eyes.

"So, Ma," Michael said. "Are you being careful, keeping your car locked? Not leaving any packages in the trunk or the backseat?"

"Of course." Her terse reply was no accident. Maggie loved all her children, and their wives and her grandchildren too. But she did not like it when they attempted to reverse the parent-child roles. She was more than capable of taking care of herself, and had been doing so for many years now.

"I heard what happened to Clare," Sara said. "How is she?"

"She's fine," Maggie replied. "I talked to her last night. She had a panic attack after it all happened, but the symptoms are so similar to that of a heart attack, she had to be checked out at the hospital."

"So was it an attempted carjacking?" Frank asked.

"No way to know for sure," Michael said. "She had what appeared to be expensive shopping bags on her backseat, and there have been a lot of thefts from cars in that area. It's probable the guy was high on something and didn't even realize she was still in the car, just thought he'd try to open the door and, if it was unlocked, take what was there." Michael bit into a piece of bacon as his brothers and their wives debated what might have happened.

"The joke was on him, though," Maggie said, explaining about Clare's rummage sale donations in the expensive store bags.

"Just be extra careful in the next few weeks," Michael told them all. "Don't leave anything in your car, even if it's parked in your circular driveway. Not even in the locked trunk."

"I'm always careful," Maggie repeated.

Michael frowned at his mother. "A couple of cars were broken into at your condo complex, Ma. You don't ever leave your car parked outside, do you?"

"No. I always put it in the garage. It's one of the things I liked most about the place, the private garages."

After a few more admonitions to the rest

of the family, Michael and Kimi said their good-byes. Kimi, a crime-scene photographer, had to work that afternoon and wanted to get home to change.

Once their youngest brother was gone, the older boys exchanged some cop jokes at his expense. Maggie didn't object, as she knew her boys were close. And they all had a good sense of humor.

When the grandchildren came up to drag her into the house to see their newly decorated Christmas tree, Maggie welcomed the diversion. Some Christmas cheer was just exactly what she needed.

CHAPTER 9

*Monday, December 7th; 18 days before
Christmas.*

Clare was back on Monday morning, and
all of the Quilting Bee women were full of
questions about how she was feeling. Most
of them had spoken to her over the weekend, but of course they had to check again.
How was she feeling? Was she getting
enough to eat? Did she sleep all right? Maggie thought that Clare looked very good,
her cheeks pink, her eyes bright — although
she did have heavy bags under her eyes.
Clare joked about that, saying how lucky
she was to need glasses, as they hid the
worst of the bags.

Maggie decided humor was an excellent
sign.

"Did someone contact you about going in
to give your fingerprints?" Maggie asked
Clare. "Michael reminded me about it yesterday."

"Oh, yes." Clare was obviously excited at the prospect. "Gerald has to give his too, for elimination purposes, they said. We're going this afternoon, after lunch. I wanted to go in on Saturday, but Gerald insisted I rest. He wouldn't even let me watch the news over the weekend."

Victoria made commiserating noises. Maggie knew how addicted Clare was to the local news broadcasts. She even watched CNN and CNBC more than the others; except perhaps Edie. But Maggie also knew that Clare and Gerald were very close and looked after one another much like newlyweds.

"Let's hope there will be a fingerprint or two, and they catch him," Theresa said. "Whoever he is."

"So, Clare." Maggie paused, holding the scissors in her hand, ready to clip a new length of thread. "Now that you've had a chance to recover . . . Can you remember anything else about the man who approached your car?"

"Did you see him touch the car?" Anna asked.

Clare drew her eyebrows together as she stopped stitching to think. "I've tried and tried to remember. But it's hopeless."

"I believe you said he wore a hoodie," Victoria reminded her.

Clare nodded. "That's all I see when I try to visualize it. The hoodie and that gun in his waistband. I think he *might* have touched the area below the window, but I'm not sure." Clare blew out a long breath as she returned to her stitching.

"These days all the thugs wear hoodies," Edie said. "Dreadful things. They pull them up and over their foreheads, and you can't see their faces at all. They should have stopped selling them after the Unabomber made them famous."

Maggie had to hide a smile at that. Imagine telling retailers they couldn't sell hooded sweatshirts because the Unabomber had used one as a disguise.

"They have their uses," Louise objected. "Vince has one he wears to work outside early in the morning. Or for early morning walks."

"You see a lot of joggers wearing them too," Theresa said. "Especially early or late at this time of year when it's so chilly out."

"That's true," Maggie said. "I've seen all of my sons wearing them at one time or another. And women wear them too. It's a handy garment; it's just too bad that so many gangsters use them."

The conversation had gotten away from

Clare. She was stitching with great concentration. Still keeping her head down and her eyes on her needle, she spoke in a small voice. "Gerald dropped me off here this morning. He didn't want me to drive over alone, and I have to say I wasn't in any mood to object."

"It was sweet of him to do that." Victoria smiled. "He takes good care of you, Clare."

Theresa nodded. "I have to admit to feeling nervous this weekend, whenever I parked the car and had to get out alone."

"That will make you more careful, and you'll be fine," Edie said with a casual shrug.

Maggie and Victoria frowned at her cavalier attitude. She was usually the first to cry out over crimes and so-called inept police work. Not that the police had anything to go on in Clare's incident, but with Edie, such details didn't always contribute to her opinion.

"By the time you got over here and we called nine-one-one, whoever it was had plenty of time to get away. All he really had to do is remove the hoodie to completely change his appearance." Edie pulled the end of her thread through and quickly knotted it.

Maggie watched Clare's hand shake a little as she pulled at her own thread. She hadn't realized it earlier, but despite looking rosy-cheeked and cheerful, poor Clare was scared and nervous. That man approaching her car must have terrified her.

As Maggie inserted her needle to begin another row of stitches, she suddenly remembered another bit of conversation from the previous day's brunch.

"Oh, dear." Maggie abandoned her needle for a moment as she looked around at her companions. "We've been so busy with one thing and another, I forgot all about something I learned from Hal yesterday."

Everyone glanced up, their faces clearly interested.

"Something about the carjacker?" Clare asked.

"No, not at all. Something about Rusty." Maggie returned her attention to her needle, but continued with the conversation. "Rusty and Hal went to school together, you know."

"I didn't!" Clare was genuinely surprised. "Were they good friends?"

"They were fairly good friends. Enough to keep in touch since graduation." Maggie snipped a thread and reached for the spool to cut another. "We were all talking about the Romelli murders of course. Not only did Rusty go to school with Hal, but Kathy was in the same class as Frank. Frank and

Kathy were good friends, and used to study together quite often."

"So did they have any insights into what may have dissolved Rusty and Kathy's marriage?" Louise asked.

"That's what we were discussing. None of us could imagine what caused that marriage to come apart. Frank said Kathy would never talk about it. And Hal said that Rusty could never figure out what happened but swore that he was a faithful husband." Maggie finished rethreading her needle, made a small knot at one end, and pushed it into the quilt sandwich. She continued speaking while she tugged gently at the thread to bury the knot. "But this is the important part. Hal said Rusty told him the argument about his cheating came right after he'd been to some kind of conference in Las Vegas. Rusty also told Hal that he *won* the expo tickets, plane fare, and hotel room. It all came in the mail as some kind of award presentation, but Rusty had never heard of the award or the organization behind it."

Edie scoffed. "And he went anyway?"

"That certainly does sound suspicious," Theresa commented.

"Oh, it's just like a mystery novel," Clare gushed. Maggie noted that she looked much improved from a moment ago.

"I thought it sounded very suspicious too," Maggie admitted, "especially since it seemed to come just before Kathy's accusations. Hal said Rusty checked on the expo, thought it looked like a good place to learn about new plumbing supplies and techniques. So he went. It's only now that it seems very suspicious."

"We'll have to ask Bridget if she knows anything about it," Louise said. "Maybe you could talk to Rusty or his parents about it, Clare."

"I will." Clare paused her stitching hand and looked around the frame at the rest of the quilters. Maggie saw that the tremble was gone, her hand steady as she held the small quilting needle. "But let me tell you about the hospital. You'll never guess."

"In that case, you'd better tell us," Edie said.

Clare looked over at Edie and sighed. "Oh, Edie, you take all the fun out of it."

"What is it, Clare?" Victoria asked.

"My doctor at the ER. You'll never guess who it was! Chad Markham! I asked him if he was related to a Dylan Markham, and he said that's his brother!" When there was no instant reaction, she hurried on. "You know, Kathy Romelli's fiancé, Dylan?"

"And?" Edie asked.

Maggie didn't know what Clare might be thinking. While it was interesting that Dylan's brother was the ER doctor, it wasn't likely she'd been able to cross-examine him about his brother while she was being treated for an emergency situation.

"You should have seen him!" Clare enthused. "He was so good looking! And he had a very nice bedside manner, I thought." She paused. "But Gerald didn't like him."

Now that could be interesting, Maggie thought. Even more interestingly, Kathy worked in the ER at that hospital.

"Why didn't Gerald like him?" Victoria asked.

"Gerald thought he should have taken more time," Clare said. "He didn't come in immediately, you see, and when he did, he said right away that it wasn't a heart attack, that it was just a panic attack. He said it was probably the stress of seeing that man with the gun outside my window."

"Don't tell me he dismissed you because he didn't think it was serious enough," Edie said, clearly outraged.

"No, he was very nice about the way he said it." Clare frowned. "At least, I thought so. But as I said, Gerald thought he should have taken more time. But I told him they're very busy in the emergency rooms, so I didn't think anything of it. It's just one of those things, where Gerald took one look at him and decided he didn't like him."

Theresa laughed. "Maybe because he could see that you thought he was so very handsome."

"You think so?" Clare thought about that, then smiled. "Well, if he was jealous, that's okay then."

Theresa laughed again, this time joined by some of the others.

Clare gave them a weak smile. "I really wanted to ask Chad about Dylan and Kathy, but I didn't know how to bring it up."

"Surely he would have known they picked you up at St. Rose, and he could have made the connection," Edie said.

Victoria's soft voice interrupted. "Some brothers aren't close."

"Also, Dylan isn't a parishioner, so Chad probably isn't either," Maggie said. "He might not even know that Kathy and Rusty were associated with the church."

"But Kathy worked there," Anna said. "Don't you think she might have mentioned it?"

But Louise shook her head. "Relationships between doctors and nurses can be complicated. He may not have talked to her about anything personal."

"You know, Norma Hyland's daughter works over at that hospital," Edie said. "And I think she works in the emergency room."

Clare smiled, a wide smile that showed off her dimples. "And Norma does love to gossip."

"Do you think she's here today?" Theresa asked.

"She's always here, unless she's sick," Edie said. "She'll probably be having a cup of coffee at ten." She glanced at the clock. "We can go check in fifteen minutes. Norma does love her coffee."

With many smiles, the women went back to stitching.

CHAPTER 10

As expected, Norma was sitting in the break room, a half-full cup of coffee in front of her, when the Quilting Bee women arrived for their midmorning refreshment. Edie got her tea and went right over to Norma's table. The others quickly followed.

Edie began by mentioning Clare's visit to the ER and her meeting with Chad Markham. "Clare said she liked Chad quite well, but that Gerald had doubts about him."

"Oh, I could tell you tales about that Chad Markham," Norma told her. She wriggled back into her chair and took a sip of her coffee. Black, Maggie noted.

Maggie and Victoria exchanged glances. Once again, Clare had proved correct in her reading of one of the Senior Guild members. Norma was settling in for a good gossip session.

"He's such a handsome man," Clare said with a small sigh. "And I thought he was very nice in explaining things to me. But Gerald didn't like him, even though he couldn't quite explain why. He said it was a guy thing."

"Sophia says he's pretty good with patients, but he's terrible to the staff. Orders them around, argues. Yells when anything isn't done just as he likes. Doesn't listen to the nurses' opinions about patients, even if they've worked with a person before and are familiar with their histories. Why, Sophia said he and poor Kathy used to fight all the time. She said they had a huge fight her last day at work."

"Really?" Maggie raised her eyebrows. "Did she tell the police about that?"

Norma gave her a puzzled look. "Why, I don't know." Then she got a gleam in her eyes. "You don't think he could have anything to do with . . ." Suddenly her pleasant face took on a crafty look. "I'll have to tell Sophia to contact the police. I'm sure she'd like to get Dr. High-and-Mighty Chad into a bit of trouble after all the trouble he's caused her over the years. That's the main reason she transferred out of the ER. She claimed to be burnt out, but she told me she would have stayed if not for him. It's pretty exciting working in the emergency room. But she's on the maternity ward now, so he isn't her boss, and he can't cause a lot of problems for her. And she just loves working among the babies. I foresee some grandchildren in my future," she added with a complacent smile.

"Oh, is Sophia getting married?" Anna asked.

"No, but she's been seeing someone." Norma smiled, her eyes sparkling with hope. "He's a male nurse she met online. He works with terminally ill patients, in their homes. I've met him a couple of times now, and he's very nice. I guess he'd have to be to work in his field. I'm hoping something might happen over Christmas. Being around all those sweet babies all day has to have her biological clock working overtime, don't you think?"

Maggie and the others wished Norma — and Sophia — luck.

"I'll say a prayer that there will be a ring for her under the Christmas tree," Clare said. "Lots of guys propose at Christmas."

"Or Valentine's Day," Theresa added. "And that's coming up quickly too."

Norma nodded. "If you want to learn more about Chad, you should talk to Dottie Taylor. The Markhams lived next door to them until *he* died — their father, you know. Then Chad and Dylan moved their mother into one of those assisted-living condos. Dottie said she was real upset about giving up her house, but they kind of ganged up on her right after her husband died. I don't think Dottie likes Chad and Dylan much."

"Is their mother still alive?" Louise asked.

"No. Dottie said making her move out of her longtime home killed her. She got real depressed and died less than a year later." She lowered her voice. "There was a rumor about sleeping pills, but then I didn't hear any more about that." She twisted the handle of her coffee mug, turning the mug from side to side. "They did have a very nice funeral for her, I'll give them that."

With much thanks for the information she'd provided, Clare stood and glanced around the room.

Seeing Clare scanning the room, Norma said, "Dottie was in here when I came in, but she was just heading back to the sewing room. She said she was finishing up some embroidered sachets, and she wanted to get back to it."

"She does lovely work," Victoria said.

"She did some of the embroidered blocks for the quilt we're working on right now," Maggie added.

"That southwestern one?" Norma asked.

"Do you mind if I come back with you to see it? I never did see it all put together. I liked those embroidery blocks. I do a little embroidery myself, and I'd like to try some redwork. Makes it simple not having to change colors, huh?"

They all laughed with her. Even Edie smiled, though Maggie was sure she didn't think it funny.

Once Norma returned to her own projects — after a suitable period of exclaiming over the beauty of the southwestern quilt — Clare proclaimed her intention of visiting Dottie.

"But we all want to hear what she has to say," Anna objected.

Clare looked around at her friends, who all agreed with Anna, though without saying a word. Silence can often convey as much, if not more, than words. "Okay, tell you what. I'll go invite her to see how the quilt is coming along. Then she can come back here with me and we can all talk to her."

"That's a good idea." Edie nodded her approval.

"And I'm sure she will enjoy seeing the progress on the quilt," Victoria said.

Which she did. Dottie was thrilled to be specially invited to view the quilt so many of them had worked on over the summer months.

"It's beautiful," she told them. "I can see that several of my blocks have already been quilted. They look so good. I hope you do another of these. I really enjoyed getting to help with it."

They assured her that they were already planning another one — a more traditional redwork quilt worked in red thread. For the past few months, they had all been bringing in favorite patterns. They told Dottie that once they had enough for a quilt top, they would contact the women about doing the embroidery.

"We had another reason to ask you to come," Clare said.

Maggie almost winced. It wasn't the most diplomatic way to lead into their interest in Dylan Markham. Dottie, who was no dimwit, would figure out why they'd invited her in.

"Oh?" Dottie turned an inquiring look toward Clare.

"Have a seat," Victoria said, offering Dottie a chair between herself and Maggie. Clare was immediately across the quilt frame.

"It's about Kathy and Dylan, isn't it?" Dottie said, taking the seat and looking around at the Quilting Bee members. "I heard that everyone has asked you to look into her murder."

"I wouldn't say we were looking into it," Maggie said, a troubled look on her face. "That's up to the police, after all. But my son did ask me to tell him if we had any insights, seeing as how we know so many people who were close to Kathy."

"I see." Dottie remained noncommittal. "I only knew Kathy casually, mostly through Bridget."

"But we heard that you lived next door to the Markhams for years," Clare said.

Dottie nodded. "I thought that might be it. Yes, I did. I liked the Markhams very much. Their two sons, not so much. Always looking for mischief when they were boys. Scaring the neighborhood dogs and cats, egging houses and cars on Halloween. Nasty kids." Dottie's lips compressed into a tight line for a moment before she went on. "They seemed to grow out of it, became quite charming teenagers. They would come around collecting money for sports teams; you know the way they do. They always managed to charm everyone into buying whatever it was they were selling." Dottie shook her head, lost in her memories. "All an act."

"We keep hearing how charming Dylan is," Louise said. "Perhaps not so much in regards to Chad."

"I met Chad at the hospital when I had to go to the emergency room on Monday," Clare said.

"I heard about that!" Dottie exclaimed. "What is the world coming to when you can't even make a quick stop at the convenience store!"

"I've been warning you," Edie pointed out. "We have to stop these young people from creating gangs. Find things to keep them busy."

"I guess it's a good thing Dylan and Chad didn't have friends their age around the neighborhood when they were running wild. I could definitely see them forming a gang, lording it over the other boys and causing even more mischief."

"When you say mischief," Maggie asked, "was it harmless, or did they cause real trouble?"

Dottie took a moment to consider. "I think it was all harmless. Just annoying. Very annoying. They were young, so perhaps they didn't have the imagination to cause serious damage. Like I said, they would egg houses and cars on Halloween, tumble trash cans.

But they didn't break windows or slash tires."

"Still, eggs can ruin the finish on a car if it's not cleaned up right away," Louise pointed out.

"Did their parents make them clean it up?" Anna asked.

"No. I'm afraid Connie and Dell couldn't control them at all. Maybe Dell, when he got really mad, then they might listen." Dottie looked upward as she remembered times past. "There were always vandalized mailboxes around too, but no one could prove who was doing that. We all suspected the Markham boys. It was a real relief when they got to high school and turned on the charm. But even then there was some suspicion that those fund-raisers for charity were more about the Markham brothers than about good works."

"You think they were keeping the money they collected for charity?" Anna tried not to show her shock.

"They probably thought they *were* a charity," Edie remarked.

"But they're adults now," Clare protested. "They may have changed. I liked Chad myself. And he's such a handsome man, just so nice to look at in that bleak place. But Gerald had reservations about him."

Dottie nodded. "And I don't blame him. The way those boys treated their mother! Criminal it was. She didn't want to leave her home. She and Dell lived there for almost forty years. And as soon as his funeral was over, her sons were right there telling Connie she couldn't live in that big house all alone, that she had to sell and move to assisted living."

"Did she need that kind of help?" Louise asked.

"No, she didn't. And in the neighborhood, she had us and all the other old-timers who knew her and were willing to help her out." Dottie frowned at the memory. "I'd thought the boys turned out well until then. A doctor and an MBA businessman. Connie was so proud of them."

"So I guess you didn't see them after Connie moved," Clare said.

"Well, you'd be wrong." Dottie moved her mouth into a kind of grimace that told her listeners she had something unsavory to share. "The house was listed, and it sold very quickly. Everyone in the neighborhood was happy to see a house move that fast, because there were others that had been listed for months and still hadn't sold. But later, we found out that a consortium of some sort bought the house. For far less than that house was worth too."

"So it wasn't that good a happening for the neighborhood after all," Victoria said.

"No. The quick sale was the result of an extremely low offer that was accepted." Dottie still looked upset over something that had happened years ago.

"Odd that Connie would have accepted a lowball offer from a consortium, instead of waiting for a similar offer from a family." Edie looked at Dottie, her needle held in her hand above the quilt top, waiting to hear what the other woman would say about her comment.

But it was Anna who spoke next. "A consortium. What does that mean exactly?"

"It means a group got together and bought the house." Edie's quick words spoke of her impatience.

"Business groups often buy properties as an investment," Victoria added. "They then use the properties to house out-of-town guests or for seminars, training, or entertaining."

"That's right." Dottie nodded. "It took us a while to find out what was what, and none of us were happy when we learned the truth. The entire so-called consortium consisted of Dylan and Chad Markham. It was hidden behind a corporation name, and law firms, but it was them all right. It seems the two brothers had formed this group themselves, just to purchase the house."

"Just to bilk their mother, it sounds like." Edie made a noise halfway between a grunt and a cough.

"But wouldn't they have inherited the house anyway?" Anna asked.

"Eventually," Dottie said. "Those of us who knew their parents were totally put off by their actions. Because of the consortium, their names weren't listed on the deed, so Connie didn't know. Neither did any of us, for that matter, not until much later. I don't know if anyone ever told Connie, poor thing. We tried to talk her out of selling, because she really did love that house, and all her memories were there. But she said it was what Dylan recommended, and he was such a smart businessman." Dottie grunted, showing what she thought of that idea! "They were the ones who talked their mother into listing it far below market value, so that it would look desirable and sell quickly, they told her. And then they still offered even less for the property when they made their offer." Dottie leaned against the back of her chair. "I was *that* surprised to hear Dylan and Chad got together to buy that house. Couldn't wait to leave it, either one of them." Dottie pushed her hair off her face, her expression still one of contempt. "They played nice together when they were little boys, you know, the way brothers do. Them against the world — or at least, the neighborhood. They loved mischief, those two."

"Like what?" Theresa had been lucky enough to always have very nice neighbors, and she wondered what Dottie meant.

"Things like spraying joggers with a hose, or scaring a dog walker. I heard from Connie that they would steal snacks from her kitchen — eat cookies she made for a bake sale, or cut into a birthday cake before the guests arrived. The worst of it was a game of mailman they devised when they were in the third or fourth grade. They took all the mail out of everyone's mailbox and redistributed it. It was a terrible mess and I worried that something important might have been lost."

"But that's a federal offense — tampering with the mail." Edie was outraged. "You should have reported them to the post office."

Dottie shrugged. "They were kids, and we didn't know they would get worse. We liked their parents and didn't want to cause problems for them. It seemed harmless at the time."

"What happened when they got older? You said they learned to bilk people by using their charm?" Maggie paused a moment to undo a tangled thread.

"With other people, especially adults, yes. But they never seemed to get along very well with each other once they hit their teens. Too competitive." Dottie nodded her head for emphasis. "Played a lot of sports, and always trying to best one another. What a pair!"

"Do they use the house a lot — for business purposes?" Maggie asked.

"*I* think they rent it out, for corporate parties and that kind of thing, you know. But they say they don't. Of course, they would have to say that. It's not zoned for that kind of use."

"Seems like you could report them," Edie said.

"The neighbor on the other side of the house did," Dottie said. "After a particularly noisy New Year's Eve party two years ago. But it didn't go anywhere, and he told me he thought Dylan managed to get it quashed through friends in high places."

Edie sniffed. Misuse of influence was another of her complaints about the political system. She didn't rant about that as often as she did rising crime statistics, but election years could be difficult in the quilt room.

"And that's not the worst of it." Dottie lowered her voice and leaned forward to impart her next bit of news. "I think they use the house for romantic trysts."

"Romantic trysts?" Anna asked.

Dottie nodded, her eyes narrowing in a kind of worldly wise manner. "It often happened that a catering truck would appear, then that evening, one or both of those boys would show up with a woman. And let me just say, it was never Kathy who accompanied Dylan. In fact, I talked to the woman across the street, and she and I agree. As often as we saw them drive in with women in their cars — well, the women were always different. Beautiful women, the kind you might remember because they were so striking. But we never saw any of them more than once."

"Wow, it sounds like the beginning of a serial-killer book plot," Clare said.

Dottie stared at her, her eyes wide.

The others laughed.

"We all like reading mystery novels, Dottie," Maggie explained. "We're always talking about various plots and how some relate to local events. And I have to agree with

110

Clare. What you just said could be the setup for a great serial-killer tale. Two handsome professional men bringing beautiful women to a house in a quiet neighborhood. And none of the women are ever seen again."

Dottie offered a timid smile. "I guess I see your point. But I'm sure the women are around, and just didn't return to the house."

They reassured her that they didn't think the Markham men were hiding murdered women on the property next-door, then Maggie asked if they only used the house for their own private dinner parties.

"Oh, no. Like I said, I suspect they rent the house out to other businesses for entertaining. Why would a doctor have to have so many parties? He doesn't have clients to entertain. Now Dylan did, and he used it a lot for that kind of thing. In fact, the neighbor on the other side thinks that there are call girls coming to a lot of the parties. He's not happy about that, I can tell you."

"Call girls," Clare repeated, her voice hushed. Maggie knew she was imaging how exciting it would be to live next door to such a venue. "How could he tell they were call girls?"

Edie eyed Clare, sitting on the other side of the frame. "How do you think?"

But Maggie laughed. "Oh, Edie, I'm sure

if there were call girls at these corporate parties, they would be high-class ones. They wouldn't look like the hookers you see on television cop shows, with their fishnet stockings and ultra-miniskirts."

"Oh, no, we never saw anyone like that." Dottie sounded horrified at the thought. In her neighborhood?

"Your neighbor's theory makes a lot of sense," Maggie said. "We all know this kind of thing goes on in Phoenix. Why, as far back as the trunk murder case, there was talk of city leaders and call girls. Why would it be any different today?"

"Probably even worse today." Edie's droll voice set the others to laughing.

"Do you suppose the beautiful women you saw Dylan and Chad bring over were call girls too?" Clare appeared taken with this new thought. "Of course Chad is single, but Dylan was engaged, so he shouldn't have been going out with other women."

Dottie seemed uncertain but decided this was a possibility, especially since they only saw the women once. "Oh, dear, wait until I tell my husband." She didn't look apprehensive about the latter, however. She seemed anxious to share the news.

"Don't be surprised if he already knows," Edie muttered.

"Did you hear that Kathy had broken off her engagement to Dylan just before she died?" Maggie asked.

"No, I didn't." Dottie thought about that for a moment. "I wouldn't think that would sit too well with Dylan. He's an arrogant man with a high dose of self-esteem. I'm sure he thinks he's God's gift to women."

"He is a very good-looking man," Theresa said. "And everyone says he can charm the stripes off a tiger."

"Chad is awfully handsome too." Clare sighed. "It made me feel better just looking at him in the hospital. He should be playing a doctor on a soap opera; he's that handsome."

"Is he like that Doctor McSteamy on TV?" Theresa asked.

The women all laughed, especially when Clare said that he certainly was.

"I hope he comes to the funeral so we can all get a look," Theresa said.

Maggie, however, was still thinking about the Markham house. "So Kathy never came over to that house," she mused. "I wonder if she even knew that Dylan was a part owner."

"It is the kind of thing that people getting married ought to share," Dottie agreed. "But I have my doubts that Kathy knew anything about it. I can't help thinking there is something secretive about that house and the ownership. Why not use your own name to buy it? Why buy it at all? They would have had it soon enough anyway."

But these were rhetorical questions of course. There didn't seem to be much else to say on the subject, so Dottie said good-bye and returned to the sewing room.

CHAPTER 11

Michael strode into Maggie's condo, placed a quick kiss on top of his mother's head, and headed straight for the kitchen. Rosy trotted happily behind him. He opened the refrigerator and took out a beer, taking a moment to stoop and pet Rosy. "It's been a day! I'm glad you stock a few beers for me. I can really use one today." He took a long sip. "How is Clare?"

"She's good, pretty well back to normal as far as we can see. As you can imagine, Gerald was very concerned. He took a dislike to the ER doctor who saw her. And you won't believe this — it was Dylan Markham's brother!"

"I'm glad she's all right," Michael said. He took a seat at the dinner table, and Rosy immediately hopped into his lap. "What didn't Gerald like about Dr. Markham?"

"Clare wasn't really sure except that he thought he was a little too slow in coming in to see her. She said it was a guy thing, so maybe it had to do with Clare thinking he was extremely good looking. I think it's sweet that he was jealous." Maggie smiled as she reached into the oven and removed a covered dish.

"Oh, Ma, that smells like heaven. Your homemade lasagna, right?"

"It is." Maggie removed the foil covering the noodles, and steam rose along with the mouth-watering aroma. "I put it together yesterday so I just had to cook it today. I thought you might bring Kimi along with you."

Michael was already tucking into the food, and Maggie suspected he'd worked through lunch again.

"Kimi is working on a series of sunset photos. She went over to Papago Park this evening to see what she could get."

"I'll make a plate for her, then. You can take it with you. Just remember it's for Kimi, not another round of seconds for you."

"Sure." Michael grinned. He knew his mother would give him more than enough leftovers for the two of them.

Maggie sat down before her plate with its smaller square of lasagna. "So, tell me what you've learned about Clare's carjacking.

Though carjacking seems like the wrong word for it since the man did not steal her car."

"The crime-scene people dusted the driver's side of the car, and they did get a few prints. They'll have to compare them to Clare's and Gerald's for elimination purposes."

Maggie smiled. "Clare said they were doing that this afternoon. She'll enjoy that, I'm sure. She's upset that she missed all that activity around her car. She told us she wasn't happy with Gerald for taking it to the car wash and getting rid of all the fingerprint powder. She would have driven it around like that until all the powder blew off on its own or got washed off by rain."

That raised a chuckle from her son. "I don't blame Gerald for taking it in. I saw the car after it was dusted, and it was a mess. I'm sure he thought he was doing her a favor."

"Maybe. Or maybe he knew what Clare would do." Maggie couldn't suppress a grin.

"Did the convenience store have any cameras? Did anyone manage to get a photo of the carjacker?" Maggie asked Michael. "With so many cell-phone cameras out there these days, that seems like a real possibility."

Michael shook his head while he finished chewing. "Not unless they haven't turned it in yet. Someone could well have gotten some video and posted it online. There isn't even a decent description of him, just a supposedly young white man in a hoodie. Clare may have gotten the best look at him, but she doesn't seem to recall any details."

"Clare was so traumatized by seeing a gun that that was all she could remember. I asked her this morning if she's remembered anything else, now that she's had time to calm down. But she says not. She was hoping there would be security footage from the convenience store."

"Oh, there was." Michael barely stopped eating to reply. "A guy in a hoodie."

Maggie sighed.

"They will be able to figure his height, calculating from the height of the car, and determine a weight from that. But that's about it."

"I guess all the young thugs wear hoodies these days. At least that's what Edie says."

"Unfortunately, so do a lot of young people who are law-abiding citizens. And lots of older people who want to stay warm. I don't think they'll be going out of style anytime soon. I have one myself. It's great for jogging this time of year."

Maggie knew this was all true. They'd said the same over their quilting.

"Will you be going to the funeral tomorrow?"

"I don't know yet. But, I tell you what . . . Would the Quilting Bee like to have dinner with me tomorrow night? I'll treat you all to the buffet at that Chinese place on Scottsdale Road. You can tell me your impressions of the various people. In fact, that might actually be better than attending myself. I'm sure Detective Warner will be there," he added, helping himself to seconds of the lasagna.

"Leave room for dessert," Maggie reminded him.

"I *always* have room for your dessert, Ma." He winked at her. "Chocolate cake, right? I smelled it before you pulled the lasagna from the oven." With a grin, he put a forkful of noodles, cheese, and sauce into his mouth. He savored it for a moment before he began to chew.

Maggie stared for a moment at her youngest son. How could he detect the smell of chocolate even over the heavy aroma of Italian food?

Then she smiled. "When are you going to become a detective? I think you're ready."

119

CHAPTER 12

Tuesday, December 8th; 17 days before Christmas.

The Quilting Bee members and their spouses filled a long pew at the funeral of Kathy and Matthew Romelli. Clare and Gerald sat at the end near the central aisle, Vinnie and Louise at the other. Clare kept dabbing at her eyes with a tissue, even before the two coffins were rolled up the aisle. Maggie had to admit to tears of her own, seeing those two coffins. Bridget and Rusty followed behind it, holding on to each other as though that was all that was keeping them upright. Behind them were two extremely attractive young men in dark suits. Maggie didn't need the pointed look from Clare to know these were the Markham brothers.

As the coffins were arranged before the altar, Maggie thought that perhaps cremation was the way to go after all. During her growing up years, the Catholic Church did not approve of cremation, so those in her age group usually opted for burial. But surely it must be easier on the family when there were only urns and photographs of the deceased in better times.

Not that there weren't photographs. There were beautiful shots of both Kathy and her son. A formal studio photograph of the two of them, and three casual poses of them having fun. Matt in his soccer uniform, throwing his arms in the air after kicking a goal. Kathy at an outdoor party, her face glowing pink from heat or happiness. Matt holding up a fish, Rusty standing behind him with the fishing pole, a broad grin on his face.

There were no grins today, only massive amounts of flowers, crowds of people. Maggie had seen media trucks outside the church representing all of the major news stations in Phoenix. A double murder made for a good lead story; and having one victim only twelve years old was a good tearjerker — a bonus of sorts.

As the familiar words of the requiem mass washed over her, Maggie hoped they were bringing comfort to Bridget and Rusty. She watched the scented smoke rise from the censer, hearing a few sneezes and coughs behind her. These days, many people claimed allergies to the incense, but Maggie loved it. She remembered the high masses of her youth, when incense was used at the altar during the service. She liked the imagery linked with it — carrying their prayers up to heaven; guiding the souls of the deceased up to God.

As the final hymn played, and the coffins were wheeled down the aisle, Clare leaned over and whispered in Maggie's ear. "Did you see Dylan put his arm around Rusty?"

Maggie nodded. "He's sad, but not devastated. Rusty looks like he's in shock. Dylan is trying to help."

"Don't you think it's a little odd? Comforting the man whose wife you stole?"

Maggie's eyes widened. "Well, I don't know that I'd put it quite like that."

Clare humphed, and Maggie remembered her loyalty to the Romelli family.

Victoria, who'd caught the gist of their whispers, leaned toward Clare. "Dylan looks like he hasn't slept for a while."

Maggie had noted the dark circles under his eyes, but Clare chose to ignore them.

"That's Dr. Chad Markham with Dylan," she told them. The procession was now outside, so she didn't feel the need to whisper any longer. "Isn't he just the handsomest man?"

Maggie heard Gerald sniff loudly, and stifled a smile.

CHAPTER 13

The Quilting Bee women carpooled to the Chinese restaurant that evening. They were all happy to meet Michael there for a free meal. Clare was even more excited about being part of the investigation into the Romellis' deaths.

"Imagine," Clare kept saying. "Our gossip might help the police find Kathy's killer."

"Michael said Detective Warner wanted our input on the people involved," Maggie told her as they walked inside. "Nothing official."

But nothing would deter Clare. "We have lots to tell him," she insisted. "Maybe something that is the *one thing* that will close the case." Her wide grin made the others smile.

Michael rose to greet them. He'd arrived early so that he could make arrangements for a large table.

"Welcome, ladies. Shall we get our food

before we begin?"

There was happy chatter among the group as they walked around the buffet tables and made their choices.

Once everyone was seated with a plate of food, Michael looked around, his face solemn. "So, how was the funeral?"

Everyone spoke at once, about the service, Rusty, and events at the graveyard.

Maggie clicked her spoon against her water glass. "We'll have to go one at a time, or poor Michael won't be able to follow."

Michael grinned at his mother. He could have taken charge, but why bother when she could handle it so well on her own?

"Why don't you start with the service, Clare?" Maggie suggested.

Clare began immediately, barely touching her food. She recounted who had been there, how they looked.

"Poor Rusty looked like he hadn't slept since it happened, don't you think, Maggie?"

Maggie agreed that he did indeed look haggard.

"And then, at the graveyard . . ."

But Maggie stopped her. "Perhaps Louise could tell Michael about the graveside ceremony." With the drama that had occurred there, Maggie thought Louise might

125

give a more balanced view than Clare, who tended to get overly emotional.

"A good number of people followed the hearses to the graveyard," Louise began. "It was the usual short service, the prayers and a hymn. And there was a man with bagpipes who played 'Amazing Grace'."

"That was *so beautiful.*" Clare dabbed at her eyes with a wrinkled tissue.

Louise glanced at her, then continued. "But the drama began when it came time to put the flowers on top of the coffins. Bridget and Rusty were not in the best shape anyway, and we could all see how difficult it was for them. Bridget's sister-in-law helped her up and past the graves, and they left their roses. Rusty came up behind them. I wondered that he could even see where he was going, as his eyes were brimming over with tears."

"Sobbing his heart out, more like," Edie mumbled.

Louise nodded, her eyes filled with sadness. "His only son, and the woman he always said was the love of his life. It was heartbreaking to watch. Rusty broke down completely when he got to the coffins. It looked like his knees just gave out. He leaned forward to put his rose on Kathy's coffin and suddenly he was on his knees

126

behind it. Dylan Markham, you know, Kathy's recent fiancé, was behind him, and he came to the rescue. I was impressed with how gently he approached and helped Rusty stand again. He led him to Matt's coffin, still supporting him. And Rusty buckled again. He almost took Dylan down with him. He fell to the ground and let out an almost animalistic sound of grief. And anger too, I think. It was dreadful."

The other women agreed.

"I've never heard anything like it," Anna said. "And I hope never to again." Her shoulders shuddered as she recalled the scene and her fingers sketched a quick sign of the cross.

"It was truly awful," Theresa agreed. "If they had lowered the caskets beforehand, I think he might have leaped right into the grave. It was definitely horror movie stuff." She too shuddered.

"I had to admire Dylan for what he did," Louise continued. "Rick and Gen, Rusty's parents, were there too, but Dylan leaped forward before they could reach Rusty. He pulled Rusty's arm around his shoulders and guided him back to the chairs. Almost carrying him, really. He was talking to him, trying to calm him down, I'm sure. We couldn't hear any of that, but whatever he said, it did seem to help. And once Rusty was back beside Bridget, she also helped to calm him."

"I was impressed too," Clare admitted, though reluctantly. "Because Dylan took up with Kathy almost the minute she threw Rusty out, I've never liked Dylan. But everyone has always said he's a very charming man."

"It seems he was exerting his charm there," Michael agreed. "And at least Rusty didn't attack him for trying to help."

The Quilting Bee women looked startled at his comment, so Michael elaborated.

"Fights are common when one man perceives another has stolen his wife, as could have been the case with Rusty and Dylan. I guess you could say that they both acted as gentlemen."

"Dylan didn't go to the luncheon at the church," Louise said. "So I guess he might have been trying to avoid all those friends of Rusty's who might have thought that."

"Wait," Edie said. "You can't tell him about the luncheon until he hears what happened when we returned to our cars after the graveside service."

Michael's eyebrows flew up, and Maggie realized he had not heard about the late morning episode.

"What happened?" he asked, picking up a piece of chicken with his chopsticks and popping it into his mouth.

"Go ahead, Edie," Maggie urged, as she too put a piece of chicken into her mouth. The sweet-and-sour chicken really was excellent.

"Well," Edie began, "people just are not listening. We've all told them again and again not to leave things in their cars. But as soon as we all headed back, a woman halfway down the line of parked cars began to shout. She'd put her purse into her trunk after the mass, and she already had a brand new computer in there. She said she had to pick it up at the store first thing this morning and she didn't have time to drop it off at home. It was a gift for her grandson, and she was really upset. She'd put her keys in her pocket, so as soon as she got back to her car, she opened the trunk to get her purse. And the trunk was empty. So everyone else quickly checked their own cars, and there were two other stupid people who had left recent purchases in their trunks. One wasn't even a trunk, just the back of an SUV. Just not smart at all." Edie finished with a click of her tongue.

"And one man who left his cell phone charging in the front seat," Maggie said. "It was gone too of course."

"And I take it they all reported the stolen items." This time Michael selected a piece of pork.

"Oh, yes. The officer who came out said the same thing. Never leave anything in your car, especially at this time of year. He thought they were foolish too, even if he didn't say so. You could tell," Edie said. She pushed her fork so hard into a chunk of zucchini that the metal tines clicked against the porcelain of the plate. Maggie almost smiled. Edie did not suffer fools easily.

"The interesting thing is that there were no marks on any of the cars," Maggie said. "How are the thieves getting inside without leaving any tool or pry marks? There wasn't any noise either, or someone in the crowd would have noticed."

"Unless it was while Rusty was having his breakdown at the graveside," Edie reminded them.

Michael swallowed and took a sip of tea before answering. "We haven't been able to figure out how they're getting into the cars. Picking the locks would probably take longer than the time period when some of these have occurred. We know they do it quickly because some people have gone into a house and come back out fifteen or twenty

130

minutes later to find their things gone."

"What about those automatic things locksmiths use?" Edie asked.

"Possible. But those are difficult to get, and more than one person has to be committing these robberies."

"There was something on the news the other night," Edie said. "Somewhere in Texas, and it was the same kind of thing. They had video from a parking garage where the thief had some kind of video gadget that he was using to break into cars. They said the police were stumped, and they asked anyone who knew what the gadget was to get in touch with the police."

Michael nodded. "I've heard about that. It's a serious problem and has been slowly spreading to other cities. It could be that it's arrived here in Scottsdale. So far we haven't gotten any video footage of the thieves. They're either careful or lucky. Maybe that's why they choose cars in the downtown area and small residential streets."

"Someone might have followed Liz from the store where she picked up the computer this morning," Edie said. "She said she put it right into her trunk the minute she got to her car. If someone there in the store parking lot saw her, they might have deduced that she was going somewhere and planned to leave it in the trunk. She even mentioned seeing a particular car several times. She noticed it because it looked like her daughter's car — her daughter in Seattle," she added, so that no one would think it was her daughter's car she'd seen.

"Then why didn't they take it while she was in church for the service?" Maggie asked. "If they followed her from the store, I mean. The service in the church is much longer than the graveside service."

"That's a good point," Anna said.

But Edie had a good rebuttal. "The people from the mortuary don't usually stay inside for the service. Well, maybe in the summer when it's a hundred and ten out," she decided. "If Liz parked close to the area where the hearses pulled up, the attendants might have been hanging out there and would have seen him breaking into the car. At the cemetery, everyone was graveside."

The other women nodded. That made sense.

Even Michael agreed that it was a good theory.

"So what did you observe at the luncheon?" he asked.

"The funeral committee really outdid themselves," Clare said.

"I don't think Michael is interested in the food," Maggie said. She turned toward her son. "There was quite a crowd at the luncheon. I think everyone who attends Senior Guild was there for the funeral and went on to lunch. Bridget held up very well, and even Rusty seemed okay."

Louise interrupted. "I think Rusty was medicated between the graveyard and the luncheon. His eyes were dilated, and he was much more mellow."

"Of course," Maggie said, wondering how she'd missed that. "And here I thought it was his parents' presence helping to keep him focused." She shook her head at her stupidity before looking back at Michael. "Dylan and Chad were not there, though both were at the church, and Dylan at the graveyard."

"What about Kathy's other relatives?" Michael asked.

"There aren't many," Maggie said. "There's her aunt from Prescott — her father's sister. She and her husband were there. I understand there are two children, but they did not attend. Bridget introduced us to her sister-in-law and her husband. They didn't seem too upset by it all, though the sister-in-law seemed rather horrified that Kathy was murdered."

Victoria agreed. "Yes, she did seem to think that people in their family should be above that kind of thing."

"She kept saying 'Murdered! Sean would be shocked, just shocked!' It was very odd, really." Theresa shook her head as she speared the last piece of broccoli on her plate. She had declined chopsticks and chosen a fork.

"They didn't appear terribly broken up about Kathy's death," Maggie agreed. "But they live in Prescott and, from what Bridget said, they were never close. I got the impression that they didn't bother with Bridget and Kathy after Sean passed away."

Michael nodded. "Anything else?"

"I think Dylan should have gone to the luncheon," Clare said. "Chad too. After all, Dylan and Kathy had been planning their wedding. And Chad worked with her at the hospital."

"Chad didn't even go to the graveyard," Louise said.

"Norma told us Chad is terrible to work with and that he argues with all the nurses," Clare told Michael.

"Norma's daughter used to work in the ER with Kathy and Chad," Maggie informed Michael.

Clare nodded absently. "She even said

something about a big argument Kathy's last day there. So you'll want to talk to the people at the hospital," she finished.

"I'm sure the detectives have already done that," Michael said. "But I'll be sure to mention it."

"Do Dylan and his brother have alibis for the time of Kathy's death?" Edie asked.

"Dylan — *and* his brother?" Michael raised one brow, and Maggie smiled. His father used to do the same thing.

"Clare took a liking to Dr. Chad at the emergency room," Edie explained. "But other people don't seem to take to him, Gerald included."

"Chad apparently does not interact well with the medical staff at the hospital," Victoria added. "And that included Kathy, who worked with him in the ER."

"But why would he want to kill Kathy?" Theresa asked.

"Any number of reasons," Edie said. "They worked together, so there could be reasons associated with that. Maybe he wanted her for himself and was jealous of his brother. Or the opposite — maybe he and Dylan are very close, and he was mad when she broke it off."

"Norma's daughter works at the hospital, and we asked her about Chad," Maggie

135

said. "She told us he has a temper and is difficult to work with. It seems he and Kathy used to fight all the time."

"Okay." Michael, glancing between the women as they spoke, seemed relieved that the back and forth was over.

"Dottie, who lived next to the Markhams when Dylan and Chad were growing up, told us the boys never really got along," Maggie continued. "Lots of sibling rivalry. And she said they were troublemakers too, terrorizing the neighborhood."

"What about alibis?" Edie asked. "You never said if they have them for the time of Kathy's death."

Michael frowned at her, then seemed to come to a decision. "This doesn't go any further." He looked around the table, meeting each woman's eye for a second or two. "They did provide alibis, but not good ones. Chad was working at the hospital. But it gets crazy in the ER, so there's no way to be certain he didn't manage to sneak out. Not impossible, though improbable."

Clare gave a solemn nod. "It was pretty crazy when I was there, and there were long waits between seeing doctors and nurses."

"What about Dylan?" Edie was trying to keep them on target.

"Dylan was at home working on his computer. He handed over a flash drive with his computer history on it, but that kind of thing can be faked. I don't know how computer savvy he might be, but the computer forensics people will be checking that thoroughly."

"Oh, good." Clare sounded so happy, Maggie stared at her in surprise. Then she realized what was making Clare so cheerful. If the police could produce evidence that Dylan had faked his computer records, her beloved Rusty would be exonerated.

"What about Rusty?" Maggie asked.

Michael sighed. "Rusty is a problem. No one could find him the day of the murder, and so he didn't learn about the deaths until he arrived home late that night. He did seem shocked at the news . . ."

"Well, of course he was!" Clare was indignant and let him know it.

"However," Michael continued, "he was very vague about where he'd been. He claimed he was just driving around and finally headed home when he realized how late it was."

"How late was it?" Maggie asked, curious.

"Almost midnight."

Clare gasped — a soft sound, but clearly audible to Maggie beside her.

"And he didn't know where he'd been?"

Edie sounded suspicious.

Michael shook his head. "He was extremely vague. One of the patrol guys thought he might have been high, but he offered to take a drug test and passed. He said Kathy agreed to attend counseling with him, and he was so happy, he just started driving to digest the news. He didn't have the radio on; he was playing CDs, so he didn't hear about the deaths."

"That would have been a terrible way to learn his son and ex-wife were dead," Victoria said.

"I agree." Michael poked at his food with the chopsticks, deciding what to eat next.

"He must have been dreaming about reuniting with his family." Clare put a forkful of rice into her mouth and chewed complacently.

No one else spoke up for a minute or two, so Michael glanced around the table. "So, does that cover everything you observed today?"

It was Maggie's turn to look around at the others. "I think so."

"Oh," Clare said, shaking with the effort of not blurting it out. "Tell him about the packages."

Michael's eyebrow shot up again. "Packages?"

"Oh, dear." Maggie almost groaned. "We heard about this on Friday, and I meant to call you. Then I was distracted. I'm so sorry. Bella Duncan, one of Kathy's neighbors, told us she saw a delivery truck leave three large boxes at Kathy's door on the day of her death. She remembered when I told everyone to watch out for thieves and to track their package deliveries."

"We wondered if the delivery person might have seen someone around the house," Louise said.

"Or, if you can discover the thief, perhaps he saw someone," Victoria added.

"Wouldn't that be something!" Clare's enthusiasm for this scenario made her eyes bright. "That would be just like in a mystery novel."

"Too much like a mystery novel," Michael muttered. "A good idea, but not too realistic," he added in a louder voice.

As they refilled teacups and passed around the fortune cookies, Michael thanked them all for coming. "You've been a big help, lending us your eyes and ears. Detective Warner will be most appreciative."

"We'll keep our eyes and ears open," Clare assured him. "And we'll pass on anything else that might be helpful."

Maggie knew that Clare would pass on

anything at all that occurred to her, whether it might be helpful or not. But she would enjoy every minute of her time as a police department snoop.

CHAPTER 14

Wednesday, December 9th; 16 days before Christmas.

The Quilting Bee women arrived at the church on Wednesday morning anxious to continue their discussion of the funeral and who may have killed Kathy and her son. Edie had promised to check online for any interesting information on Dylan Markham, and that was another thing they hoped would prove helpful.

But any plans flew like doves from the church steeple when they arrived at St. Rose to find the parking lot filled with emergency vehicles.

"Oh, my," Victoria said as she drove slowly to the back part of the lot where there were some spaces available. "What do you think has happened now?"

"This is how it looked when Clare had her episode on Monday," Maggie replied.

Worried that another parishioner might

be injured, they hurried from the car, anxious to learn what they could. Hoping it wasn't another carjacking. Hoping no one had been hurt.

As they approached the rear entrance to the church courtyard, Maggie spotted Michael's tall form standing beside one of the police cars. She turned that way, hoping he would see her and approach.

Michael, it turned out, had been watching for her, and met her to one side of the courtyard gates.

"What's happened now?" Maggie asked.

"Some cars were broken into during morning mass. When the thief was seen by someone coming out, he attacked the man and took his car."

"Was he hurt?" Victoria asked.

Michael frowned. "He's an older man, but in good physical shape. The paramedics think he'll be all right, but he probably has a concussion."

"Is it someone from the Senior Guild?" Maggie asked.

"No. I didn't get his name, but he's a businessman who comes for morning mass before work every day. He's still a bit young for the guild, I think," Michael added with a smile at his mom. Heaven forbid any of her children called her old. She was much too vital for a word like that. However, they often hinted that she wasn't as young as she once was.

"The man was knocked unconscious?" Maggie asked, her brow furrowed as she thought about the information her son had provided. "How did the thief manage to get his car?"

"From what I've learned, the man apparently left the church right after communion. He said he had to get to the office for an early meeting. He walked out, saw what he described as a 'scruffy young man' trying to open the door of a car in the lot. He recognized the car as belonging to a friend of his, and he shouted out. His mistake was running toward the car and the kid. The kid got spooked, I guess, ran at him, and knocked him down. The man had his car keys in his hand and they might have fallen on the ground. The kid grabbed them, probably clicked on the open button to see which car it was, got in, and took off. A good car too, a year-old Mercedes."

"So you know the license number," Victoria said.

"We do," Michael said.

"You don't look happy, though," Maggie said. "So I'm assuming he hasn't been caught."

"He has not." Michael frowned, two deep lines appearing on either side of his mouth.

"The media is going to have a field day with this," Maggie said with a frown of her own. "Not to mention Edie. Two carjackings in less than a week, and in close proximity. And no one in custody."

"Speak of the devil," Michael muttered.

Edie was tromping toward them — there was no other word for it. Her face was set in hard lines as she looked from one emergency vehicle to another. She began to speak before she even came to a stop.

"What is it this time?"

Maggie and Michael explained as she frowned at them.

"Two carjackings in less than a week!"

At her exclamation of disgust, Maggie exchanged a look with Michael and Victoria. They had to work to keep from smiling. Maggie had certainly called it, but this was no laughing matter.

"Do you think it's the same person who accosted Clare on Monday?" Victoria asked.

"I wouldn't be surprised," Michael said. "Same general description. But then, all these young hoods dress the same nowadays. Hoodies pretty well keep anyone from seeing their faces, and general physical descriptions can apply to hundreds of young men."

"I thought you said there would be extra patrols in this area after Monday's attempt," Edie said. Her eyes accused him of lying to them.

"There *have* been extra patrols. But they don't drive through the parking lot of the church. The hijacking took place in the back lot here, where a car on the street would not have seen a thing. I'm sure that's what made it perfect for going through cars looking for items to steal. Even after all our warnings, people are still leaving cell phones, packages, even computers in their cars, and in plain sight."

Clare approached them then, her whole face sparkling with excitement. "What's happening? Can we go inside?"

The rest of the Quilting Bee members were trailing along behind her.

"It would be best if you went on with your usual routine. None of you were here when the crimes occurred, so you'd only be in the way. The detectives are still talking to everyone who was at the morning mass, and having them all check their cars to see if they were broken into."

Maggie turned, leading the way into the church courtyard, then on to the quilt room. But Victoria stopped her before she'd taken more than a few steps toward the central fountain.

"We should go to the break room," Victoria said. "Everyone will be there talking about this."

"You're right." Edie turned toward the social hall. "Besides, I'd like a cup of tea."

Maggie had to agree with them both. A cup of tea would be nice after hearing the distressing news. And Victoria was correct — *everyone* not scared off by the multitude of emergency vehicles would be there.

Maggie took her mug of tea to one of the tables, wondering how she could have thought even for a minute that the sight of the emergency vehicles would scare off any of the Senior Guild members. Looking around the room, she thought that some of them had probably called friends to tell them about the excitement and those friends had then driven over to join them. The room was filled to capacity, with some of the men standing along the side wall, coffee mugs in hand. Maggie noticed faces of members who had not been to Senior Guild mornings since before the bazaar.

"We're lucky to find these seats," Clare told her, as they pulled some chairs together

146

at one of the tables. "Everyone is here. Even Bridget!" she added, nodding toward a table filled with women from the knitting circle.

Bridget was indeed there, sitting between Yolanda and Dottie. Bridget was pale, and the circles under her eyes could have been mistaken for bruises. But she seemed content being there with her friends, and Maggie was happy to see her making an effort to resume her normal activities.

"It's just terrible!" one of the women at the next table complained. "It's not even safe to park in the church lot anymore. What is this world coming to!"

Edie came over, pulling a chair with her and squeezing it into place at the table. "It's those gangs," she declared. "They're invading Scottsdale, and they're always looking for some kind of mischief. Illegal mischief."

"Now, Edie." Maggie gave her friend a pained expression. "There's no reason at all to think a gang has anything to do with this. It's during school hours, for one thing."

"Gang members are often dropouts," Edie informed her. "And they wouldn't have any problem playing hooky either."

Dottie looked toward Clare. "Do you think it's the same person who tried to take your car on Monday?"

"Oh, it must be!" Clare said. Maggie

thought she seemed very confident for someone who had not seen the person this morning and had nothing more than a general description that could match any of a dozen men in the room right now. "Maggie talked to Michael and he said the description matches."

The buzz of conversation grew as everyone began to talk about the danger of carjackings and how these were too close for comfort.

"And as senior citizens, we're often targets," one of the men said, nodding briskly as he finished. "These young gangsters think they can overpower us."

"I heard that man this morning was hurt real bad," one of the men standing behind their table said.

"No," Maggie assured them. "Michael said he'll be fine." No reason to mention the concussion. He probably hit his head when the thief knocked him down. He'd talked to detectives, given them a description. He couldn't be too badly hurt.

Just then, one of the woodworking men came in, cell phone in hand. "The local news says there's a car chase on, and they think it has to do with the carjacking here this morning."

All around the room, cell phones began to

appear. Maggie heard one elderly woman asking how to find the news station app. She didn't bother pulling out her own phone. She'd hear the results of the chase soon enough.

It took only minutes, though it seemed much longer. A patrol car had spotted the stolen car a few blocks away, and the chase was on. It didn't take the media long to get on it. One of the news helicopters had been doing traffic reports and was right over the area.

With so many Senior Guild members glued to their phones, the room turned quiet. Only the occasional "what's happening" from those without Internet access broke the silence. The news station had a helicopter up, doing a street-by-street play-by-play, warning drivers to steer clear of the desperate carjacker. Maggie feared that things would not end well. Her premonition proved too true. Speeding up Hayden at over ninety miles an hour, the carjacker lost control of the car. It sped across the median, flipped over into the oncoming lane, was hit by a pickup truck, and pushed down an embankment. Phones passed from hand to hand so everyone could see the mess that resulted. From the helicopter overhead, the Mercedes looked to be nothing more than mangled steel. Maggie wondered if the young man had survived.

"Oh, dear," Clare moaned. "I wanted him caught, but I didn't want him dead."

"He might not be," someone said. Maggie recognized the man as a former Scottsdale police officer. "I've seen people survive accidents worse than that. He could be injured pretty bad though."

The helicopter remained hovering above the accident site while police cars and then an ambulance arrived. The seniors watched the entire time — mesmerized. It looked like the young man had survived. They saw him being wheeled toward an ambulance.

"They got him!" Clare breathed out the words, but Maggie heard them clearly. And the relief in her friend's voice.

CHAPTER 15

Maggie and the other quilters waited until Bridget was alone, then approached her en masse, each of them hugging her in turn.

"How are you managing?" Victoria asked. "You just let us know if you need any help."

Bridget swallowed hard, touched by their kindness. Her voice cracked as she thanked them. "Thank you. I appreciate it."

"Are you eating?" Louise demanded, checking her with a searing glance. "You've lost weight."

Bridget pressed a hand to her stomach and managed a wavering smile. "I'm well on my way to finally losing those ten pounds I've wanted to drop for years."

Maggie admired the strong character that allowed Bridget to find humor at such a difficult time.

Louise smiled. "Remember that you do have to have some nourishment. You just let us know if you want some meals dropped by."

"Between you and the knitting group, I'll be gaining back those ten pounds in record time." Bridget attempted another smile, but failed, her mouth pulling down into what appeared closer to a grimace.

Bridget gestured to Maggie and the others as she rose and went out into the courtyard. "Why don't you all join me out here. There are some tables set up, and it's a bit more private." As she lowered herself into a chair, she also lowered her voice. "Are you working out who might have killed my Kathy and our precious Matt?"

"Of course," Clare quickly seated herself in a chair next to Bridget.

"We've been talking about it," Maggie admitted. "Clare has known the Romellis for years, and she's been concerned from the start that Rusty will be blamed."

Bridget nodded eagerly. "That's my worry too. But Rusty would never . . ." Bridget's voice broke and she stopped as though unable to discuss the murder itself. She took a deep breath, swallowed.

Louise, who had just seated herself, instantly arose. "You look about ready to collapse," she scolded. "I'm going to get you some sweet tea. The sugar will replenish you. You know Kathy wouldn't want you to get sick over her loss. You have to stay healthy."

"I know." Bridget patted Louise's arm. "Thank you."

They made weather-related small talk until Louise returned with Bridget's tea. The previous night's temperatures had dipped into the low forties, but with the sun shining, it was quite comfortable outside. People continued to pass through the courtyard on their way to and from the break room, but no one interfered with their little group.

"Here you go," Louise said, placing the mug on the table before Bridget. "I put milk and sugar in the tea, and even brought a selection from the snack table."

Louise sat, but when Bridget didn't reach for something, she took a sugar cookie sprinkled with yellow and blue sugar crystals and shaped like a star and put it on a napkin in front of her.

Bridget smiled weakly. "Thank you, Louise." Bridget glanced around the table. "Please, tell me what you think about all that's happened. The police don't tell me anything, and I'm at a complete loss. Everyone loved Kathy." Tears gathered in her eyes.

"We don't really have anything, at this point," Maggie said. "Michael said the same thing — that everyone loved Kathy. It's a tribute to her memory."

Bridget didn't comment, but Maggie thought she seemed a little brighter.

"There's not a lot of information available about what happened," Clare said, her disappointment evident in her voice. "We hoped one of her neighbors might have seen someone, but no one did. No one even heard the shot."

Bridget winced at the final word, and Maggie's heart went out to her.

"Do *you* have any suspects in mind?" Maggie asked. "Maybe someone Kathy had trouble with?"

Bridget shook her head. "Everyone loved Kathy. She was such a good person." Bridget ended with a sigh. "A little naïve perhaps, but always ready to help someone out. I'm afraid people took advantage of her sweet nature."

"Rusty says Kathy agreed to attend counseling with him that last day," Clare said.

"That's true." Bridget stared at her mug, turning it in circles with gentle touches of her finger. "I talked to Kathy earlier that week." She lowered her voice and looked up. Her hand dropped to her lap. "I'd learned something about Dylan that I thought she ought to know. I wanted her to

154

be aware of the kind of man he really was — a different person from the man she thought she knew."

This news excited Clare, who was anxious to hear it for herself. "What did you learn about Dylan?"

"Do you know Bill Gallagher?" Bridget asked.

Most of the women nodded.

"Not personally," Theresa said. "But I know who he is."

"He was a good friend of Sean's, my late husband," she added, glancing at Theresa, the newest and youngest member of the quilt group. "He's been a good friend to *me* since I lost Sean. He would have been at the funeral except that he had knee surgery on Monday, and I told him he was not to show himself or I'd be very upset. The surgery had been scheduled for quite some time and if he'd tried to reschedule, it would probably have been a couple of months. You know how all the snowbirds have their elective surgery while they're here, so the surgery schedules fill up. I know he's been in pain, so I told him he didn't need to appear. I know how he feels, and there were others there to offer support. Like all of you," she added, tears appearing in her eyes.

Maggie noticed Edie tapping her fingers

quietly against the table. She wanted Bridget to get on with it, while Bridget felt the need to explain the absence of her dear friend.

Bridget took a sip of her tea, swallowed, and looked up and around the table, her eyes resting on Maggie. "In any case, Bill called me that week before Kathy died."

Maggie noted the delicate phrasing for the terrible fact, and exchanged a sad look with Victoria.

"Bill was invited, along with several others, to meet with Dylan about an investment opportunity."

Edie scoffed.

Bridget looked her way, surprised at her reaction. "Are you aware of Dylan's projects?"

"No," Edie replied. "I'm just naturally suspicious of anything called an investment opportunity. I guess it's that the word 'opportunity' suggests a special honor, when really they just want you to give them your money."

Bridget stared at her for a moment. "I do believe you have the right of it," she finally said.

"Was there something odd about the investment?" Victoria asked.

Before she began her story, Bridget took a bite of the star cookie and put it back on the napkin, then washed it down with a sip of the sweetened tea. Louise patted her arm in approval.

"As I said, Bill has been a good friend to me since Sean died. He knew Kathy was engaged to Dylan — knew they were already planning the ceremony for the New Year. So when he was invited to this meeting, he thought it would be a good chance to finally get to know Dylan. He also said that with interest rates so low, he's open to new investment opportunities."

Bridget paused to take another sip of tea. "You were right about this sweet tea, Louise. It actually tastes good. It's been a while since something tasted good," she added. Maggie's heart went out to her. The sadness in Bridget's voice was palpable.

"What about Dylan's investment plan?" Edie asked.

Bridget swallowed more tea before continuing. "Bill said it sounded good. Dylan asked several potential investors to dinner at a nice restaurant. It was in a newly developed area, one of those places where there are lots of stores scattered around, and they call it a marketplace."

The listening women nodded. There had been a lot of talk at the Quilting Bee about whether these new shopping areas were better than malls. While they seemed to have a wide variety of stores and restaurants, most of the Quilting Bee women preferred indoor shopping in the aging malls, as it got so hot in the Arizona summers.

"Bill said that kind of situation can make for a good investment because it's often done in segments, so a later investor can evaluate how well the first segment is doing."

"Seems sensible," Edie acknowledged.

"Bill said the dinner was good, the food outstanding. Dylan was a good host and an excellent conversationalist. He didn't make his sales pitch until the coffee and dessert course. Bill said it was all very well done."

"Everyone has always said that Dylan really knows how to pull out the charm," Louise acknowledged.

"Oh, he does," Bridget agreed. "That's how he won Kathy over so quickly. I never thought she'd want to marry again, unless it was to remarry Rusty. Of course, she was so broken up over the divorce, she was an easy target for a smooth-talking man."

"You sound like you don't really care for Dylan," Maggie suggested.

"Oh, I like him well enough," Bridget said. "But I've always been very fond of Rusty, you see, so anyone else would be a hard sell.

The thing about Dylan . . ." She paused as though collecting her thoughts. "I guess I always felt that there was more to him than the charming face he showed the world. Nothing I could ever put my finger on. Until the call from Bill."

"So what was the problem?" Edie prompted.

"Bill said that Dylan made his pitch very skillfully. It sounded like a good deal. A *very* good deal. Dylan said he would be developing the property adjacent to the existing one, the one where they'd just had that lovely dinner. Bill said they could all see that it was a successful venture. The place was full of customers — the restaurants and shops both."

"So what was the problem?" Maggie asked.

"He showed some professional drawings of his proposal, mentioned some companies that showed an interest. Good, solid companies. It was as they left the restaurant that Bill began to wonder about Dylan. They stood outside for a while, near the undeveloped area, and commented on all the activity at the adjacent complex. Dylan was going on about how the two would complement each other. How he'd planned it that way from the beginning. And that was the problem."

Edie raised her eyebrows, but refrained from speaking.

"Bill said he was surprised and asked Dylan if he owned the first property. His understanding was that he only owned the new, adjacent site. Dylan claimed it was all his, all the way down to the next intersection, which gave at least a quarter of a mile of undeveloped potential. But, he told them, he already had all the investors he needed for that first segment, so only the new section was open for investment. He called it stage two, with a stage three planned sometime in the future."

The women listened carefully.

"Bill said that's when he became suspicious," Bridget continued. "Because Bill knew the man who had built that particular complex — a friend from his days at Stanford. And as far as Bill knew, his friend had been the one to develop the property. But he hadn't spoken to his college friend for some time, so he figured he'd give Dylan the benefit of the doubt. Maybe his friend had sold the property to Dylan, and he was merely exaggerating his participation to make the new opportunity sound better."

"It sounds like Dylan may have a bit of the con man in him," Theresa said.

"Yes, I'm afraid he does," Bridget affirmed. "And more than a bit, after what Bill learned. I must admit it was hard to greet him politely at the funeral. I'm glad he didn't come back for the lunch. He said he had a meeting he had to get to."

"I saw him and his brother at the church," Clare said. "Chad treated me at the ER the other day."

"Yes, I heard about that." Bridget put her hand on Clare's arm. "I'm so sorry." Then her face clouded. "Chad worked with Kathy for years. He's the one who introduced her to Dylan, you know."

"Did he?" Maggie threw a quick look around the table. No reason to let Bridget know they already had this information.

Bridget nodded. "It was at one of those gala charity fund-raisers for the hospital. She and Rusty were there and seated at a table with Chad, Dylan, and their dates. Chad later told Kathy that his brother was totally smitten with her. She reminded him that she was married. She said Chad got irritated and said he thought she would be flattered that a handsome, wealthy man like Dylan would be so taken with her."

"Humph," Edie muttered. "He doesn't sound like a prize."

"No wonder Gerald didn't take to him."

Theresa winked at Clare.

"He and Kathy didn't really get along. She was always pressing him about what would be best for the patients, and Chad felt he knew it all." Bridget frowned, and Maggie imagined she was remembering the conversations she'd had with Kathy over this same topic.

"It's that old God complex that some doctors have," Louise said.

"Let's go back to Dylan and his investment opportunity." Once again, Edie was impatient with the constant diversions. Still, Maggie was glad she'd managed to use the tactful "opportunity" rather than investment "scheme."

"Yes, what did your friend learn from his college friend?" Louise asked.

"This is the part I learned early that week, before . . ." Bridget swallowed hard, and her listeners all knew what words she could not bring herself to say. For her to utter the words "before Kathy's murder" was just too painful for Kathy's mother to articulate.

"Bill managed to connect with his old friend and learned he had *not* sold the property. But Bill had also checked county records and learned that Dylan's company was listed on the title as the owner."

"Wow." The soft word escaped from an

excited Clare.

"The plot thickens." Edie slid a glance at Clare, as though offering the words for her friend.

"So *did* he own the property?" Maggie asked.

"Bill's friend swore he didn't. But it took him a while to figure out what had happened. Apparently Dylan had filed a transfer of title just the way you would if you'd purchased the property. Except that he hadn't. Bill said he'd heard of this once, on some cable television show that was covering a story of large-scale financial fraud."

"Wow," Clare said again. "Do you think that's where Dylan learned how to do it?"

Edie's brow furrowed. "I don't recall hearing about this. Dylan's a well-known developer; it should have made the news."

"No. You haven't heard about it because it hasn't come out." Bridget paused. "*Yet.* Bill reported it to the attorney general's office, and he was told they would investigate. I'm sure they'll try to keep it quiet while they do that."

"It's interesting that *Chad* introduced Kathy to Dylan." Maggie leaned in toward Bridget. "Because Hal told me something the other day that has had us wondering. Hal remembered that Rusty told him he never knew where Kathy got those ideas about him cheating, but that it happened right after he returned from a plumbing expo in Las Vegas. The remarkable thing is that Rusty hadn't been planning to go to the expo — didn't even know about it. He got everything in the mail — plane and expo tickets, hotel reservations — all packaged up as some kind of award. He said he'd never heard of the group, but he checked on the expo, found it was legit, and thought it sounded like a good opportunity — so he went."

Bridget stared at her. "It's so long ago now, but I think I remember that. Kathy thought about going with him — she asked if I was available to stay with Matt. But then she had to work an extra shift to cover for someone."

Maggie, Clare, and all the others exchanged significant looks.

"Don't you find that odd?" Maggie asked. "That the tickets appeared out of nowhere, then Kathy suddenly has to work when she was supposed to be off? And right afterward, she decides Rusty is cheating on her?"

"It's more like a mystery novel than real life," Clare said.

"Oh, dear." Bridget wrung her hands, the first time Maggie ever remembered seeing a person actually do what so many novels described. "If only Kathy was here to explain these things. She never would talk about the divorce, you know. She thought that if she ignored bad things, they would go away. It was her biggest flaw. If something bothered her, she just ignored it, acted like it didn't exist."

"Did that work?" Theresa sounded amazed.

"Not really, but she claimed it did." Bridget sighed. "Kathy was a wonderful daughter, a wonderful person. But everyone has a few faults."

The number of people passing through the courtyard had lessened and then stopped, and they hadn't seen another person for quite some time.

Clare glanced at her watch. "Goodness, the morning is half gone already."

Maggie thought it best that no one succumbed to speaking the old adage: "Time flies when you're having fun." None of this had been "fun."

"Has there been a reading of Kathy's will?" Clare looked directly at Bridget. "Any indication there as to who might benefit from her death?"

Theresa looked from Clare to Bridget, her eyes sparkling. "Do they really do that? Get

165

everyone together and read the will, like in an Agatha Christie novel?"

"Nothing so formal," Bridget replied. "I'll be seeing her lawyer — well, *our* lawyer — later this afternoon. But we think we know what's in the will."

Bridget's brows drew together in a troubled frown. "We *think* we do," she said again. "The truth is, Kathy was planning to change her will."

Maggie frowned. "Did she not get a chance to actually do the changes?"

Bridget tilted her head forward and lowered her voice. "I know she met with her lawyer to draw up a new will before the wedding. Kathy said that it was time she took Rusty out and left everything to Matt and her new husband."

Clare gasped. "She wrote Dylan in as her heir?"

Maggie knew exactly what Clare was thinking. Motive. A quick glance around the table told her that all the other Quilting Bee members were thinking the same way.

But Bridget shrugged. "I'm not sure. I don't know if she ever signed a new will. If not, then Rusty will get everything." She sighed. "And he deserves to. They had almost fifteen years together, most of them very good. It was only there at the end . . ."

Maggie and Victoria exchanged a sad look. There was no doubt in Maggie's mind that Bridget still cared deeply for her former son-in-law.

"Of course, Kathy wanted Matt to have everything." Bridget's eyes overflowed with tears. "Who would have ever suspected that they would die together?"

The women looked down at the table, at each other, at the tubs of chrysanthemums in the courtyard — anywhere except at their friend on the edge of losing her composure. So Maggie was shocked to hear Edie begin speaking in the pedantic style she adopted when she wanted to impart what she felt was important information.

"It is actually something that must be considered, especially by young families. Parents *do* sometimes die together in car accidents or even in plane crashes, and they should have provision for underage children. They should also consider who they want their estate to go to if their children predecease them."

Bridget gaped at Edie, and Maggie wondered if Edie had forgotten that Bridget lost her parents in a small plane crash. She had been an adult at the time, but it still seemed indelicate somehow.

"Do you know what time Rusty dropped

Matt off at Kathy's that day?" Maggie asked. No need to specify she meant the day of the murders. That dreadful day was uppermost in all their minds.

"They were returning from a Boy Scout meeting, so it must have been around four. Why, is it important?"

Maggie explained about the package delivery Bella remembered, and them wondering if the delivery man or even a thief might have seen something important.

"I'll try to remember to ask Rusty," Bridget replied.

As they all rose to head back to their respective craft rooms, Bridget checked her watch and sighed. "Wednesday was Kathy's day for a manicure. We'd sometimes go together, maybe have lunch beforehand. I don't know if I'll ever be able to go back there."

"She had a regular manicurist?" Theresa asked, excitement in her voice. "Is it near here? My regular person moved, and I don't care to travel all the way to Pinnacle Peak to get my nails done. I've been looking for someone closer."

"It's right over here on Indian School," Bridget said, giving Theresa the name and location. "Ask for Julie, and you can tell her I recommended her. She was a good friend to Kathy too. I know she used to talk to her and claim to feel better afterward. Nail therapy, she called it."

Maggie exchanged a look with the others. This might be exactly what they needed.

As soon as they were back in the quilt room and seated at the frame, Theresa glanced eagerly around at the others. "What do you say about having a girls' day out and getting our nails done? It will be lots of fun."

CHAPTER 16

The morning had been tiring, with the excitement of the robberies and police chase, then the long conversation with Bridget. Maggie was relieved to be home, relaxing in her favorite chair, Rosy curled up at her feet. She was working on a pillow top for the gift exchange, a thirties-era pattern with appliquéd flowers and embroidered leaves and stems.

"Now, who can that be?" she asked Rosy when her doorbell rang. Not waiting to hear if Maggie had a suggestion as to who it might be, Rosy raced for the door, barking — though whether in greeting or alarm, Maggie could not tell.

To Maggie's surprise, Rusty Romelli stood at her door. He immediately squatted, to better pat Rosy. And probably so as not to scare her, Maggie realized, as he was a big man.

"Matt was always asking for a dog," he

said, stroking Rosy's head and back. "Maybe if I'd gotten him one . . ." He paused, shaking his head. "The might-have-beens can kill you, you know? Kathy was never keen on a dog, especially one that would be large enough to qualify as a real watchdog."

Maggie smiled as she lifted Rosy into her arms. "Oh, I don't know. Even a small dog like Rosy here can make a lot of noise. She has the potential to scare off a casual burglar, I'm sure. And she always lets me know when someone approaches the door."

Rusty frowned. "You're right. Sometimes the little ones make even more noise than the big dogs." He stood and gave Maggie a beseeching look. "May I come in?"

"Certainly. I'm sorry. I didn't mean to leave you standing at the door."

Maggie ushered him into the living room, reaching for the remote to turn off the television as Rusty took a seat on the sofa.

"Bridget told me the Quilting Bee is looking into this for us, and suggested I come and tell you about the will." He ran a hand through his thick hair, making it stand up in all directions. He needed a haircut, but he'd probably been too busy — and too grief stricken — to notice, Maggie thought. "Bridget was right about Kathy planning to redo her will. She *had* talked to her lawyer

171

about changing it."

He paused, and Maggie thought he expected her to say something. "Did she want to include Dylan, as Bridget thought?"

Rusty nodded. "But before she was due to go in and sign the new will, she called him again and said she didn't want to have Dylan in the will after all. Told him she had broken off with him." He paused, swallowing hard. "The new plan was to leave everything in trust for Matt. Bridget and I would be guardians of the trust until Matt graduated from college or turned twenty-five, whichever came first."

Maggie nodded. "It was a good plan. But was that new will not signed either?"

Rusty shook his head. He sat forward in his chair, raking his hand through his hair once more. Maggie noticed that he was starting to look a bit shaggy. In addition to the need for a haircut, he had a two-day growth of beard, and his shirt was a wrinkled mess. The poor man, she thought. With everything he'd had to handle in the past week, haircuts and ironing were probably very far down the list. She was surprised at Gen, though. Surely she would iron his shirts for him.

"Kathy hadn't been in to sign the new will because she had just talked to him about it.

Just a few days before . . ."

Maggie noted that he, like Bridget, could not mention the terrible way Kathy died.

"So . . ." Rusty swallowed, and Maggie could see his Adam's apple move with it. "He was having the new will drawn up when she . . . when she died. So the old will is still in effect, the ones we drew up when we got married and amended after Matt was born." He sighed. "I figure this makes me the number one suspect in her murder, though I don't understand how they could ever think I would kill my son." He sighed again, a deep rumble that must have emptied his lungs. Rosy, ever alert to the feelings of those around her, ran over and jumped up beside him. Rusty patted her, attempting a smile that never reached his eyes. "Even that prissy lawyer eyed me suspiciously and said it might take a while to probate. I'm sure he meant until he sees whether or not I'm arrested." He frowned, then broke down completely. Great racking sobs came from deep in his chest.

Maggie didn't know what to do. Finally, she decided doing nothing was probably best. Just let him cry it out. She picked up the box of tissues she kept near her chair and crossed over to him. With his hands over his face, Maggie didn't think he was even aware of her nearness, so she put the box on the table beside him and returned to her chair. Rosy put her paws on his thigh and tried to comfort him, but he was too deep in his grief to even notice. But Rosy was not easily discouraged. She licked his chin, then his tears, and eventually her canine kisses seemed to break through to him.

Maggie indicated the tissues she'd placed beside him, and he pulled several from the box.

"Thank you."

"Don't let his attitude get to you," she told him. "You have to go on as best you can. And meanwhile, we'll talk it out the way we usually do and see if we can turn up any good news for the police."

CHAPTER 17

Thursday, December 10th; 15 days before Christmas.

Theresa greeted the other quilters with a smile on Thursday morning. "I've made the arrangements for our manicures this afternoon." Maggie thought she had the look of a child announcing a birthday party as she looked at the others seating themselves around the frame. "I called Clare and Victoria yesterday to make sure it was okay. Julie had a cancellation, or we would have had to wait *two weeks* to get in with her. She must have a lot of regulars."

"That's good," Edie said. "The sooner we hear what she has to say about Kathy, the better."

"I thought we might have lunch together beforehand, what do you think?"

Clare and Victoria agreed that that was an excellent idea.

"There's a salad bar just down the street

from the nail salon," Theresa told them. "If that's all right with you, we can go there. They advertise organic ingredients. And that way we only have to park once."

"Sounds good," Maggie said. "I'll join you for lunch."

"I wish I could join you," Louise said, "but Vinnie and I are doing some Christmas shopping after Senior Guild. It's hard to get him to go shopping, so I don't dare cancel. But if you decide to go again, I'll join you for sure."

"It's also getting too late to put off shopping much longer." Maggie grinned at Louise. "What is it with men and shopping, especially at Christmas?"

"Carl is good about going with me if I ask him to." Theresa smiled, a bit on the smug side, as she knew how lucky she was. "And he always takes me dress shopping for my birthday. He comes along and gives his opinion on what I choose. It's nice."

While the others exclaimed over Theresa's luck to receive such a special gift each year, Maggie watched Clare. Clare continued to stitch quietly, not commenting on Carl's gift or how lucky Theresa was to have him. Maggie wondered if she'd even heard Theresa's comment. There was evidently something lying heavy on Clare's mind. Maggie had to address her twice before she responded.

"I haven't been sleeping well," Clare complained — or perhaps apologized. "There are too many things going on." She squinted at the needle she was trying to re-thread, as if lack of sleep was affecting her eyesight.

"Clare, you have to let this go." Maggie stopped stitching to give Clare one of her no-nonsense looks. "You're worrying too much about the Romelli murders. I'm sure the police will work it out. And we're doing all we can to help them out with the personalities involved. You know that's your strong suit."

"I *am* worrying about Rusty," Clare admitted. "He's really the nicest young man. He's always polite, and he comes right away if we have any plumbing problems, no matter the time." She pushed her needle into the quilt top and turned it with her thimble, taking three small stitches. "I always thought that he and Kathy had such a wonderful family. Like everyone else, I was shocked at their divorce."

"It was the same on Kathy's side, if you recall." Maggie snipped a thread before continuing. "Bridget and all her friends were just as shocked. We all thought they were the perfect couple."

Clare passed Maggie a spool of thread. "I just wish we could do more to help. Rusty won't be able to relax until he knows what happened to Kathy and Matt."

"And everyone stops looking at him and wondering if he did it," Edie added, receiving a pained look from Clare.

"They always talk about closure," Theresa said, tugging at her thread to bury the knot in the quilt sandwich. "I've always wondered about that. Do you really need what they call *closure*? Or could you deal with an unsolved murder and get on with your life?"

Being the best qualified to answer since she'd had some psychological training, Louise replied. "Every person is different, but lots of people do deal with it. Not every murder is solved, and the family members left behind don't shrivel up and die. I'm not saying it's easy for them to deal with not knowing. That has to be incredibly painful. Perhaps Rusty needs to see a professional. I can give you some names to pass on to him," Louise offered.

"Maybe I could pass it along to Rusty's parents." Clare sighed, a deep, heavy exhalation of breath. "We saw Rick and Gen last night. They were still *very* upset."

"Was Matthew their only grandchild too?"

178

Victoria asked. Maggie silently thanked her for moving away from Edie's comment — which had annoyed Clare.

"No, but he was the only boy. It's going to be really hard on Rick — Rusty's father, you know. They're both named Richard, so Richard senior goes by Rick and Richard Junior by Rusty." Clare shook her head after this, as though she had to remind herself where she'd been going with the conversation. "Rick used to do a lot with Matthew and Rusty. They would go camping and fishing a lot in the summers. I don't think Kathy was the outdoor type."

"She did always seem very elegant and stylish," Victoria said. "Though that doesn't preclude her from enjoying a campout."

Edie harrumphed. "Elegant and camping rarely go together."

"What did Gen and Rick say about Rusty and how he's coping?" Maggie asked.

"Gen says Rusty is just devastated. He was upstairs — we didn't see him. Gen said he'd finally agreed to take a sleeping pill. She says he's barely slept at all in the past week, and she's really worrying that he might kill himself — and someone else — on the road by falling asleep while driving. And she's really mad about the way the reporters are making it sound like Rusty is to blame."

"Do *they* have any idea about who might want to kill Kathy?" Edie asked. "Because it seems obvious that someone wanted to kill Kathy, then probably shot Matthew when he saw it happen."

Clare's eyes were bleak. "They don't have any idea. Everyone loved Kathy. Gen said it's driving Rusty crazy trying to figure out what happened. Of course, he's thinking it must have been Dylan, but I doubt he has any proof. He just doesn't like Dylan because Kathy was planning to marry him."

"Everyone says Dylan can be very charming," Maggie said. "But perhaps his kind of charm appeals more to women."

"Good point." Theresa reached for a needle grabber, one of the little rubber circles that would help her pull a reluctant needle through the fabric. "Why would he want to kill the woman he planned to marry?"

"Probably because she didn't want to marry him anymore," Anna said.

Clare shrugged. "According to Gen and Rick, Rusty told the police he thinks Dylan did it. And Michael said his alibi isn't foolproof."

As Clare thought this over, Maggie thought she looked more like her old self — definitely an improvement.

"Bridget thought Matt and Rusty got to the house about four." Clare looked around at the others, clarifying that was what they remembered also. "Then he and Kathy talked for a while. The early news shows didn't have the story, it wasn't on until ten. That's not a huge time frame for the murders to happen."

"And it's even less than between four and ten," Victoria said. "It would have taken some time for the TV stations to get the story. As you say, Rusty spent some time there at the house talking to Kathy. And by the time the ten o'clock news came on, all the news stations had reporters standing in the street outside the house. It's actually quite a narrow time span, perhaps no more than three hours."

They stitched quietly for a few minutes as they considered this small window of opportunity. It wasn't a great deal of time.

"Speaking of information that would help . . ." Edie looked over at Clare. "We should find out who profits from Kathy's death. She was a wealthy woman. I would think a will would leave everything to her son, but now that's all changed. So who will get her house and her money?"

"Don't look at me," Clare said. "I would have told you already if I knew."

"Bridget seemed to think it would still be Rusty." Victoria snipped a thread and reached for a spool.

"I forgot to tell you — with so much happening all at once." Maggie paused in her stitching to look around apologetically. "Rusty came to see me yesterday, to tell me about the will." She went on to tell the others what she'd learned.

"Wow, so that really does make him the prime suspect, doesn't it?" Theresa's hands stilled as she stared at Maggie.

"But he won't inherit if he *is* guilty," Louise reminded them.

"What if Rusty is so torn up because he *did* kill Kathy and Matt?"

Edie's question plunged the room into silence — except for an irate Clare.

"What?" Clare's outrage propelled her up and out of her chair. If Louise hadn't reached out to steady it, her chair would have landed with a bang, its back flat on the floor. "How can you *say* that! He lost his only child, and the woman he still loved. Of course he's devastated."

Louise, helping Clare back into her seat, tried to calm her down. "Clare, please, think of your blood pressure."

"I'm sure Edie is just playing devil's advocate," Victoria said. Her quiet voice was

182

often enough to calm everyone down after an emotional discussion. "There is a statistical reason that the police always look at the husband first in these cases. Or, in this case, the ex-husband."

Theresa smiled. "The ex-husband is probably a more popular suspect than the husband."

Sitting once again, Clare did not pick up her needle. She continued to stare belligerently at Edie.

"I'm not saying Rusty *did* murder Kathy and Matt," Edie said, unfazed by Clare's reaction. "But married couples often get into terrible fights. Suppose Kathy and Rusty got into a fight over Matt — or because she didn't want to get remarried — and things got out of control. If he shot Kathy in a passion, then turned around and saw Matt watching him . . . Rusty could have shot him before he even realized what he'd done."

"Kind of a knee-jerk reaction, you mean," Theresa suggested.

But Maggie shook her head. "He would have had to chase Matt out of the house and onto the patio. That's not the kind of mindless reaction you're describing."

Edie frowned, considering Maggie's comment. "I'm thinking of a man reacting emotionally. If he shoots a woman in a haze of passion, he would be slightly out of his mind at that moment. I even wonder if he'd remember doing it afterward."

"That makes a strange sort of sense," Louise admitted. She glanced quickly at Clare. "I'm not saying Rusty did it; I'm just saying that Edie's idea about a crime of passion and temporary insanity followed by amnesia about the event is a plausible explanation."

Theresa nodded. "It sounds like something a defense attorney on a television show would come up with."

Clare could barely speak, she was so upset with this line of inquiry. Louise and Victoria conversed quietly with her, explaining yet again that they were merely speaking of possibilities, and it was good to look at it from all sides. But Rusty and his parents were old friends; Rusty called her Aunt Clare. She refused to consider him a killer.

"What about Dylan?" Maggie took a few stitches as she thought this over. "If the husband is a prime suspect, the new fiancé has to be as well. And there is that business about Rusty's free trip to Vegas and what happened immediately afterward. You know Rusty claims he and Kathy were getting back together, so Kathy must have decided to break if off with Dylan."

"Do you think she'd already done it?" Theresa asked. "Broken it off with Dylan, I mean?"

"Bridget seemed to think so," Louise said.

"The same crime of passion/temporary insanity/amnesia thing could work in regards to Dylan," Maggie said.

Clare seemed appeased by this new theory. "You're right," she finally said. "If Kathy called it off unexpectedly so close to the wedding, Dylan could be upset enough to go into a rampage. Didn't Dottie say he had a temper? And that he liked to get his way? He might have shown up at the house to confront her and gotten into an argument." Clare pulled her needle through and tugged at the knot she wanted to hide. "I heard that the police think she was shot with her own gun."

"I'm not sure we know enough about Dylan's personality to make any suppositions about him," Victoria said. "Many men are capable of harming or even killing their loved ones. But none of us knows Dylan, not even casually."

"According to Bridget, he's nothing but a con man," Clare said.

"And Dottie sure isn't fond of him." Theresa shook her head. "It sounded like Dylan and his brother bilked their mother out of her lifelong home. And when she didn't want to move too."

"Neither of which are violent crimes," Louise reminded her. "It's the kind of crime that a con man will claim harms no one. A victimless crime, they call it. But of course, that's not true, as we all know from the Bernie Madoff disaster. Many, many people were harmed in that case."

"And look at all the people here at the church who lost money with Julian." Maggie still didn't understand that. "They don't seem to be as upset with him as they should be."

"Most of the church investors that Carl and I talked to said they didn't lose any money," Theresa said. "The later investors didn't make much, but they didn't lose either."

"I guess that explains it," Louise said. "It's like that old saying, you know, 'don't poop where you live' — to put it into a more genteel language," she added with a smile.

Clare continued to stitch with a morose expression pulling the corners of her mouth downward.

"Is there something else bothering you?" Maggie formed a small knot at the end of her thread and glanced at Clare as she prepared to stitch.

Clare shrugged, but there was frustration in her reply. "I guess I'm nervous. There's so much happening, and I keep worrying over whether it involves me or not."

"Have you been following the story about the carjacker?" Theresa asked. "That certainly involves you."

"I have. At least as much as I can on television and in the newspaper."

As she watched Clare study her stitches in silence, Maggie realized how downhearted her friend must be. This was the kind of topic that would usually have Clare practically bouncing in her seat. Today, however, she was sitting slumped over and dejected.

"I keep thinking the police will call me in to identify him, but so far I haven't heard a thing." A slight frown marred her expression.

Maggie knew Clare was terribly disappointed not to have heard anything. Maggie imagined that Clare saw herself standing at one of those two-way mirrors so often seen on television police shows, peering through the glass at a lineup of young men in hoodies.

"But how will you identify him?" ever-practical Edie asked. "You said you barely saw him, that he had a hood pulled up over his head."

"You also said that all you really saw was the gun stuck in his waistband," Louise reminded her.

Clare's frown deepened, and her eyes clouded. Maggie felt a sudden wave of sympathy for her friend. Clare, like most of them, led a sedate lifestyle suitable for a retired couple of moderate means. But unlike Maggie and a few of the others, she had no other family in Scottsdale. Or even in Arizona. Clare looked forward to delving into local crimes with the Quilting Bee to add some excitement to her days. She liked to pretend she was an amateur sleuth, like the women in her beloved mystery novels. Jessica Fletcher was her hero, Henrie O and Amelia Peabody close seconds. However, in most cases, the quilters examined crimes they heard about through television or the newspaper. It was unusual to have this kind of personal involvement, although it *had* happened before. And all too often too, Maggie thought.

"The carjacker is still in the hospital, Clare. Michael mentioned it when I spoke to him yesterday. The police haven't even talked to him yet. From what Michael said, I don't think he's been *able* to talk."

"He's lucky to have survived that accident," Louise said.

Anna concurred. "I saw the pictures of the accident scene on the news, and it was terrible." She shuddered. "Just terrible. You couldn't even tell what kind of car it was; it was just a twisted pile of metal."

"The papers said he's a student at ASU," Theresa said. "I wonder why he would try to steal someone's car. Why take a chance on ruining his future?"

"Drugs?" Louise suggested. "So much crime can be traced to drug use."

"The papers also said he was from Yuma," Edie reminded them. "That close to the border, he might be part of a gang, stealing cars here and taking them across the border to sell."

"Have they released his name yet?" Theresa asked.

"No." Maggie was glad they had not. If his name had even a hint of a Latino sound, Edie was sure to begin a rant about illegal immigration. It was bad enough she'd used the word "gang." But, however much Maggie hated to admit it, this time Edie's supposition made a lot of sense. Groups, or "gangs," did indeed steal cars, then drive them across the border to sell. It was one reason why older cars and pickup trucks made desirable targets; the older cars and trucks had less computerization and therefore less security, making them much easier to steal.

"The police will probably approach you later," Victoria assured Clare, "when the young man is recovered, and you might have a chance of recognizing him. They can't take you to the hospital and let you look at just the one person. I believe they have to give you a choice, to be sure you actually do recognize him."

"That must be it." Clare's face softened. "It would be nice to know they have him under arrest. I've been very nervous about driving alone since it happened." She ducked her head, apparently embarrassed by her newfound fear. "Maybe if I could be sure he was off the streets, I'd feel better."

"Oh, Clare, I had no idea you were feeling that way. How awful." Theresa paused in her stitching to look across the quilt frame at Clare. "How did you get here this morning?"

"Gerald dropped me off," she admitted.

"Well, I'll drive to the nail salon this afternoon," Theresa assured her. "And if you need a ride somewhere, you just give me a call."

The others quickly joined in, offering their services as drivers, happy to help Clare out until she regained her confidence and could once more manage to drive alone.

How sad, Maggie thought, that Clare no longer felt safe driving around her longtime neighborhood. That young man in the hospital — if he was the one — had a lot to answer for.

Chapter 18

Sharlene bustled into the break room just as the Quilting Bee women were settling at a table with their preferred drinks. Tea for Maggie and Victoria, Edie and Anna. Coffee for Louise and Theresa. Clare had opted for a cup of hot chocolate. Sharlene's entrance was heralded by jingling sleigh bells she had taken to carrying everywhere. Although almost everyone looked forward to the Secret Santa gift exchange, the bells were definitely becoming tiresome.

Sharlene lifted her arm, waving a clear plastic jar over her head and shaking those irritating bells even harder. There were some slips of folded paper visible at the bottom of the jar. "Not everyone who signed up for the Secret Santa has pulled a name, people. I have ten more names in here. That means you've lost a whole week when you could have been working on a nice gift for the person whose name you pulled."

She began working her way around the room, stopping at each table to speak and cajole. The sound of sleigh bells followed her, letting everyone know where she was at any particular moment.

"She needs to have a master list with all the names on it, then have them check off their names after they pull one," Edie said. "Actually, she should also be keeping track of who has who so that if something falls through, she'll know who to cover."

"It sounds as though you've done this before, Edie," Victoria commented.

"I have done it for another group I used to belong to," Edie said. She tightened her lips as she finished speaking, as if daring anyone to ask what group. It was obvious to them all that she didn't want to talk about it.

Sharlene approached them at that point, and Maggie couldn't help thinking that Edie was probably glad to see her.

"I don't recall seeing you draw a name, Edie," Sharlene said, waving the jar at Edie. Maggie noticed that there were only four pieces of paper in it now.

"I didn't sign up for the Secret Santa," Edie stated, a bit of defiance in her tone.

"Whyever not?" Sharlene said. "It's going to be such fun."

"I have my reasons," Edie said. And before Sharlene could ask about them, Edie went on to tell Sharlene how she should be keeping track of the participants.

Sharlene looked impressed. "You're absolutely right. Obviously, this is my first year trying something like this, and I have some things to learn. Maybe you could help me with it next year, Edie."

Maggie almost laughed at the look on Edie's face. But, to her surprise, Edie was quite gracious in her answer.

"I'll think about it," she said.

Sharlene appeared to believe that meant yes, and moved on to the next table with her jar.

"Is everybody working hard on their gifts?" Sharlene finally called out, apparently done with her circuit. As people around the room called out their progress, she beamed at them, continuing to shake her bells at all the good news. Finally, she waved at the room in general and exited, singing "Jingle Bells" in a pretty soprano voice. To Edie's dismay, she shook her bells in time with the tune.

As they took their places around the quilt frame back in the quilt room, Edie sniffed in disgust. "I don't know if I'm going to be able to make it through the next week with all of Sharlene's good cheer. And those bells!"

"She just loves Christmas," Anna said. "At least she hasn't been in dressed as Mrs. Santa this year."

"It's early yet," Louise said, laughing. Sharlene had been known to appear at the craft mornings in one of her Mrs. Santa costumes. She enjoyed playing the part and didn't see any harm in sharing her joy of the season.

"I think the gift exchange is a fun idea," Theresa commented. "Aren't you enjoying making your gift? That's the idea, isn't it?"

There were murmurs from around the quilt frame indicating that all was well, and yes, they were having a good time with their gift choices. Except from Clare. She frowned. Stitching paused as they all looked over at her.

"That's another thing I'm having trouble with," Clare said, heaving a big sigh.

"I thought you were making a lap quilt for the exchange," Theresa said.

"Oh, I am. Or rather, I started a lap quilt. Then I wasn't sure about the pattern and I put it aside." Clare looked very unhappy.

"I thought you decided on a nine-patch quilt with hearts," Maggie said.

"Like the one we made for Candy," Louise added.

"That's what I started." Clare concentrated on her stitching as she talked, her face down and her words almost swallowed by the quilt. "I did all the nine-patch blocks in Christmas greens, and then I started the hearts. But then I wasn't sure that was the right pattern for Bridget. Or maybe not the right colors."

The other women exchanged looks across the quilt top. Clare continued to look down as though concentrating on her stitches.

"So, did you start something else?" Victoria inquired.

"I was doing the red-and-green theme because it's a Christmas exchange, you know? I used a white-on-white for the contrast."

"That sounds nice," Anna said.

"It was looking good," Clare admitted, finally looking up at the others. "But then I thought it just wasn't Bridget. You know what I mean?" She looked pleadingly around, silently begging them to understand something she found difficult to express.

"But why?" Theresa looked puzzled.

"She's not a red-and-green person." Clare shrugged, not finding the proper words to tell them how she felt when she looked at

196

her quilt. "I don't know. It just didn't look like something that would appeal to her. Like making a black-and-white optical illusion art quilt for Victoria." Clare looked around as several of the women winced.

"You see what I mean? Maybe Bridget would like it because it's a Christmas quilt, but I can't help thinking I could make something she would *really* like. With all she's gone through recently, I want to make her something special." Clare put her needle aside and reached down into the tote bag she'd placed beneath her chair. "Anyway, I started this. See what you think."

Clare brought out several quilt blocks, laying them out on top of the quilt they had in the frame. There were four nine-patch blocks, each done in a different shade of mint green. The contrasting fabric was a tone-on-tone cream that brightened the green even more.

As the women paused in their stitching to exclaim over the pretty fabric and lovely color, Clare uncovered the final block in her small stack. A pretty turquoise bird sat on a narrow brown branch.

"It's a pattern from the nineteen-thirties," Clare told them, and several of the others nodded, apparently in recognition. After years of quilting, they were all well versed in the various patterns. "I decided that the Christmas greens were too harsh a shade. Then I remembered that Bridget likes birds. So what do you think?"

"It's beautiful," Victoria said, and everyone else agreed.

"Bridget will love it," Louise added. "And I think you're right. This is a better color combination for Bridget than Christmas reds and greens. It's perfect."

"That green-and-turquoise combination is just gorgeous," Theresa said. "I'd be thrilled to get a gift like this."

"What will you do with the other blocks?" Maggie asked. "The first ones you made?"

Clare finally smiled, reassured by her friends' reactions. "I guess I'll have a Christmas lap quilt for Gerald and me. Or I might send it to my daughter as one of her gifts. But, you know, I've never made myself a Christmas throw. So this may be my opportunity to have one. Add a little cheer to the family room."

They continued to talk about Clare's quilt and what fabrics and patterns she would use for the rest of the bird blocks. Should they all be the same, or vary the pattern somewhat? Or use different bird patterns for each block? Then they reminisced about other quilts they had done, brought to mind by Clare's quilt.

Maggie, still reflecting on a thirties-style bird pattern she'd once used for a children's quilt, smiled to herself. She thought how pleasant this conversation about quilt patterns had been. So much nicer than murder.

But it seemed they weren't quite finished with bad news this morning.

"Maggie."

At the unfamiliar voice, the women all looked toward the door. Bridget's friend Yolanda stood there blinking rapidly as she made her way slowly into the room. The sun was very bright out in the courtyard, and it could take a few minutes for a newcomer's eyes to adjust to the dimmer lighting inside the workroom.

"Yolanda, come in," Victoria said, rising to offer her a chair at an open spot along the frame. "Did you come to see the quilt?"

"No, I didn't come to see the quilt." Yolanda's cheeks turned pink, and she appeared flustered. "I mean, yes, I'd *love* to see the quilt, but I wanted to talk to you about this latest news."

"What news is that?" Louise asked. "Sit down," she urged, gesturing toward the empty chair between herself and Victoria. Although Victoria had immediately brought forward the extra chair, Yolanda had not taken advantage of it. Or perhaps she'd not even noticed it, Maggie thought, as Yolanda looked at the chair indicated as if seeing it for the first time.

"Thank you." Yolanda sat gingerly on the end of the folding chair, gripping her hands together tightly over her knees. "I came to talk to you about the other bit of news — about that carjacker they caught." She paused long enough to lick her dry lips. "They said he goes to ASU and lives in a fraternity house off campus, one not recognized by the university," Yolanda said.

The others nodded. They had heard the same in the various news broadcasts the previous evening.

"The thing is . . ." Yolanda licked dry lips once again, pausing as she considered what to say next. "You know my grandson Joe is at ASU now."

The women all nodded. "Of course we know," Maggie replied.

"How is he doing?" Victoria asked.

"He's been doing well," Yolanda said. "He's on a baseball scholarship, you know."

The quilters all made the appropriate congratulatory remarks, and Yolanda glowed with grandmotherly pride. "His father was always good at sports too. I'm sure he gets it from him."

"Did he love the quilt you made for him?" Clare asked. Early in the year, Yolanda had approached the Quilting Bee for help. She wanted to make a graduation quilt for her grandson, something special for his dorm room that would keep his grandma in his thoughts. But since she had never done any piecing, she went to her friends in the Quilting Bee for advice. They suggested a simple design of flannel blocks that would have a masculine look and be easy to wash and dry. Clare and Louise took her to choose fabrics, then instructed her on prewashing and preparing the fabrics. When it was time for the cutting, Maggie and Victoria joined them, the four quilters bringing rotary cutters, mats and rulers to lend. Rotary cutters had revolutionized the cutting of quilt blocks, making it fast and easy to cut multiple pieces at once, and Yolanda was duly impressed. Once Yolanda had pieced her top, Edie gave her advice on how to do some simple machine quilting. The result was a beautiful and practical quilt in grays, reds, and blacks with plaids, solids, and prints mixed into a quilt suitable for a hunting lodge — or a young man's dormitory room.

"He *loved* the quilt," Yolanda told them. "He said right away that it would be perfect for his room at school. He said he would think of me every time he saw it — and remember all of you too. I told him how you taught me to make it."

"Aww," Clare said, her eyes suspiciously bright. "He's a great kid."

Joe had been attending the Senior Guild's All Hallows' Eve Bazaar since he was a toddler, so all the women knew him. As a teen, he had helped with set-up and clean-up tasks. He was a tall, athletic boy, and strong, so his help was always appreciated. He was also part of the parish youth group and participated in their quarterly pancake breakfasts and with the Lenten fish fries. All of the Quilting Bee women liked him, which was why they had been so willing to help his grandmother with his special quilt.

"He would have thanked you all himself, but he's been so busy with schoolwork that he didn't make it to the bazaar this year. He told me he missed it."

Then Yolanda's expression changed. Where earlier her face had flushed with pride for her grandson, it now paled to a ghostly white. A small mole high on her cheekbone that Maggie had never noticed before stood out in stark relief.

"One of the reasons he was so busy then was that he decided to do rush week this fall. He was anxious to have the fraternity experience." She ended with a heavy sigh.

Oh, dear, Maggie thought, suspecting where this might lead. "Did he join the house that was mentioned in the news?"

Yolanda nodded. Unshed tears filled her eyes. "He called last night — called his parents, and my son called me. They haven't released the name of that young man yet, but Joe knows." A tear trickled down her cheek, and Louise passed her a tissue. "Joe didn't make the final cut at the house he was really interested in, so he decided to go on with this group. It's a very small house, and he liked that. He says they are great guys — friendly, always willing to help their brothers." Yolanda shook her head at the final word, obviously not very thrilled by the whole fraternity thing.

Maggie wondered if "always willing to help" meant help with studying, or with giving out old exams. She'd heard that fraternities and sororities kept files of old exams for their members' reference.

Yolanda continued to explain. "The fraternity does a lot of good works, according to Joe. They tutor in the inner city, and they had a fund-raiser for the family of that police officer who was killed — the one with the four young children."

There was a brief moment of silence as they all remembered the sad case of the police officer in Phoenix who was killed on his way to work by a drunk driver speeding the wrong way up a thruway exit ramp. The young father had been killed instantly.

"Joe is sure his fraternity brother is the young man in the hospital?" Maggie asked.

Yolanda nodded, her tears gone, but Maggie noticed her knuckles turned white as she gripped her hands even tighter together. "My son put through a conference call so we could all talk together — Joe, my son and his wife, and me. I thought we should go right down and pick him up. Bring him home. There's only another week of classes — or of exams, I should say. Classes are already done. But my son went along with Joe when he said he needs to stay. Something about study groups and getting good grades on his exams."

"You can't fault him for that," Victoria said.

"No, of course not." Yolanda was quick to reply. "But I worry about peer pressure. If that man is one of his so-called brothers . . . well . . ."

"You're right to be concerned," Edie told her. "Peer pressure can get kids into a lot of trouble. They start by getting a friend to shoplift with them, then before you know it, the friend is an accomplice to a murder."

All hands stilled over the quilt. All seven of the other women stared at Edie in shock.

"Edie!" Louise exclaimed.

"How on earth did you get from shoplifting to murder?" Maggie clicked her tongue in annoyance. "You're scaring Yolanda to death."

Surprised, Edie looked over at Yolanda's white face. "Well, I didn't mean to. I'm sorry Yolanda, but you just don't know what might happen when they join these gangs and start to go wrong."

"You think his fraternity is a gang?" Yolanda's voice barely rose above a whisper. Her eyes were wide and frightened.

"It *could* be." Edie wasn't ready to give up on her theory. "Any group of young people can become a gang. It just takes one bad apple to goad the others into doing something wrong."

Yolanda's eyes widened even more as she stared at Edie. "And you think the man in the hospital was a bad apple, influencing his friends to engage in criminal pursuits?"

The Quilting Bee members were stitching once again. But Maggie paused for a moment to look up at Yolanda. "Edie is just talking, Yolanda. She has no idea about those boys. I'm sure most of them are fine young men."

Edie's lips tightened, but she did not comment. She kept her eyes trained on the quilt top as she placed her tiny stitches.

"Your Joe is a good boy." It was Clare's turn to pause in her stitching. She sent Yolanda a reassuring glance. "He knows right from wrong, so I'm sure he wouldn't consider breaking the law."

Somewhat comforted by this, Yolanda tried to smile. "Joe did say everything was fine. He swears his fraternity brothers are all great guys and says he doesn't want to desert them now when there's some trouble."

"That just goes to show his strength of character," Clare assured her.

Smiling now, Yolanda took some time to admire the quilt before returning to the knitting room. Maggie felt sure the entire conversation would be repeated and rehashed there, to the accompaniment of clicking knitting needles.

CHAPTER 19

After their lunch with Maggie and Edie, Theresa, Victoria, and Clare set off for their manicures, laughing like teenagers about their afternoon together. Maggie went home to Rosy, just as happy that the others were ready to enjoy their afternoon, despite the grim occurrence that had led to its setup.

Once home, Maggie discussed dinner plans with Rosy, petting her all the while.

"What should I have for dinner this evening, Rosy?" She put her down while she checked the refrigerator and freezer. Rosy watched carefully, just in case something good should come her way. She already knew that the refrigerator was filled with good things to eat.

"It looks like there's some leftover stew," Maggie finally said. "That might be good for a cold night. What do you think?" She looked at her pet. Rosy's ears perked up and she tilted her head to one side. Her pink tongue peeked out of her mouth, taking a quick swipe at her nose. Maggie had to smile. "You can smell it already, can't you? Okay, stew it is. Good choice." She patted Rosy on the head and closed the refrigerator door.

With her dinner plans settled, Maggie turned on the television and picked up her current stitching project — the appliqué block of blue morning glories with embroidered stems and leaves. It was one of a set of floral blocks from the nineteen-thirties, and she was almost done with the stitching. She thought she'd make it into a pillow for her Secret Santa gift.

It was at least an hour later when her afternoon talk show was interrupted by the station's "breaking news" banner with its urgent-sounding musical tones. Quickly, the screen cut to a serious young woman sitting at the news desk.

"We have just learned of a heavy police presence at a home in Scottsdale." The screen switched to an overhead shot of a large home, police cars, an ambulance, and a fire truck all parked on the street, emergency lights swirling. "We have learned that it is the home of well-known Phoenix businessman Dylan Markham. For now, all we know is that there is a dead body inside.

Police will not be releasing the name of the victim until family can be notified. You may remember that Dylan Markham's fiancée and her son were murdered recently in their Arcadia home, and that case is still under investigation."

Maggie put aside her stitching to look at the screen. Sensitive as always to Maggie's moods, Rosy leaped up into her lap. Her little tongue licked Maggie's chin, and she watched her mistress to see if this small action would help her feel better. Maggie put her hands on the dog, running her hands along the warm, quivering body.

"Yes, Rosy, you are a lovely little dog, and I don't know how I ever lived without you."

There were times when a warm body was infinitely better than a handful of stitching.

Maggie was still trying to process this new information, wondering how it might impact the investigation into the Romelli murders, when her doorbell rang. The others had agreed to stop by when they dropped Victoria off after their manicures, to share with Maggie anything they might learn from Julie.

Her three friends were too happy with their afternoon adventure to notice at first that Maggie was quite solemn. They flashed their hands before her, showing off bright colors and shiny nails. Clare had opted for a lovely shade of pink on her close-cropped nails, Theresa had gone a bit wild with a deep maroon, and Victoria showed off an elegant French manicure.

Victoria was the first to notice that Maggie was barely smiling. "What's wrong?" she asked, putting an arm around Maggie's shoulders.

"Dylan Markham may be dead," she told them.

"What?" Clare's eyes widened, and her mouth fell open for a moment before she snapped it shut.

"They broke into the program just now to announce a dead body at his house. They haven't said as yet whose body it is. But who else could it be?"

"His brother? Another girlfriend?" Clare looked ready to go on with her guessing, but the television was once again breaking for a news flash. Victoria, Theresa, and Clare crowded into the living room just off the entrance, Maggie trailing behind.

Theresa and Clare sat down on the sofa, their eyes on the television screen, which once again showed the overhead shot of the house and the emergency vehicles.

"So that's his own house, not the one

where he grew up?" Clare asked.

"Oh, yes," Theresa commented. "Look at that place. He couldn't have grown up there. It's one of those new McMansions. Much too modern for an older house. I'd say that house isn't more than five years old, tops."

The others must have agreed, as no one objected to her observation.

Maggie took her seat in her favorite chair, and Victoria sat on the matching chair on the other side of the lamp table. As they listened to the onscreen reporter recount the same sparse information in several different ways, Victoria reached over to pick up the quilt block Maggie had set aside.

"I see you're still working on thirties-style blocks. This is really lovely, Maggie."

As the newswoman droned on about a body found in a Scottsdale home, Clare and Theresa looked over. Victoria held up the almost completed quilt block for them to admire.

"I just have to finish up the French knots," she told them.

"That's beautiful, Maggie," Theresa said. "What a lovely pattern."

"I enjoy mixing embroidery with the appliqué," Maggie said, taking the square of fabric from Victoria and picking up her embroidery needle. "It was a fairly popular technique in the thirties, so there are lots of patterns."

As the news briefly changed to "our regularly scheduled program," Clare turned to Maggie. "Wait until you hear about our afternoon," she said.

"Did you enjoy yourselves?" Maggie asked.

"It was very nice," Victoria said, glancing down at her white-tipped nails. "I'd forgotten how pleasant it is to have a manicure. The salon was charmingly decorated, and soothing music played. I found it very relaxing. We should do it more often."

Theresa nodded. "Let's. I liked Julie very much. She was really torn up about Kathy's death, poor thing."

Clare nodded. "Julie's been doing Kathy's nails since before Matthew was born. They were pretty good friends."

"She's a very friendly person," Victoria agreed. "It's a lovely shop. I liked my tech very well too. Leigh. She said she did Kathy's nails a few times when Julie wasn't available. She also said everyone there loved Kathy."

Theresa laughed. "They said she was a good tipper."

"That's not a bad epitaph," Maggie said,

joining the laughter.

"And wait until you hear what they told us," Clare said, almost bouncing in her seat on the plush sofa.

"Well, tell me," Maggie said. She couldn't hold back a smile. Clare was so delighted, and she hoped that meant there was some good information that would lead to the discovery of who killed Kathy.

"Well," Clare began, unconsciously echoing Maggie, "Kathy talked a lot about her breakup with Rusty. Everyone else said she never talked about that at all, so it was a good thing we learned about Julie."

Theresa nodded eagerly. "And you'll never believe who told Kathy that Rusty was cheating on her."

"I've always assumed it was Dylan," Maggie replied. "Though it could have been Chad. But I only learned about him recently." She watched both Theresa and Clare lose that smiling glow of anticipation at sharing something exciting.

"How did you know?" Clare asked.

"I didn't. It just seemed the most reasonable explanation. Dylan was right there to comfort her afterward, and to take advantage of her loneliness. It just seemed likely he was involved. But after learning about Chad and the fact that he worked with

Kathy, I thought he might be a more likely suspect."

Theresa nodded. "Kathy told Julie all about it. Chad attended a conference of some kind in Las Vegas at the same time Rusty was there for a big plumber's expo. He came back with photos of Rusty and some woman, and showed them to Kathy."

Clare was anxious to pick up the tale. "Chad not only showed her the photos he had of them eating in a restaurant, he told her he'd followed them upstairs and saw them enter a room together."

"But did he stay outside the room all night to see how long he stayed in there?" Maggie inquired.

"Oh, I doubt it," Clare said. Then she saw the expression on Maggie's and Victoria's faces and realized Maggie was being sarcastic. "Oh." She laughed, a light titter of a laugh that made the others smile.

"What I don't understand is why Kathy didn't ask Rusty about it," Theresa said. "All she had to do was tell him that someone saw him eating with a strange woman in Vegas and see what he had to say. It was probably nothing at all."

Maggie nodded. "That's all he had, photos of Rusty eating in a restaurant with another woman?"

Victoria shook her head, her expression solemn. "There were also a couple of them hugging and kissing. One in the restaurant, one in a hallway."

Maggie could see what might have happened. "It begins to sound like Chad was as much of a fraud as his big brother."

"Just what I thought," Victoria said.

Theresa and Clare looked from one to the other, puzzled.

"What are we missing?" Theresa asked, gesturing from herself to Clare and back again.

"Chad could put any kind of spin on those photos. Maybe not so much on the one with them in the restaurant, but one taken in a hallway? Unless Kathy was very familiar with the hotel — and there are so many in Vegas — there's no way for her to know if he's telling the truth about where that particular hall is located. Is it outside the restaurant? Outside a room? Right beside the slots room? She would have to take his word for it that the photo was taken wherever he said it was. And the woman could easily be an acquaintance he ran into there. People often exchange a hug and a casual kiss when greeting one another. And then again when parting."

"Oh, I see." Clare sat back, thinking this over.

"But that would be too chancy." Theresa's brows drew together as she thought this over. "If they set Rusty up with free tickets and hotel room and everything, they couldn't just take a chance that he would run into an old friend and kiss her. And that Chad would be there to record it."

"You're right." Maggie frowned. How did she miss this aspect? "It had to be a bigger conspiracy. It's all so over-the-top, but it all makes such perfect sense. Why not find an old female friend of his and offer her the same amazing deal with free tickets and reservations."

They all thought about this for a minute, while the guests on a talk show droned on in the background.

"Julie also told us how Kathy first got together with Dylan," Victoria said.

"Oh, yes," Clare said. "Julie said that Kathy told her she was really upset after Chad showed her the photos . . ."

"Well, who wouldn't be?" Theresa said, interrupting Clare's sentence.

Clare nodded absently and continued. "When Chad showed her the photos, he swore Rusty was visiting this woman in her room. Kathy said Chad told her at the end of their shift — he must have known she would be too upset to do any more work. So afterward, he invited her to come to dinner with him, telling her that she needed some time to calm down. Turned out, he was meeting Dylan for dinner."

"I thought Bridget said they met at a charity event," Maggie said.

"They may have," Victoria said. "So many doctors go to those, and of course, Kathy donated to a lot of charities with medical ties. Perhaps she didn't want to admit all this to Bridget. Both she and Rusty have said that Kathy never would talk about her reasons for the divorce."

"Oh, Kathy had met him before." Theresa picked up the story. "Julie said that Kathy had met Dylan before that night but hadn't really liked him. But that night he really turned on the charm. Gave her a shoulder to cry on, commiserated with her about her cheating hubby. And most important, he didn't try to come on to her, which was the problem in the past."

"Interesting," Maggie murmured.

"Julie thinks they gave Kathy quite a bit of wine," Victoria said. "Maybe told her it would calm her nerves."

"Julie said Kathy hardly ever drank, and she said she didn't think Kathy could handle alcohol because of that." Theresa frowned, her eyebrows drawing together as her forehead furrowed. "Though maybe Kathy didn't drink because she knew she didn't have the head for it."

"In any case," Clare said, "don't you think it sounds like a conspiracy? Dylan wanted Kathy, and he set out to get her, and his brother helped."

"But why would Chad go along with that?" Maggie asked. "He had to tell such a tall tale to Kathy, a woman he worked with. And when she got home, slightly drunk from the sound of it, why didn't Rusty tell her she had it all wrong?"

"Oh, that was the beauty of their plan," Clare said, leaning forward. "I forgot that part. Rusty was still in Vegas, you see. His conference went through the weekend, and Chad had been there for only one day at the seminar he was attending. So Kathy didn't get to see Rusty for another couple of days. By then, I suppose Chad and Dylan had brainwashed her."

There was a moment of silence as they all thought this through, broken only by the drone of the television. The anchors were still repeating what little was known about the situation, though there was now a split screen, with a reporter standing down the street from the Markham house. Emergency vehicles filled the space immediately in front of and around the large house, and Maggie felt sorry for any neighbors just arriving home from work. They were going to have a devil of a time getting through.

"Did Julie know about Kathy calling off her engagement to Dylan?" Maggie asked.

"No, she didn't." Clare sat back up, eager to share. "Kathy went in every two weeks, so she wasn't due in for another week when she died. But Julie said Kathy was really happy when she first got serious with Dylan."

"Yes, Julie said she was delighted to see her that way, because she had been so depressed after throwing Rusty out." Theresa smoothed out her skirt, briefly admiring her newly done nails. "The really interesting thing is that she said that as time passed, Kathy seemed less happy about her relationship with Dylan. Julie thought she was regretting the divorce."

"Now that is interesting," Maggie agreed.

"Julie did say she didn't expect Kathy to go through with the wedding," Victoria said.

Clare was happy to pick up the story. "Julie said that when Dylan proposed, Kathy was over the moon. She talked about a new start and how she might do things differently. But as time passed, she talked less and less enthusiastically about the wedding. They were planning that fancy do at the Desert Botanical Garden, you know."

Maggie nodded absently.

"What was interesting was that Julie said Matt wasn't happy about the wedding, and that had been bothering Kathy. That's why she didn't think she would go through with it. And at her last appointment, she told Julie she might have made a mistake," Theresa said.

Clare spoke so quickly in her excitement to get the words out that Maggie almost missed what she said. "Remember, Bridget said that Matt was going to be best man. Well, I guess he made a big fuss, said that would be a betrayal of his father, and he wouldn't do it."

Maggie ran her hand over Rosy's back, pausing to scratch near her tail. "Do you think Bridget knew?"

"I don't think so." Clare shook her head. "She might have felt embarrassed admitting that to her mother."

"With all Bridget has shared with us, I think she would have mentioned it," Victoria agreed.

"Yes," Clare said. "The last time she was in, Kathy told Julie she might have made a mistake about her ex. That she might have *wronged* him. That's the word she used, 'wronged.' Wait until I tell Rusty. He'll be so glad to hear that." Clare frowned. "Not that anything will make him happy right now, but at least he'll know that she finally believed that he hadn't cheated on her."

"I'm sure it will be a comfort to him," Victoria agreed.

"But so sad that he didn't hear it until after her death." Theresa sighed.

Clare echoed the sigh. "It's a real tragic love story. It's like one of those sad romantic movies that are so popular nowadays."

"Personally, I prefer a love story with a happy ending," Maggie said. "And, while it is sad that Kathy and Matt are gone, I'm sure Rusty must have known she believed in him. After all, she did tell him her engagement was off, and agreed to counseling."

Clare brightened. "That's true. Still, I'm going to let him know what Julie said. He ought to know the truth about that whole episode."

"I just hope it doesn't get too much like a novel," Theresa said. "You know, where the wronged man goes after the guy who victimized him. I'd hate to see him land in jail because he was trying to get revenge."

"Oh." Clare's eyes had widened into large circles. She turned her gaze toward the television screen.

"Maybe you should wait until the murders are solved before you tell him the whole story," Maggie suggested, glancing pointedly toward the television and the station's continued coverage of whatever had happened at the Markham house.

Clare quickly agreed.

Finally, as the four o'clock news began, the news anchor announced that they had just learned the identity of the dead body found in the home of Phoenix businessman Dylan Markham. To no one's surprise, it was the body of the businessman himself.

"The police have not released any other information at this time," the anchor concluded. He and his female counterpart went on to discuss the unsolved murder of Markham's fiancée and her son, and the possibility of a connection between the two.

"This is going to complicate the investigation into Kathy's murder," Clare announced. "It has to. After all, he was our favorite suspect." She ended with a sigh.

Maggie merely raised her eyebrows. Victoria mimicked her expression, adding a small grin, and Maggie had to return a much larger grin. Good grief, she thought.

"I'm turning into Edie, aren't I?" she asked Victoria in a low voice. "Heaven forbid."

Victoria laughed. "Don't worry, dear, you're a long way from that." She reached across the table to pat Maggie on the arm. Then she rose. "We'd better get going. It's getting late. Gerald will be looking for you, Clare."

With the news anchors moving on to other stories, the women said their good-byes and headed for the door.

CHAPTER 20

Friday, December 11th; 14 days before Christmas.

As Maggie expected, the women could barely wait until they were seated around the quilt frame the following morning to begin talking about the death of Dylan Markham. There had been frightfully little information on his death, just the announcement that it was an apparent suicide. The television reporters also included brief summaries of his business career. Interviews with neighbors turned up little except "He seemed nice" and "He kept to himself." Damned with faint praise, Maggie couldn't help thinking. Dylan might have been charming, but it appeared he didn't exert said charm on his neighbors. Maggie suspected that most of them would have had worse to say if they didn't think he had killed himself.

"What do you suppose his suicide means?"

Anna asked. "Can there be a connection with the death of the Romellis?"

"That is the sixty-four-thousand-dollar question," Louise said.

Clare was quick to fill everyone in on all that they'd learned from Julie during their manicures the previous day.

"There must be a connection, don't you think?" Clare looked eagerly from one friend to another as she held her threaded needle above the quilt, ready to begin sewing as soon as the others answered. "Dylan and Chad must have set Rusty up during that trip to Las Vegas, just so Dylan could date her."

"That still seems such an extreme thing to do." Victoria shook her head. "Although I will admit it makes sense that he would be the instigator."

"But why?" Theresa asked. "Dottie said he's always got beautiful women with him at that house that he and his brother own. Why on earth go to all that trouble to get one married woman when he can have his choice of beautiful single women?"

"The one you *can't* have is always more desirable," Maggie said. "The grass is always greener, and all that."

Clare frowned. "They said on the news it was an apparent suicide. I think it means

Dylan killed Kathy and Matt and then couldn't live with himself, so he committed suicide."

Maggie knew Clare wanted them to agree with her, but she also knew that nothing was that simple. "If he did kill himself," Maggie said, "that would be a very neat solution."

"So you don't believe it either?" Dottie had entered the room while they were immersed in their stitching and the provocative conversational topic. No one was aware of her presence until she spoke. "Neither do I."

Maggie rose, gesturing Dottie toward an empty chair. "Come in. Join us for a bit."

"You don't think he killed himself?" Clare asked. Her voice had risen an octave since her previous statement. "But they said it was suicide."

"They said *apparent* suicide," Edie reminded her, and Dottie nodded vigorously. "That just means it *looks* like suicide, but they can't be sure until they investigate. Someone else could have killed him and staged it to look like he killed himself."

"Oh, my gosh," Clare said. "That's just like a mystery novel."

"He was too much of an egoist to kill himself," Dottie told them. There was no doubt in her voice that her theory was the correct one. "Thought very highly of himself, Dylan did."

"I wonder how long it will take for the autopsy and a decision on how he died." Theresa seemed to be thinking out loud, but she did look around at the others to see what they thought.

"If it was murder, there are *a lot* of possible suspects," Louise said. "Bridget told us about his investment schemes, so there are sure to be disgruntled investment partners out there. And Dottie," Louise said, nodding toward their guest, "told us about the rotating girlfriends at their party house, so there might be unhappy girlfriends."

"I'm still not sure we know enough about him to come to a sensible conclusion about his life and death." Maggie frowned down at the line of stitches she had just laid. They looked fine. If only this case was as clear as the line of small, neat stitches. And like Edie, she wondered at the choice of words. To her, "apparent suicide" meant there would be more information coming at a later date. But how much later?

"He was being investigated by the state attorney general's office for fraud," Edie reminded them.

"Really?" Dottie glanced around and the

others confirmed it. "Not that I'm surprised, mind you," she added.

"Bridget told us," Maggie said.

"It hasn't come out yet, about that investigation, but it will. After all, *we* know about it." Edie frowned as she began her next sentence. "Of course, other fraudsters have committed suicide upon being discovered, feeling it is better than being arrested and going to jail."

"The thought of going to jail has to be scary," Anne said.

"Oh, Dylan wouldn't like *that,*" Dottie agreed. "I'm sure of that."

"I grant you suicide is a possibility," Louise said. "From all we've discovered about him, I think Dylan was a proud man, and he would not have liked his financial shenanigans unveiled on the front page of the newspaper. Still . . ."

Louise didn't say more, but she appeared to be thinking about the suicide angle, and Maggie had a feeling she too had doubts.

"The news programs will have the information about the investigation soon enough," Victoria said.

"I think he has — had," Dottie said, stumbling over the change in tense, "the kind of arrogance that would let him feel sure he could beat any fraud charges. I find

228

it hard to believe he would actually kill himself."

"These days it's not the newspapers that create problems," Maggie said. "It's all about multimedia. Television and Internet coverage are the things that upset people now. They can't escape the stuff that's on the Internet, and it keeps getting repeated ad nauseam; it never goes away, even if the person is later cleared. I'm sure Dylan would be familiar with the problems that could cause him in the future. He'd have a hard time getting any more investors. I'm sure."

Theresa agreed. "Now that Dylan is dead, and a probable suicide, the story will be even juicier. Whether it's suicide or murder, the journalists and bloggers will love it."

"Meanwhile, we can't assume that there's any relation to Kathy's murder," Victoria insisted.

"But it *is* a strange coincidence," Clare insisted. "And you know what all the mystery books say about coincidences."

"There aren't any," they all said together, then laughed briefly. Dottie glanced around the room, smiling wryly at the intimacy the group enjoyed. There was a similar camaraderie in the sewing rooms, but it was not the same as here. These women were *very* close; Dottie felt they were much more than sewing friends. Suddenly, she felt like an intruder. But she did want to let them know how she felt about that suicide designation.

"I'll have to be getting back to my own sewing, but I wanted to let you know that I don't believe for a moment that Dylan killed himself." She rose as she said this, but remained standing there beside the quilt frame. "He was an arrogant man, just full of himself. Nothing will make me believe he would take his own life. I'm glad to hear that you have doubts too."

And with that, she fled the room.

Clare looked after her, then around the quilt frame at her friends. "There's so much going on right now. Maybe that's a good thing. I almost forgot about the hijacker." She raised her head. "Maggie, have you heard anything new from Michael?"

"No," Maggie replied. "But perhaps he'll have some news at our brunch on Sunday."

"It would be nice if Dylan killed himself and left a note confessing to killing Kathy." Clare sighed in satisfaction at this neat wrapping up of two cases.

"Like Maggie, I wonder if he did kill himself," Louise said. "Dylan sounds like the worst kind of egoist. The way he bilked all those businessmen. And a narcissist of that caliber is usually too in love with himself to commit suicide. It's the more timid souls who manage to dredge up some courage and actually do it."

Maggie agreed. "I keep going back to the word 'apparent.' Why do they say *apparent* suicide? Why aren't they certain it *was* a suicide?"

"I've wondered that too," Edie said.

"Perhaps they suspect murder but must await the autopsy results," Victoria suggested.

There was a quiet moment of stitching while they all digested this.

"Very likely," Louise finally said.

"And it means there wasn't a suicide note," Theresa said. "Otherwise there wouldn't be any doubt, would there?"

"Oh, no." Clare immediately protested this conclusion. "Some murderers leave fake notes, or even make the victim write one so that the handwriting is theirs. Mystery stories are full of fake suicide notes."

The others had to agree with Clare. For a while they talked about stories they'd read with fake suicide notes and how the killers had created the notes. And whether the investigators had believed in the notes.

"What if Dylan was shot with the same

gun that killed Kathy?" Clare suddenly asked.

"Was the gun missing from the first crime scene?" Victoria looked up from her stitching.

"Now that you bring it up, I don't believe there has been any mention of the gun." Edie drew her brows together as she considered this. "All the reports just say they were both shot."

"If Dylan did *not* commit suicide, and the same gun was used, that will only complicate matters," Victoria replied.

"Complicate it? How?" Clare looked up from her stitching. "Wouldn't that settle both cases?"

"Because, our earlier conjecturings — if there is such a word," Louise said, "had us looking at Dylan as the possible killer of Kathy and her son. So, if he committed suicide with the gun that killed Kathy, then the Romelli murders are solved. But if he did not kill himself, why would he have been killed with the same gun?" Louise looked over to Victoria, to see if she had interpreted her comment correctly, and Victoria nodded.

"Unless Rusty killed all three of them," Maggie said.

"No!" Clare stopped sewing and stared

into space for a moment. "Well, yes, I see what you're getting at." She poked her needle back into the quilt. "But we *know* Rusty didn't kill Kathy and Matt," she insisted. "We'll just have to pray that this was a suicide."

"There's still Dylan's brother," Theresa pointed out. "He knew Kathy, and even fought with her at work. So he can be a suspect. And as far back as Cain and Abel, brother has killed brother for one reason or another."

"Too true," Victoria agreed.

Clare sighed. "What a shame if that beautiful young man killed his brother."

"Beauty is just skin deep," Theresa reminded her. "And after what Julie told us about their shenanigans with Rusty in Las Vegas, he doesn't appear to be a sterling character."

Clare merely sighed again.

"Why do you think Chad might want to kill Dylan?" Anna was puzzled, and her face showed it.

"Well, Dottie said they didn't get along as teenagers," Theresa said. "Remember, she was surprised that they cooperated to buy their parents' home. And once they had the place, they seemed to use it as a party house. So they could have had disagreements about women. Women can really cause trouble between brothers."

"And it's always possible that Chad invested with Dylan," Louise said. "From what we've heard, Dylan's investments were on the iffy side. Chad could have lost a lot of money if he did invest. And I'm sure he would not be happy to learn his brother was scamming him. Money is one of the top motives for murder. And it can definitely cause trouble among family members."

"Too true," Edie said.

They all laughed when Theresa began singing the "Money" song from *Cabaret*. Laughter brought a more relaxed atmosphere to the room and pulled the conversation away from talk of murder. They spent the rest of the time until their break chatting about seasonal plans, taking time to discuss favorite recipes. As they left for the break room, hearts were lighter than they had been for days.

CHAPTER 21

Bridget poked her head around the door of the Quilting Bee room. Since returning from their break, the women had been trying not to discuss Kathy and Dylan, trying for happier stories as they approached the Christmas holiday. Settling back into their stitching after their morning snack — there had been a delicious loaf of Italian bread dotted with fruit, a real holiday treat — Theresa was explaining her plan for a Hawaiian quilt wall hanging, her favorite type of quilt.

"It's too late for this year, of course, but I thought I'd do white poinsettias on a red background." As usual when talking about her passion for Hawaiian quilts, Theresa's face shone and a happy lilt appeared in her voice.

"You may have to line the white fabric so the red doesn't show through," Edie commented. "Otherwise, it sounds very pretty. Bring in the pattern when you have it drawn out. I'd love to see it."

"That does sound pretty," Louise concurred. "And if you don't line the white fabric, the flowers would probably look pale pink, which would still be a lovely look. Poinsettias come in a very pale pink color. Of course, then the seam allowance will show through, and some people dislike that."

"Lining the petals with a light batting would be nice too," Victoria said. "It would give the quilted blossoms a padded look and make them stand out from the background."

It was at this point that Maggie caught some movement in her peripheral vision and looked up. Bridget stood, hesitating, half in and half out of the door.

Maggie stood. "Bridget, come inside. It's chilly out this morning."

There had been a cold rain falling when Maggie took Rosy out for her potty break that morning. By the time she picked up Victoria, it had stopped; however, the sun was struggling to release itself from the grip of thick gray clouds, so the temperature wasn't as warm as might be expected on a sunny winter's day.

Bridget came inside. "Actually, it's warmed up some." She sat in the chair Maggie indicated. "The sun even made a brief appearance." Still, she pulled her jacket close across her chest as she spoke.

They spent a few minutes discussing the weather before Bridget commented on what she'd overheard before stepping inside. "I had no idea so much planning went into your quilts. I guess I thought you just chose a pattern from a book and started to cut."

The Quilting Bee women all laughed.

"I suppose it could be that simple," Maggie said. "But a lot of us prefer appliqué work, and with that, we spend a lot of time deciding on fabric."

"The fabric can make a world of difference to how a design will look," Louise agreed.

"Well . . ." Bridget cleared her throat, and looked over toward Clare. "Actually, I came in because I wanted to talk to Clare."

"Oh?" Edie arched a brow as she looked between the two women. "Can you speak in here? Or do you need to step outside?"

"What is it?" Clare asked. She placed her needle down on the quilt top and waited expectantly.

"I guess I can tell you all," Bridget said. "I decided to step into the church on my way back to the knitting room after my tea break. I've been doing that — popping into the church, to light candles for Kathy and

Matt. It's comforting to light the candle and say a prayer to the Blessed Virgin before I join my group after my break."

"That's nice," Anna said.

Clare agreed. "Did you want me to go in with you?"

"No, no, you don't understand." Bridget stopped Clare from getting up out of her chair. "I've already been inside the church. I lit two candles and said some prayers. I find it very peaceful sitting in the church. The lighting is dimmed, and it's so quiet. And it has that special churchy smell. I'm sure you know what I mean."

"Oh, yes," Clare said. "It used to be melted beeswax and incense, but nowadays it's different."

"Probably furniture polish and carpet deodorizer," Edie suggested in her droll voice.

Maggie frowned, thinking that Edie sure could take the romance out of a setting. Carpet deodorizer indeed!

"Maybe," Clare agreed. "But I like the quietness of it myself. It's so nice if you just want to go in and pray over some decision. Or over something you can't quite understand." Her voice softened at the latter statement.

Bridget nodded as she realized that Clare

understood.

"Anyway, I saw Rusty in there. I'm sure it was Rusty. I don't think he saw me. I was over by the Blessed Mother's statue and the racks of candles, and he was on the other side of the church and toward the back. He was kneeling with his head down on his arms. Clare, his body was shaking. I'm sure he's crying."

"Are you sure it was Rusty?" Edie asked, although Bridget had already said she was. But Maggie thought she might have asked the same thing if Edie had not. If the man had his head down as described, Bridget wouldn't have been able to see his face. How could she be certain of the man's identity?

Bridget didn't hesitate. "I'm sure." Her voice was so decisive, no one else questioned her identification.

There was a moment of silence as they digested the information.

"He's had such a difficult time of it recently, he may find some comfort being in the church, just as you do," Anna suggested.

Bridget nodded uncertainly. "Do you think we should try to see what's wrong? Try to help him? Or do you think we should let him be?"

Clare's forehead wrinkled in sympathy. "Oh, dear. Do you think we should try to comfort him?" Clare directed the question to Louise.

"The poor man lost his son and the woman he claimed was the love of his life. And just before getting her back too. You've both said how upset he's been. Let him be. He's probably praying, same as you. Perhaps he's asking God to help him find some peace."

The others agreed.

"More like railing at God for taking his family," Edie said. When the others stared, she shrugged. "Anger is one of the early responses to dealing with death."

No one had anything to say to that. They all knew she was right.

"He's just very discouraged right now, and it probably makes it harder that it's the Christmas season," Louise told her. "In all probability, it makes him feel even worse to see everyone else celebrating with their families when he no longer has his own."

Bridget sighed. "I have to sympathize with him there. I have no Christmas spirit this year either. It makes me cry every time I see the things I had already purchased for Kathy and Matt."

"If you'd like," Victoria offered, "I could

come by and pick up and return those things. It might be good to get them out of your house."

"Thank you, Victoria, that's very kind. But I've already decided to donate them to the St. Vincent group to distribute. They should be picking them up soon."

"Aren't you doing the Secret Santa exchange?" Clare asked. "Didn't you sign up right after Thanksgiving, when Sharlene first suggested it?"

"Yes, I did. It was before . . ." Bridget stopped, but they all knew what she left unsaid. She took a deep breath and continued. "I tried to tell Sharlene I couldn't do it." She ended with another sigh.

Louise understood the latter sigh. "She wouldn't let you, would she?"

"No, she wouldn't. Said it would cheer me up, give me something to do."

"She has a point," Maggie said.

"I tried, Maggie, really I did. But I just could not get up the energy to start a new project, even a small one."

But Edie had an idea. "Surely you have something you've made in a closet, something that might be perfect. I know I have lots of finished projects stashed away."

Bridget remained silent as she thought over Edie's suggestion. Then her eyes brightened. "I do have several simple afghans that I keep to give out to sick friends. I pulled a man's name from the jar, so an afghan would probably work well. Thank you, Edie."

"It will be good to see you at the gift exchange party on Saturday," Louise told her. "You need to start getting out. Staying at home just allows you to brood. It's not healthy. And you're still losing weight."

Bridget agreed that she would probably enjoy the party, then left after asking what they would be bringing for the potluck.

"Bridget seems to be showing more interest in food," Maggie said. She knew Louise was concerned about Bridget's weight loss.

"It will take her a long time to recover from losing Kathy and Matt," Victoria said. "But I agree that having her ask about potluck recipes is a good sign."

Maggie would have preferred to return to talk of recipes, but Clare had other ideas.

"That poor man," Clare said, pausing in her stitching as her thoughts returned to Rusty. "Are you sure we shouldn't try to go to him in the church, Louise? See if we can help?"

"I don't think anything we do can help him right now," Victoria said.

"And he knows where to find us if he

wants to talk," Maggie added.

Louise agreed. "He's grieving, Clare. Just allow him to do it in his own way."

Clare sighed, but finally nodded her agreement. She pushed her needle into the quilt top and began laying a line of stitches.

"It never stops hurting, losing a spouse," Maggie said. "But, over time, you learn to go on. You have to. Rusty will discover that, but he has to do it himself."

"Or, you can take the easy way out, like Dylan Markham did, and kill yourself," Edie commented.

Clare gasped. "You don't think Rusty . . ."

"Edie was just thinking out loud," Maggie reassured Clare, shooting Edie a not-now look. One side of Edie's mouth pulled down, but she didn't say anything more.

"Dylan Markham wasn't a Catholic," Anna reminded them. "He probably didn't know that suicide is a terrible sin. One of the worst. That's why they wouldn't bury suicide victims in the consecrated cemeteries years ago. But Rusty knows. He wouldn't do it."

Clare seemed comforted by this.

"He will get over this terrible grief," Victoria assured Clare. "But it will likely take a very long time. He's lucky to have his parents and Bridget — and you and Gerald too. You all care about him, and that's sure to help."

Clare nodded, but the sadness remained in her eyes.

CHAPTER 22

Sunday, December 13th; 12 days before Christmas.

As soon as the Browne family sat down for brunch on Sunday morning, Michael's brothers bombarded him with questions. They wanted to know about Dylan Markham, and how his death affected the investigation into Kathy's murder. And what about that carjacker — was he still alive? Why was there so little information about him?

"Let the poor man eat before you interrogate him," Kimi urged. As Michael's girlfriend for the past several months, his brothers didn't object to her standing up for him. So they reluctantly held off on their questions until the meal was almost over. That also allowed the children to finish eating and head off to play, eliminating the danger of them hearing something unsuitable.

With the main topics of interest put on

hold, Maggie turned to Frank. "Did I see you at Kathy's funeral? Near the back of the church?"

"Yes. It was a nice service. But I didn't go to the graveyard or the luncheon. I had to get back to work."

"It's a shame you missed the luncheon," Maggie told him. "The funeral committee outdid themselves."

"I heard that Rusty broke down at the graveside," Hal said.

"He did. It was terribly sad. It happened when he went to drop the roses on the caskets. His legs just gave out and he fell to his knees." Maggie bowed her head as she remembered his pain.

Sara and Merrie both murmured at how difficult that must have been.

"Just dreadful," Maggie agreed. "To our surprise, Dylan Markham stepped up and helped him. He put his arm around Rusty's shoulders and helped him up and back to the seats at the graveside. I would have thought those two would not get along at all, but it was quite a touching scene." With a little shake of her head, she took a sip of her coffee. "The ex-husband and the fiancé. Though, according to Bridget, Dylan was the ex-fiancé."

"And now he's dead too," Sara said. "Do

you think he killed Kathy and Matt and that's why he committed suicide?"

When neither Michael nor Kimi provided an answer, Maggie added her comment.

"I'm not convinced he *did* kill himself. That word 'apparent' could mean that the police suspect foul play and are awaiting test results."

"Good call, Ma," Hal looked to his brother. "You may be right. What about it, Michael?"

With a heavy sigh, Michael continued to eat. He'd finished his waffles, eggs, and bacon, but he'd taken another bowl of fruit. He stared down at it as if eating melons and kiwi were the most important thing in the world.

Bobby chuckled. "I don't think he wants to talk about it."

Kimi, sitting beside Michael, put her arm around his shoulder and squeezed. Watching them, Maggie hoped again that Michael might finally settle down. She'd love to have Kimi as a daughter-in-law, and there was always room for more grandchildren. But she'd never ask Michael his intentions; he could not be rushed. She would have to wait until he made a decision and decided to share the news with her.

"It would tie up both cases nicely if he *did*

commit suicide." Hal checked the other family members for agreement.

Michael remained stubbornly silent.

"I suppose that would be a good movie ending, but real cases probably don't tie up so nicely." Maggie spread some jam on her last piece of toast. "This prickly-pear jam is excellent, Sara."

"Thank you." Sarah asked her to pass it along, and Maggie started it on its way down the table. "And you're probably right about the murder/suicide thing being too theatrical to be real." But she looked again toward Michael and Kimi. "So, how does Dylan's death affect Kathy's case? There must be a connection, don't you think?"

"It's pretty damned complicated," Michael replied, surprising Maggie. She knew her boys used swear words, all men did. But, like their father, they usually did not use foul language in her presence. Granted "damn" wasn't especially foul; she used it herself at times. But it was still uncharacteristic. And it must mean that the case was more difficult than usual. "And I'd rather not say anything more about it," Michael finished.

"Of course." Maggie looked carefully at her younger son's face, then motioned to her other sons to leave him be.

"In other news," Maggie continued, "we learned that Kathy had regular manicures. So Theresa decided to make an appointment and go over to check it out. She, Clare, and Victoria did a ladies' afternoon and went for manicures."

"Don't tell me," Michael said. "And they interrogated the poor nail tech while they were there."

"The 'poor nail tech' was eager to share information," Maggie informed him. "And we finally got the story about her breakup with Rusty."

She went on to tell them about Rusty's trip to Vegas, Chad Markham, and the photographs he'd shown Kathy.

"Wow." April's eyes had widened as the full story came out.

"I'm kind of surprised Kathy bought that," Frank said.

"We wondered about that too," Maggie admitted. "But the brothers apparently ganged up on her and gave her a lot of wine, which she was not used to drinking. Julie said she did not hold her liquor well, and that's why she rarely drank."

"That's true," Frank said. "I seem to recall an incident at a class reunion." He glanced quickly at his mother and did not elaborate. "Kathy was naïve and gullible. If they told her Rusty was cheating and showed her some photos, she would probably take them at their word."

"So we were right to think that trip sounded suspicious." Hal sipped his orange juice, looking over the glass at his mother.

Maggie nodded, glancing over toward Michael. "We think Chad and Dylan arranged that elaborate hoax just so Dylan could get a foot in the door with Kathy. It seems extreme, but I remember someone saying that Dylan was very arrogant and always got what he wanted. He might have gotten his brother to help him seduce Kathy. I'm sure she wouldn't have given him a second look while she was married. And the one you *can't* have always seems more desirable than the one who's available."

"On second thought, this whole thing does sound like a movie script." Sara looked at her sisters-in-law for confirmation, and they both nodded their agreement.

"And poor Rusty." Maggie picked up her coffee cup, but did not take a drink. "Bridget came into the quilt room on Friday. She'd stopped in at the church to light a candle, and found Rusty in there. She said he was at the back, on the other side of the church. That's a rather dark corner when the lights are low during the day, and he was kneeling with his head on his arms. She thought he might be crying."

"He was probably praying for his lost family." Sara brought the coffee carafe over to Maggie to heat up her cup.

"I've tried to call him a few times, and he never returns the calls." Hal frowned. "Maybe I should try to drop in on him."

"I think he's been staying with his parents," Maggie told him. "Clare says his mother has been trying to get him to eat and sleep regularly, but it's a difficult job."

"I can't imagine that kind of loss, much less coping with it." Sara had tears in her eyes as she looked at her husband and sons.

Hal stood, put his arm around her, and kissed her cheek. "We're all fine," he assured her. "And we will remain that way. Ma and Michael will see to it."

General laughter softened the mood, while Sara continued her round with the coffeepot.

"What about that carjacker?" Frank said. The car chase and smashup were still appearing on local news broadcasts, although little information had been released by the police or the hospital.

"Yes, what's happened to him?" Merrie asked. "Is he still alive?"

"It was a horrid crash." April shuddered,

arms crossed on her chest, hands gripping her upper arms.

"It's amazing that no one else was injured in that accident," Sara added. "The car went across three lanes of oncoming traffic, didn't it?"

"Oh, yes." Michael looked satisfied that the man was in custody and that no one else had been hurt. With the change of subject, Michael had dropped his intense interest in his food, and he seemed willing to participate in the conversation once again. "He's still in the hospital, but Detective Warner told me I can go with him to interview him in the morning. His doctors think he'll be well enough to talk then."

"I hope you're being careful, Ma," Bobby said. "I hate to think that happened right there in the St. Rose parking lot. You were there too, weren't you?"

"Actually, I was not," Maggie replied. "Victoria and I arrived after it happened. And I'm always careful; you should know that." Maggie was beginning to feel like a broken record when it came to reporting on her own safety. But even that brief thought made her sad. Would her sons even know what a broken record sounded like? Her grandchildren certainly would not. She might be able to take care of herself, but there was no arguing that she was getting old. Even her clichés were out of touch with today's youth.

Megan, who had returned to the table briefly for another bowl of pudding, glanced at her uncle. "She has Rosy to protect her."

The others smiled at the child's confidence in the pet she'd chosen for her grandmother.

"Maybe if we'd gotten a guard dog, like we meant to," Bobby muttered. But his sisters-in-law all shushed him. To a woman, they felt it was too cute the way Megan had found the perfect dog for Maggie, and now her complete confidence in Rosy's ability to protect Maggie. They could all see that Maggie and Rosy had taken to one another. Rosy currently lay beneath Maggie's feet, napping after a romp through the pasture with Hal's elderly Golden Retriever. Rosy opened her eyes briefly at the sound of her name, then closed them when no one called her over. She was already back into her nap. Dreaming of lizards and dog biscuits, more than likely, Maggie thought. Rosy did love to chase lizards.

"The news said the carjacker was a student at Arizona State," Merrie said.

"Yes. I heard that too," Sara agreed. "They said he's from Yuma."

"That's near the border," Frank observed. "Maybe he has a contact in Mexico who can sell the cars for him."

"Now you sound like Edie," Maggie told him with a grin.

"Heaven forbid!" Frank looked horrified and everyone laughed.

"Well, Edie's been saying the same thing. And she started before she even heard the young man's name. She's convinced it must be a gang working together on either side of the border."

"Let's hope we'll find out tomorrow," Michael said.

Sara passed around a platter of waffles for seconds, and for a moment, all the men were busy with butter and syrup. Most of the women passed on seconds, sipping on coffee or nibbling on fruit.

Maggie looked over at Michael. "Yolanda Grant came to see us the other day. It turns out her grandson — you remember Joe, don't you, Michael?" Michael nodded. So did Hal, who often worked with the youth group as well. "It seems Joe joined the same fraternity as the man in the hospital. He called his parents to let them know, and they called Yolanda. She was quite upset. And Edie didn't help any, telling her the fraternity boys comprise a gang and would be leading him into a criminal life."

The other women laughed, and Maggie had to convince them that Edie hadn't been joking.

"Joe's a good kid," Michael said. "But good kids often get caught up with not-so-good friends. It's a shame he got involved with that particular fraternity. It's not recognized by ASU, you know."

"Yolanda said he was turned down by the one he really wanted to join, and he liked that this was such a small group. He swore to his family that they're all nice guys who do a lot of good social projects."

"I hope it all works out," Michael told her, and she wondered if he knew more about that situation too.

"It sounds like you're agreeing with Edie, Michael," Hal said. "About the fraternity brothers drawing Joe into their web of crimes." With the final phrase, he dropped his voice to a low bass to better narrate his idea and create the proper atmosphere — rather like the voice at the beginning of an old radio suspense program. Her sons might not remember those, but Maggie did. Another sign of her age, Maggie thought, with an internal sigh of resignation.

Michael put a piece of waffle into his mouth and shrugged. "No way to know.

Time will tell."

Hal and Frank laughed. "Got any other clichés for us?" Frank asked.

Once again everyone laughed. Maggie was glad that the atmosphere was lighthearted even though the subjects were so serious. So close to Christmas, it should have been even more so, she thought, releasing her breath in a soft sigh.

"Meanwhile, has there been any progress in finding out who is stealing from the parked cars?" Merrie asked. "Do you think this man in the hospital is involved?"

Michael frowned. "No, there's no progress, and it's damned frustrating. I took four reports yesterday from people who had parked on the street or in their own driveways and lost things from their cars." He shook his head. "I'm still baffled as to why no one has ever seen anyone suspicious around the cars."

"You're right," Hal agreed. "With the large number of thefts, the odds should be in your favor. *Someone* should have caught sight of a person or of people at least hanging around, or attempting to break into their cars."

"I hate the paperwork," Michael told them, and his brothers all laughed at his mournful expression. "I have to be nice, but

I have to admit I had no sympathy at all for the idiot yesterday who parked in his driveway and left his cell phone and laptop plainly visible on the front passenger seat. He kept shaking his head and saying, 'but it was in front of my own house,' like he actually had a fence and a security system."

"Dumb," Frank agreed. "You've been warning people for over a week. I always put my car in the garage, and I *still* don't leave stuff like that in it. Why take chances?"

"Asking for trouble," Hal agreed.

"Happy holidays," Michael said with a sigh.

"Is this kind of thing only a problem around the holidays?" Merrie asked.

"No," Michael admitted. "It's always a problem, but it's usually worse around Christmas because there's so much shopping going on. And people will put large shopping bags in their cars and then just leave them there while they go in and eat dinner." He threw out one hand in frustration at the idiotic way people could behave, and almost knocked over a glass of iced tea. He quickly steadied it with his other hand. "This year, it's completely out of hand. For once, I'll have to go with Edie and say there has to be a gang of people involved."

"Someone has obviously perfected a

method of getting into the locked cars," Hal said. "Solve that, and you'll have your man. Or men."

"Oh, is that all?" Michael threw a small tangerine at his brother.

Hal caught it without even blinking and lobbed it back at Michael. Before it could spread to the others, Maggie stepped in.

"Boys!" Maggie brought out her no-nonsense voice, and both of her sons suddenly sat up taller and became busy with the rest of their meals. "Honestly," Maggie muttered. Beside her, Sara stifled a giggle.

"Hal." Maggie stacked her empty plates and looked toward her oldest son. "Have you learned anything about Julian Chasen?"

Relieved to be out of the doghouse, Hal grinned. "Oh, did I." He glanced over at Michael. "It turns out your federal investigation isn't exactly a secret. Everyone I talked to seemed to know about it. I broached the subject by implying that you were concerned about him, Ma. I said you thought he might have cancer as he'd gotten so thin. That's when they all said, oh, no, not cancer. Just worry over whether he'd be going to jail for the next twenty years."

Maggie frowned. "Did they all know he was running a Ponzi scheme?"

"Not until they heard about the investigation. But word about that kind of thing spreads quickly in the financial community, so once someone suspected it was a Ponzi scheme, everyone heard about it. And the Feds can never keep information from leaking out; you must know that, Michael."

"So it's just stress causing him to look so thin and run-down?" Maggie frowned. "I still think he looks ill."

"I'd think that facing twenty or more years in jail could do that to a person," Sara said.

"The white collar–criminal diet," Frank said, and everyone except Maggie laughed.

Maggie frowned. "He had a *lot* of clients over at St. Rose. Do you think they'll be able to get their money back?"

"It's too late now," Hal said. "With an ongoing investigation, they'll have frozen all his accounts."

Michael nodded his agreement. "Eventually the court will work something out and try to distribute his assets. But they won't be able to recover much."

Hal agreed. "Sad but true. They'll be lucky to get ten cents on the dollar."

"What a mess," Maggie said. She pulled her cup of milky coffee closer and took a long sip.

CHAPTER 23

Monday, December 14th; 11 days before Christmas.

The Quilting Bee women had not been stitching for long when a weeping Yolanda entered their room. Bridget came in behind her, hand on her arm for support.

Clare rushed forward. "What's wrong?"

Bridget led Yolanda toward an empty chair, glancing up at Clare. "It's her grandson. She thinks he's been arrested."

"She only *thinks* he's been arrested?" Edie asked. "She doesn't *know*?"

"I'm not sure," Yolanda replied, her voice soft and reedy.

Bridget patted her friend on the back. "Yolanda, tell Maggie and Clare and the others all about it. They'll know what to do."

Yolanda dabbed at her eyes with a damp tissue and looked up. Her eyes were puffy and bloodshot, and Maggie wondered how long she'd been crying.

"Oh, Maggie. I don't know what to do," Yolanda wailed. "They raided the fraternity house this morning. It was on the news while I was making breakfast. I couldn't eat after I heard. I think they arrested all the young men. And Joe . . ." Her voice broke, and she was unable to continue.

Maggie had turned on the morning television news show while she had her breakfast, and the lead local story was about a police raid on the off-campus fraternity house Yolanda had told them about. Much had been made over the fact that ASU had expelled the fraternity two years ago for alcohol and hazing violations. Also, the fact that the raid had taken place at four o'clock that morning. The reporter speculated that the police wanted to be certain all of the members were at home when they arrived, and fraternities had a reputation for late nights.

The women made sympathetic noises, which seemed to help Yolanda. Bridget handed her some dry tissues, and she wiped her eyes and cheeks.

"Joe called his father from jail." At the final word, she wailed once again.

"From jail or from the police station?" Maggie asked.

"Those are two very different things," Edie told Yolanda. "And it's an important distinction."

Victoria, who had slipped out of the room shortly after Yolanda arrived, returned carrying a tray of mugs. Steam rose leisurely from the mugs as she handed them around, beginning with Yolanda and Bridget, and ending with herself and Maggie. Maggie accepted the mug and took a tentative sip. Comforting fragrance tinged the steam that rose from it, the aroma of chamomile, if she wasn't mistaken. Victoria always knew just what to bring for comfort. It was a shame she'd never had children, as her mothering instinct was good.

The Quilting Bee women had pushed their chairs back from the quilt and were sipping their tea, listening eagerly to all Yolanda had to say. Yolanda tasted her tea, holding the warm cup in both hands, and appeared to calm down.

"Oh, dear, now I'm confused. I think he said the police station. But I heard about the raid on the news, and they showed some of the boys in handcuffs. In their pajamas!" She gulped, and quickly put the tea mug back to her lips. Maggie wasn't sure if she was sipping or merely inhaling the aroma, but whichever it was, it seemed to be working to relax her.

"Did your son get him a lawyer?" Clare asked.

"He said he was going to, but I haven't heard back from him." Yolanda glanced at her watch. "Not since around six thirty or so."

Everyone wearing a watch checked on the current time, even though there was a clock prominently displayed on the wall above the closet. Nine twenty.

"Have you tried calling him?" Victoria asked.

Yolanda shook her head. Both hands remained wrapped around her mug of tea but she did not attempt another sip. Aromatic steam still rose from the mug. Yolanda raised it to her lips, but then pushed it back down without taking a sip.

"I didn't know if I ought to bother him." Yolanda picked up one of the damp tissues littering her lap and once again dabbed at her damp cheeks.

"Perhaps you should call now," Louise suggested. "If he's busy, you can leave a voice mail."

"Good idea," Bridget murmured.

Yolanda looked into Bridget's eyes. Bridget nodded, taking the mess of damp tissues from her hand and disposing of them in the wastebasket. Then she took her mug so that her friend's hands were free.

Yolanda reached for her phone; Maggie hadn't realized her purse was still hanging on her shoulder. The women listened as Yolanda placed the call. To her obvious surprise, her son answered right away. "Jerry," they heard her say. Then she didn't say anything for a full ten minutes as she listened to her son. They could hear the squeak of his voice, but no distinct words.

The women trying to eavesdrop felt better as they saw the tension ease from Yolanda's face. As her body relaxed, they too began to unwind. When she touched the screen to end the call, Yolanda smiled at all of her friends.

"Oh, thank you all for being such good friends. You were right, Edie, about distinguishing between a call from jail and one from the police station. Jerry says Joe was just taken in for questioning and hasn't been arrested." Yolanda slumped in her chair with relief — as much as one could slump in a metal folding chair. "And he doesn't think he will be."

"The news said the raid had to do with the recent thefts in Scottsdale," Clare said. "The Tempe and Scottsdale police are working together on it, they said. That has to make it complicated, having two jurisdictions involved."

"Did Jerry say whether Joe knew anything about the thefts?" Bridget asked.

"He said he doesn't."

Maggie sipped her tea, marveling at how much better Yolanda looked since hearing from her son. It would take time for the puffiness around her eyes to disappear, and the redness too. Though there were eyedrops that could take care of that, if she had any. But aside from that, she appeared to be back to her usual self. Amazing how worrying over our families can affect us, Maggie thought.

"I wonder what the police learned from the man in the hospital," Clare said.

"Michael told me they weren't going to interview him until this morning," Maggie told them. "Perhaps they had information from someone else leading them to suspect that the fraternity was involved in the thefts."

"It would be wonderful if they can find the people responsible for the thefts and stop them," Clare said with a wistful sigh. "Michael thought perhaps that man who came up to my car was only trying to steal my bags, remember, Maggie?"

"He did."

"So they may have caught him now," Bridget told Clare. "He may be one of those men they picked up this morning."

"Wouldn't that be nice." The wistfulness in Clare's voice made Maggie's chest tighten.

CHAPTER 24

As the women returned to the quilt room after their break, Clare stopped suddenly. Anna almost walked into her, and might have fallen if Louise hadn't been quick to react and grab her arm for support.

"Clare!" Edie's indignant voice scolded. "What on earth are you thinking, stopping like that with no warning? If you were driving, you'd have been rear-ended, and serve you right. It's a good thing I didn't have a cup of tea in my hand, or it would be all over the floor — or down the back of someone's dress."

But Clare was staring out the open gate into the parking lot. She raised her hand, pointing. "That's Rusty's truck out there."

Maggie's gaze followed Clare's pointing finger. "That white pickup? Clare, there are dozens of white pickups just like that around here. All the contractors seem to have white trucks."

"No, she's right." Victoria was squinting toward the vehicle in question. "You can just make out the words on the door. See? He has one of those magnetic signs. 'Romelli and Son Plumbing.'"

Clare grabbed hold of Maggie's wrist, her fingers digging into the soft flesh. Maggie hoped she wouldn't end up with a bruise.

"Do you think he's in the church again? Like Bridget told us about the other day?" Without waiting for any agreement or argument, Clare headed for the church. Maggie, still held by Clare, was carried along beside her. The other women exchanged glances and followed.

There's nothing like a big, almost-empty church, Maggie thought. The air is cool and sweet, the atmosphere quiet and holy. Clare finally released Maggie's wrist as they entered the wide doors and stopped to bless themselves with the holy water. As quietly as possible for a group of seven senior citizens, the women entered the nave. Since Bridget had been lighting a candle when she spotted Rusty, they turned automatically toward the statue of the Virgin Mary with its attendant rows of candles.

Now it was Maggie's turn to take Clare's wrist. She led her into a pew, and the others followed. Kneeling briefly, the women quickly said a short prayer, signed themselves, sat, and looked around. Because the church was built in the form of an arc, from their vantage point at one end they had a good view of the entire space. There in the opposite corner, barely visible in the dim light, was a man doubled over in a pew. He appeared to be praying, and praying hard. If Maggie had come upon him unawares, she would have guessed he was asking forgiveness. Since she knew it was Rusty, she wondered if he was asking God how he could take his family from him. Blaming the Almighty was one of the stages of grief. She just hoped Rusty could get past it and manage to return to his regular life. Things would never be the same, but he was young and should be able to overcome this terrible ordeal. Eventually.

With a pat on the arm and a gesture with her head toward the door, Victoria brought Maggie back to the present. Maggie nodded briefly to Victoria, then took Clare's arm. "Time to go," she whispered.

Back in their room, once more seated around the quilt frame, the women stitched soberly and quietly for a long moment.

"It breaks my heart." Clare swallowed a

sob and rapidly blinked to hold back her tears.

Louise, seated beside her, patted her shoulder in sympathy. "It's a terrible thing, but he has to work it out for himself."

"It's just like Bridget said." Anna's voice remained soft and low, as if they were still seated in the church.

"The poor man is trying to find his way," Victoria said. "No one can do it for him. He'll work it out, and asking God's help is a good thing."

CHAPTER 25

Maggie sighed when she let Michael in that evening. He looked exhausted. She gave him a hug, pulling his head down so she could kiss his cheek. When had her baby grown so tall? Rosy danced around their feet, anxious for her turn at some affection.

"Were you working that bad accident at McDowell and Hayden?" Maggie asked. "I saw some overhead pictures on the news. It looked bad."

He nodded, leaning down to pat Rosy. "Traffic control. Lots of looky-loos." He straightened, following his mother into the kitchen. "It was terrible. Three teens are dead. None of them were wearing seat belts. The driver is in critical condition. And if he survives, he'll have to live with the fact that he killed three of his friends." He sighed. "And the parents have to deal with losing their children barely a week before Christmas."

"Oh, Michael." Maggie looked over at her son, knowing that it must have been hard on him seeing three young lives snuffed out, and for no real reason. Her heart went out to him and to the parents whose children were gone. The teens would be celebrating Christmas with Mary and Jesus this year, and she hoped that would bring a measure of comfort to the families. It would be a difficult holiday for all of them, just as it would be for Bridget. And Rusty.

Michael took a deep breath, and Maggie could see his body physically relax. "Ma, your kitchen always smells so darn good. Good kitchen smells always say home to me."

"You're sweet." Maggie chuckled as she removed a pan from the oven. "I hope you enjoy this. I got the idea at the funeral luncheon on Tuesday. Comfort food," she added.

Michael peeked over her shoulder at the bubbling brown contents. "Are those pork chops with mushroom gravy?"

"They are." Maggie smiled. "And I also have macaroni and cheese, apple sauce, and broccoli. What do you think?"

Michael grinned. "After a day like today, nothing could be more perfect." He glanced around the kitchen. "There's dessert too, right?"

Maggie swatted him with a dish towel. "It's a surprise. You'll have to wait like a good boy."

Laughing, they sat down to eat. Maggie took a mouthful of macaroni and cheese, savoring the nostalgic flavor as well as the thoughts it provoked. She'd made many a pot of mac and cheese when her boys were growing up. It was one thing that they all ate without complaint, and that everyone in the house enjoyed. Even Harry, her late husband, had liked macaroni and cheese — as long as there were pork chops or a steak to go along with it. Maggie smiled at the memory.

She looked up just in time to catch Michael slipping something to Rosy, sitting sedately beside his chair.

"Michael! Don't feed her from the table."

"Aw, Ma, it won't hurt if I give her a little something. I'm not here that often."

Only every week, Maggie thought. But then, she spoiled Rosy too, even if she did not feed her during her own meals. So she had to forgive Michael, albeit grudgingly.

Then she noticed that his plate was already empty. The poor boy had probably missed lunch again. He reached for the pork chops, and she passed him the bowl of apple sauce. As she returned to her meal, she checked out her son's face once more. Not only had his features relaxed since his arrival, his eyes had a sparkle in them now that he had good food in him.

"Were you able to have lunch?"

"I got a hamburger. Things didn't get crazy until later."

Maggie had not forgotten that Michael had been asked to join Detective Warner when he questioned the injured carjacker. She'd wanted to give him time to enjoy his dinner before she quizzed him about it. His implication that the morning had started out well made her think it was okay to begin. "So what happened this morning at the hospital?"

Michael finished chewing a bit of meat before replying. "Now that went pretty well." His lips curved into a slight smile. "Better than expected actually. With all that happened later, I'd forgotten that the day got off to a good start."

"I'm glad to hear that." Maggie placed her fork and knife on her empty plate and rested her arms on the edge of the table while Michael told her about the visit to the hospital that morning. And continued to eat. Her sons all had good appetites.

"Apparently young Cody was just having some *fun*." The sarcasm in his voice was unmistakable.

"Terrorizing people by stealing their cars was his way of having fun?" Maggie's eyebrows rose.

"He says he wasn't trying to steal the car, that he was robbing cars in the parking lot when the man came out of the church and saw him; shouted at him. He ran, shoved the guy out of the way, saw that he'd dropped his keys, picked them up, and took the car. As he took off, he could see that the guy didn't get up right away, so he was scared. Then he was spotted and pursued by an officer in a patrol car and panicked. That's how he ended up losing control of the car."

"If he was scared, he should have stopped and turned himself in," Maggie commented.

"That's too logical for a young kid in the midst of a crime. The adrenaline rush probably added to his bad choices."

"How old is he?" Maggie asked, wondering at his word choice of "young kid."

"Eighteen. He's only a freshman."

"Like Joe," Maggie said with a sigh. "That's young, but still . . ." She ended with a sad shake of her head.

"The stealing was some kind of dare

275

among his fraternity brothers." Michael put some meat in his mouth and chewed.

"Unbelievable." Maggie shook her head in disbelief. "Does the university know how they're having *'fun'*?" She didn't have to place quotation marks around the word "fun" with her fingers; her voice did it for her.

"I checked on that myself. The fraternity is part of a nationally recognized group, but they've been in trouble before. They live in a house off campus, and the university doesn't recognize them. Personally, I'm thinking that they don't get the best pick of incoming freshmen for that reason. It sounds like only half of them are involved. In any case, we'll be talking to all of the other brothers."

"I'm sure you're already doing that. Yolanda was very upset about the raid this morning. She thought Joe was under arrest. She looked like she'd been crying for hours."

"You know it was the Tempe police who raided the fraternity house."

"Of course I know. The house is obviously in Tempe. I assume the university police may also be involved. But the news said it was a joint effort with the Scottsdale Police Department. It seemed like it had to be a joint operation, since they also said it had to do with the recent thefts in Scottsdale."

"Joe hasn't been arrested," Michael reminded her. Or perhaps he didn't realize she knew that and was *telling* her.

"I know, Michael. Yolanda called her son and learned that. She was sobbing her heart out, thinking that Joe was languishing in jail. We told her he was probably just taken in for questioning, but she didn't really believe it until she talked to her son. She said he got a lawyer for Joe."

"Then you shouldn't be concerned." Michael said. "He's in good hands. As for Mister Cody Garcia, he's scared stiff and talking as fast as he can."

"Garcia, huh? And does he have relatives in Mexico?" Maggie gave Mexico the Spanish pronunciation.

Michael nodded. "His mother is Anglo. His father's family has been in the United States for many, many years, mainly in the Tucson area. But he does have a few relatives in Mexico." Michael used the American pronunciation.

"So it wasn't a case of stealing cars to sell across the border? Like Frank suggested? And Edie," she added with a smile.

"No, nothing like that."

"It sounds like he was very cooperative,"

Maggie said.

Michael appeared to have finished with his seconds, so Maggie collected the dirty plates and took them to the sink. On her way back to the table, she retrieved dessert from the warming oven. "Since I had all these comfort food dishes, I thought I'd make some apple turnovers for dessert. I used to make them all the time when you were young, remember? But it's been a long time. They smell good."

"I remember," Michael said, helping himself to two of the warm pastries. "Is there vanilla ice cream?"

"Of course," Maggie said, bringing the carton of ice cream and a scoop.

As soon as she returned to her seat, she went back to asking about his morning interview. "Were Cody's parents there with him?"

"Hmm-hmm," Michael mumbled, his mouth full of apples and ice cream. "They've been here all week. Cody's aunt — his mother's sister — lives here in town. His parents came as soon as they heard about the accident and are staying with her. They seem like good, law-abiding people who are bewildered by their son's bad choices. She works for a day care, he sells cars. They engaged a lawyer for Cody, and had him there this morning. They all urged Cody to cooperate." Michael frowned. "His father told him that everyone knows the first to talk always gets the best deal."

Maggie had to smile. "That's true, isn't it?" She'd passed on dessert herself, being full from the meal, and was just watching her son enjoy his. But she would have one of the turnovers later, after her dinner settled. They must have turned out well; Michael certainly seemed to like them. She'd send the rest home with him and keep just the one for herself. His buff physique could deal with the extra calories much better than her aging body.

"This is delicious, Ma. You should make some for the Sunday brunch. I'll bet they would go over really well."

"Why, thank you for the compliment, Michael." Maggie was surprised to see her big strong son blush.

"You know how much I like the meals you make for me, Ma. I hope I tell you often enough."

It was Maggie's turn to get emotional. She felt tears dampen her eyes. Of course she knew how much Michael appreciated her meals. Just the way he attacked the food — as he had just this evening — proved that. But there was something special about hearing the words spoken.

Maggie was sure Michael would be uncomfortable if this conversation got any sappier, so she tried to remember what they had been discussing before the compliments began.

"It can't just be on television that the first to talk gets the best deal."

"No, that *is* usually the case. But the police can't promise a deal; that's up to the prosecuting attorney. In any case, the lawyer agreed with the father, and Cody told us all that he knew. At least, that's what he claims."

Maggie was sad to hear her son's cynicism, but she supposed it went along with being a cop. "Was he the one who tried to steal Clare's car?"

"He says not."

"Do you think it might have been someone else from the fraternity? Having *fun*?"

"It's quite possible. From what he said, I think at least half of the fraternity is involved in the thefts. There are only a dozen of them; the house isn't very big, so it limits membership."

"If that's the way they have fun, that's a good thing," Maggie said. "So how did they know to raid the fraternity this morning? The news said it was about the thefts in

Scottsdale. But you didn't talk to Cody until this morning, and the raid was at four a.m."

"It turned out Cody was able to communicate earlier, but his lawyer put off his formal interrogation until this morning. He felt he should be stronger before he had a formal visit with the police. However, the lawyer did provide information about what was going on at the fraternity. Detective Warner said they wanted to get there as soon as possible, in case the brothers decided to get rid of all the evidence."

"That makes sense."

"Cody did say one thing that I found particularly interesting," Michael told her. "He says there was someone *not* in the fraternity who was involved. He doesn't know who. He thinks it's an older man and that he's the one handling the sale of the merchandise they stole from the cars. We don't know if that's true, or if it was a ruse so that the record keeper could take a larger share. They had some elaborate system of record keeping and spreadsheets, so that each man profited according to what he brought in. He gave us the name of the fraternity brother who kept the records of their fun little enterprise. Jude Chasen," he said, watching carefully for her reaction.

"Jude Chasen?" Maggie repeated. "I'd say

that has to be Julian's son, wouldn't you? Chasen isn't that common a name."

"I heard that they removed a lot of stuff from the fraternity house," Michael went on. "The guys said there was a TV news truck there recording it all, so you may see it on the news tonight. We all hope it's the stuff taken during those car thefts, but Cody claims a lot of it has already been sold. Your friends who lost things should be hearing from the SPD, getting calls to come down and see if they can identify what they lost."

"That should raise spirits," Maggie said. "And we could sure use some cheering up. There's still a lot of talk at church about the Romelli family and how nothing seems to be happening in that case."

"The detectives are still working on it." Michael frowned. He'd finished his dessert, and Maggie could see that he did not want to talk about this.

"Did the information about the package delivery help at all?"

"I really don't know, Ma. But I did pass it along to Detective Warner along with all the other observations provided by the Quilting Bee."

"Now that Dylan Markham has committed suicide, surely there must be something new? Clare was just saying that his suicide

282

should wrap up the whole case, especially if he killed himself with the same gun that killed Kathy and Matt."

When Michael didn't reply right away, Maggie asked. "Or did Dylan Markham commit suicide? That word 'apparent' has been bothering me from the start."

"Ma . . ."

"You don't have to give me that poker face. I still don't believe that Dylan Markham committed suicide. And I know you don't want to talk about it. But you have to realize that everyone at church is talking about this. All the time we didn't spend with Yolanda this morning, we ran through ideas about the Romellis. None of us can imagine who would want to kill Kathy. But it seems like there are dozens who might have wanted Dylan dead. The investors he bilked, the women he took to that party house he and his brother had. And while he was engaged to Kathy too!" Maggie looked indignant. "We even wondered if his brother might have killed him, especially if he invested with Dylan. Their former neighbor says they never got along as boys, especially as teenagers." Maggie took a breath, surprised that she'd ranted on for so long. She took another deep breath. "As if there wasn't enough going on with the murders and the thefts and the carjacking . . . And now this thing with Joe. We all know and like him."

Michael sighed. "Shouldn't you all be busy planning for Christmas?"

Maggie knew when he was hinting that she should stay out of a police investigation.

"We are. I am. We're having a Secret Santa exchange at the Senior Guild, you know. We're all supposed to make crafty gifts to exchange. Sharlene Eckhold planned it all and had us pull names."

"Mrs. Santa?"

Maggie could hear the smile in Michael's voice. As far back as Michael's childhood, the Eckholds had entertained the parish youth by appearing one Sunday in December as Mr. and Mrs. Santa. In fact, the parish children routinely referred to them that way no matter the time of year.

"That brings back memories," Michael said.

There was a short pause as Maggie imagined he was reminiscing about his own visits with the Santas/Eckholds.

"Well, I'm glad to hear you're busy with that. I assume you're making some kind of quilt."

"A pillow, actually." No need to tell him about the pattern and why she'd chosen it. To most men, all flowers looked the same.

"Good. You all should spend more time with your quilts and less trying to solve all our crimes for us."

Maggie grimaced, and her son smiled. "Very funny. I seem to recall a phone call asking for our input."

"You're right." Michael's smile faded and he rose. It was time for him to go.

Maggie walked Michael to the door, a towel-wrapped plate with the warm turn-overs held in his hands.

"Now you be sure to share those with Kimi," she admonished.

Michael gave her a warm hug — one-handed — and a kiss on the forehead, along with his "Goodnight, Ma. Thanks for a great meal."

She hugged him back, holding on to him a bit longer than usual as she remembered his sweet compliments earlier that evening.

When she returned to the kitchen, she pondered the way Michael had closed himself off when she asked about Dylan. He'd done the same yesterday at brunch when his brothers asked. She was sure there was more there than he could reveal. But why? Maggie knew that he often shared work-related stories that should be kept quiet, and she had never given him any reason for concern there. So why wasn't he sharing this time?

As Maggie filled the dishwasher, she considered again how Michael had looked when he said he'd rather not talk about it the previous morning at the brunch. Also, the way he'd sworn when she'd asked how Dylan's death might impact the Romelli case. Michael had put on his "cop face" — that expressionless countenance they must teach at the police academy. Michael often resorted to it when he didn't want to talk about a case. Or when he scolded her for getting involved in some ongoing investigation.

Once the dishwasher was full, Maggie started it up, then plugged in the kettle. A cup of tea would be just right with her late dessert. While she waited for the water to boil, she considered how Dylan's suicide might affect Kathy's death. It seemed to her that it *could* tie it up nicely. If there was a suicide note — well, that would be the icing on the cake. A newly discarded fiancé seemed the perfect suspect in a murder case. And it made more sense that Dylan could shoot Matt than his own father. Hopefully, this new wrinkle would put Rusty in the clear.

The loud click as the kettle turned itself off brought Maggie out of her reverie, and she quickly poured the steaming water into a mug where she had already placed a tea bag. Decaffeinated green tea for a late-night drink. She sniffed appreciatively as she waited for it to steep. Sitting down, she picked up her fork and sliced into the apple turnover. Cinnamon-scented steam rose from the warm pastry, and Maggie dipped her fork in, snagging a slice of spicy, sweet apple. For now, she decided, she would forget about murder and just enjoy the results of her baking.

CHAPTER 26

Tuesday, December 15th; 10 days before Christmas.

When Maggie and Victoria arrived at the church on Tuesday morning, they discovered most of the Senior Guild members milling in the central courtyard. Again. But this time, the milling crowd was in a good mood. Talk was all about the raid of the fraternity house, especially about all the things they'd seen the police carrying out of the house on the evening news.

It was a beautiful winter morning, crisp and cool, but with a bright sun already warming the day. Maggie knew that by the time they left at noon, she would be much too warm in the cardigan she wore so comfortably now.

"Did you see all the bags and boxes they brought out of that house on yesterday's news? And I'll bet they didn't show half of it. I just hope my things are in there." It was the woman who had lost her purse and newly purchased computer at the graveyard on the day of the Romelli funerals. "I called my insurance company, and they said I could file a claim, but then I'm sure my rates would go up. I've been praying ever since it happened that I'd get that computer back, but this is the first time I felt like my prayers might be answered. I went in the church just now and lit a candle."

Maggie heard variations of this from people all around her. The victims of the thefts were asking one another if they'd heard from the police, and shouldn't they hear soon? Those not involved as victims were nonetheless listening intently, eager to learn more. There hadn't been this much excitement at the church since the carjacking that led to Cody Garcia's arrest.

Clare was in the midst of it all, even though she had not lost anything to the thieves. But, after all, she'd been involved and in a more direct way than those who had lost goods. Except for that man who was attacked after morning mass, she was the only one who had seen an actual person, even if she was unable to identify him.

As soon as she spotted Maggie and Victoria, Clare hurried over.

"Isn't it exciting?" She pushed her tote

bag back up onto her shoulder. "Everyone is hoping to recover whatever they lost, but so far only Jim Stolz has heard from the police. He lost his laptop when it was taken from his car — that was parked in his own driveway!" Indignation threaded her voice. To think that a man's goods would not be safe parked in his own driveway! "He thinks he heard so quickly because he had engraved his social security number right on the computer case."

"Did he get it back already?" Edie had joined them during Clare's dialogue and was quick with her question.

"No, not yet. He said they told him he'll have it back in a few days, as soon as they can check it over and get the photos they need for their case. He's going in to ID it after Senior Guild this morning. They told him their computer forensics people have to check it out before he can get it back because they think one of the fraternity boys was using it, and they want to see if any of Jim's files were compromised. His identity could have been stolen if they got into any of his personal or financial stuff."

"That's great," Theresa said. "I had a friend at work who had her identity stolen and it's the most awful hassle. And it can take years to straighten out."

Another woman was also excitedly reporting that her father's pocket watch had been found. It was stolen from her car after she picked it up from the jeweler who'd cleaned it so she could gift it to her son that Christmas. "I'm sure it was because we had good photographs of it, for the insurance company. There was a personal inscription too. I'm *so* happy they found it. It's a family heirloom."

"I sure would like to hear what Julian Chasen has to say about his son's involvement in all this," Maggie said. "Have you seen him, Clare?" Maggie was still stretching her neck, trying to see above the crowd. Julian wasn't particularly tall, but since the group was largely composed of women, she thought she might catch a glimpse of him. While not especially tall for a man, he was still taller than most women.

But before Clare could reply, a short woman with too-dark hair pulled her away. Her new companion was speaking rapidly, a big smile on her face. Must be another one whose stolen goods had been recovered, Maggie thought.

"Julian's son is involved?"

Louise's voice brought Maggie's thoughts back to her friends.

"Didn't I tell you?" Maggie was surprised.

With so much going on, she was losing track of what she'd shared with whom. She quickly brought the others up to speed on what little she knew about the fraternity and the brothers.

When she finished, she headed for a group of men from the woodworking group. Since they worked with Julian, they were more likely to know if he was about.

"He was here earlier, but he said he couldn't stay," the first man she approached told her.

"Had something to do with his son," another man told her.

"That's what I wanted to talk to him about," Maggie said. "I heard his son belongs to that fraternity that's been in the news. Yolanda Grant's grandson is also a member."

"Oh, yeah, Julian was so proud of him. Each house gets to elect a president, and Jude was elected to head that group. Julian said he felt like he should be passing out cigars, except that you can't smoke anywhere anymore."

"I heard about the raid," the first man said. "Didn't realize it was Jude's house. No wonder Julian didn't come in yesterday. Of course, he doesn't come every day, but he's been in a lot this month." He shook his head. "He's had some trouble with that boy in the past, but recently things have been real good between them. I figured the boy had finally matured."

"Really?" Maggie said in her most encouraging voice, hoping he would go on.

With a nod, he did. "Yeah, for one thing he's been attending ASU for six years now. Julian told him he had to stop changing his major and finish up already, and I guess he's been trying. He was supposed to graduate this month, but Julian said he needed one more class, so he'll be done in May."

"What's his major, do you know?" It probably didn't matter to their little investigation, but Maggie was curious.

"I think it's economics. Or maybe accounting. It's something with numbers. Surprised the heck out of me when I heard. After all his dithering around, I thought he'd have a major in something like phys ed."

"Or basket weaving." This brought a round of heavy laughter from the group. Must be a private joke, Maggie decided.

However, the information on Jude's major was *very* interesting, Maggie thought. She remembered Michael saying that the fraternity kept track of the stolen goods and who was owed what through a sophisticated computer spreadsheet program. She would bet it was the kind of thing accountants used.

"He's good with computers too," another of the woodworkers commented. "*I* thought he might be majoring in computer science. When my laptop got all wonky on me, Julian took it home, and Jude fixed it right up. Worked as good as ever. Better even."

Better and better, Maggie thought. Whatever had been going on at that fraternity house, it looked like Jude Chasen might be in it up to his ears.

CHAPTER 27

Clare caught up with the rest of the quilters outside the door of their room. "Wait until you hear!" She rushed inside, gesturing impatiently for the others to join her.

"Yes, I have some information about Jude Chasen," Maggie said, putting her things into the closet for safekeeping.

Clare turned to face her, surprise plain on her round face. "Me too!" Then the sparkle left her eyes. "What did you hear?"

Once seated, needles in hand, Maggie repeated her information about the fraternity house and Jude's place in it.

Clare's face brightened as soon as Maggie indicated that she was finished.

"Well, the courtyard wasn't as full of people when I got here, just a few groups here and there. I saw Pixie Price over by the church office, looking kind of stealthy. You know how she loves to gossip, and I thought she must be eavesdropping on someone."

Edie clicked her tongue. "Of course she was. Goes without saying where Pixie is involved."

"Did you see who it was?" Theresa asked.

"Oh, yes." But Clare wasn't ready to reveal that yet. She knew she had her audience's full attention. "I tried to be quiet, but she heard me. That woman might be old, but she has the ears of a teenager!"

Clare pushed her needle back into the quilt and began to rock it before returning to her story.

"She gestured frantically — that's the only word for it. You know, that kind of hand-flapping movement that means 'don't make a sound.' Anyway, I looked over her shoulder, and it was Father Bob and Julian Chasen. They were talking in that little garden area beside the office door."

"You shouldn't have been eavesdropping on Father Bob's conversation, Clare." Anna's eyes were wide with horror. "What if they were discussing something really private, you know, kind of a confessional thing?"

"Well, they shouldn't have been doing it out in the open like that." Edie nodded firmly. Maggie could see that she was anxious to know what Clare had learned.

"I did try to pull Pixie away from there."

Clare pulled her needle through and began another row of stitches. "I really did, even though I was dying of curiosity. But Pixie wouldn't move, and she's stronger than she looks."

"So what was Julian saying?" Theresa had abandoned her stitching, watching Clare so as not to miss a word. Any doubts she had about eavesdropping on a priest's conversation with a parishioner were wiped away by her curiosity.

"He was telling Father that Jude had had a serious lapse in judgment, and was asking his advice. He sounded like he might be crying when he explained how Jude decided he had to help his father out of his financial mess. Then Julian admitted he knew Jude was into something illegal — that he'd seen some stuff on his computer around Thanksgiving but hadn't followed up on it. He was blaming himself for not alerting the police last month."

"He thought he could help with his father's financial mess?" Edie's incredulous voice rose an octave. "Julian must owe millions!"

Good point, Maggie thought. But then, young people were often unrealistic in their expectations.

"How is it they didn't see the two of you

lurking there? You must have been fairly close to have heard so much." Victoria raised her eyes from the quilt top momentarily.

"Oh, Pixie is so tiny she can hide behind a bush and not be seen." Clare's mouth tilted down on one side in envy. "We were to the side of them, but not really hidden. The truth is, they were so involved in their conversation they wouldn't have seen anyone. And I wasn't actually there for very long. Father started to pray with Julian, and I pulled Pixie away. That was when I saw all of you at the door here. I couldn't believe how full the courtyard had gotten in that little while that I was with Pixie!"

Maggie wondered about that. It was probably much longer than Clare realized, and really quite bad of her to be listening in on such a private conversation.

"So it sounds like Jude thought up this thievery to get some money for his father's bills." Theresa mulled this over. "I guess it's nice that he wanted to help his father."

"You don't sound too sure of that." Louise laughed.

"And it's flawed reasoning, in any case." Victoria looked up. "Remember the fraternity brothers were sharing in the profits — Maggie learned that from Michael. So he wasn't exactly Robin Hood."

"And where did they get the fancy equipment to break into the cars?" Maggie asked. "Remember, the police were very anxious to find an eye witness so they could learn how they were doing it? Unless one of those boys was some kind of electronic genius and invented some new tool to pick car locks."

"That's not as far-fetched as it sounds." Louise snipped off a thread and reached for the spool. "So many of these young people are geniuses when it comes to electronic gadgets. They've grown up with computers and are comfortable with the way they work. Unlike the old fogies like Vinnie and me, who have so much trouble with the darn things."

"No wonder Julian has lost so much weight." Maggie passed Louise the needle case. Louise was eying her needle critically, holding it up in the light. There was a definite curve to it. Time to toss it and get a new one. "Sara and I were thinking it must be stress from his financial dealings and the thought of jail time. But if he knew about his son also getting into something illegal . . ."

"Well, the apple doesn't fall too far from the tree," Edie intoned. Unlike so many others in the Senior Guild, Edie had turned against Julian as soon as she heard about his financial shenanigans. Edie had been very interested in Julian's investments initially but had finally decided against it. Then regretted it for some time when others reported such excellent returns. Later, she played up her decision to stay away. Maggie thought she recalled her denouncing his scheme as "lacking foundation." She'd turned out to be correct, even if she might have benefited from hindsight.

"I wonder if the fraternity brothers will reveal the source of their breaking and entering prowess." Victoria pondered out loud as she threaded a needle.

"Let's hope so," Maggie replied. "Michael indicated that they were being very cooperative. This whole business needs to be put behind us."

"Amen," Clare said. And the others agreed.

CHAPTER 28

Wednesday, December 16th; 9 days before Christmas.

"I feel so good about some of the robbery victims getting their things back," Victoria said the next morning as they began their stitching. There had been a number of people milling around in the courtyard again that morning, and with happy news. Many of them had received calls from the police about their stolen goods, and they would be getting them back in a day or two.

Everyone agreed on this being a wonderful thing, since so many of the stolen items had been intended for Christmas gifts.

"I wonder if they found the goods taken from Kathy's front door among the things at the fraternity house," Edie said.

"Wouldn't that be good to know," Theresa commented, drawing her thread through the quilt top. They were almost done with the redwork quilt, and there was a certain anticipation rife in the room. It always felt good to finish up a quilt, just as it did to start a new one.

"Except that no one knows what was taken," Maggie reminded them.

"You don't think one of those fraternity boys killed Kathy during a robbery?" Anna asked.

"Oh, no," Maggie replied. "I don't see any reason why the fraternity thieves would kill someone, even if they were caught red-handed. Michael said they seem like good kids who were drawn into something that got out of control. If one of them was taking the boxes and was seen, he could have just run off, the way Cody did when he was caught here at the church."

"We were thinking more along the line of the thief seeing someone on the property, maybe even the killer," Louise told Anna. "That's why we hoped to identify the thief."

Anna blinked once, then nodded, finally grasping the importance of a possible witness.

Victoria tugged at a thread to finish off her line of stitches by burying the knot. Once the knot slipped into the batt, she looked up at Clare. "With all the news about the stolen property yesterday, Maggie never got a chance to tell us what she learned from Michael on Monday night. Clare, he interviewed the carjacker."

"I don't know how much interviewing Michael may have done, but he was there while Detective Warner did the interrogating. That's how I learned that Jude Chasen is a member of the fraternity. I don't know if Yolanda was aware of that." Maggie snipped off a thread and reached for a spool as she continued speaking. "In fact, I learned from one of the woodworkers yesterday that Jude was the president of that little group." She went on to remind them of what else she'd learned about Jude and his studies.

"Not that it makes much of a difference," Edie commented. "Perhaps father and son will go to prison together — the father for the Ponzi scheme and the son for common thievery."

Clare, however, was impatient to hear what Michael had to say about the carjacking. "Did the man in the hospital admit he tried to attack me?"

"No. He said he never had a gun, and he didn't know anything about your episode."

"He said he *didn't* try to take my car?" Clare sounded lost. "Then who did?"

"I don't know." Maggie tried to say it as calmly as possible. She knew Clare had been counting on the interview with Cody putting closure to her episode. Clare wanted her attacker behind bars, and she thought he might have been these past few days. Now she was no longer sure.

"If the man in the hoodie was part of the fraternity, I'm sure they'll know soon enough," Maggie assured Clare. "Michael said Cody is being very cooperative."

"Probably figures he can cut a deal if he talks first." Edie's cynical attitude was apparent in her voice as well as her words.

"Michael said the young man's parents have been there with him the whole time, and they engaged a lawyer for him."

"So, did he accept his right to remain silent?" Edie's mocking voice told them all that she assumed he had.

"No." Maggie took a perverse pleasure in telling Edie she was wrong. Edie was determined to cast the young man as a gangbanger, and from what Michael had shared, Maggie was sure he was not. "He was anxious to cooperate." She went on to explain what Michael had told her about the young man's explanation of why he and the others had participated in the robberies.

"Fun!" Edie's face was a picture of indignation. "Of all the . . ."

But Clare interrupted her.

"And he didn't know who attacked my car?"

"I'd hardly say you were attacked, Clare." Edie looked over at her with dreary tolerance. "He merely *approached* your car, though I know he scared you."

Clare's face turned red and her eyes bulged. "How . . ."

When she was unable to get the words out, Louise stepped up to her side and put an arm around her shoulders.

"Edie, why don't you get Clare a hot cup of tea. With sugar." Louise's tone left no room for dialogue. "Right now," she added, as Edie hesitated. "Clare needs something, and she needs some quiet time to compose herself."

By the time Edie returned with the cup of tea, Clare was sitting calmly at the quilt frame, though her hands were not stitching, but clasped tightly in her lap. Unfazed, Edie handed her the cup. "I put in one teaspoon of sugar, Clare. I know you don't usually take it sweet, so I didn't want to overdo."

Clare, her cheeks still red with indignation, accepted the cup and nodded her thanks.

Victoria tried to steer the conversation toward Christmas doings, and was successful for some time. Long enough to learn

305

that Clare would be in the valley throughout the holiday period, and that Edie would be spending Christmas day with a niece in Cottonwood. And Anna shared a yam recipe that she had tried out over Thanksgiving and found delicious.

Theresa was asking about gravy when Clare broke in.

"I just can't stop thinking about Rusty," she said. "The sight of him there in the church! I saw him again this morning, you know." Clare frowned. "He's in so much pain. I'll bet if we could figure out who killed Kathy, it would help him get on with his life. Don't you think?"

The others agreed that it might.

"I still like Chad for it." Theresa frowned down at her latest line of stitches, decided they were fine, and continued. "He might be lovely to look at, but I think both of those brothers were seriously flawed."

"Well, I certainly like him for it better than Rusty," Clare said.

"But why would he have killed Kathy? And her son?" Anna asked.

"I told you before," Clare said. "He could have gone over to talk to her about her breakup with Dylan, and things just got out of hand. It *could* have happened."

"Lots of things *could* have happened,"

Edie said. "I still think Dylan is the most likely candidate. Then he suddenly discovered his conscience and took his own life."

"I'm still not convinced he took his own life," Maggie said. "There's never been an official statement from the police about just what happened in his home."

"We have to stop talking about this," Victoria said, clearly frustrated. "We just keep going around in circles. We aren't getting anywhere, nor are we liable to. Not without more information."

"She's right," Maggie conceded. "And all the discussion of murders and possible suicide is turning this holiday into a depressing season. We need to get back our usual holiday spirit."

Theresa immediately took up the challenge. "Is everyone done with their Secret Santa gifts?"

"Oh, yes," Anna said. "I even have it all wrapped and ready for Saturday. I'm trying to decide on what to bring for the potluck."

Their holiday spirit soared as they began to talk about their favorite potluck recipes, and Theresa once again asked about gravies.

It wasn't until they were leaving for home that Maggie's spirits sagged once more. Still nervous about driving on her own, Maggie and Victoria were taking Clare home.

Clare was apologetic about taking them out of their way.

"Don't be silly," Maggie told her, as she turned out of the St. Rose parking lot. "You're our friend, and you need a little help. We're happy to give you a ride."

"I feel silly," Clare admitted. "There's no reason for me not to drive myself. Except that every time I get behind the wheel, I start to shake. And my heart races."

Even from the front seat, Maggie could hear Clare gulp. Then Clare took a deep breath and held it.

"It's ridiculous," Clare went on. "But I can't seem to control it. And I don't want to have another one of those panic attacks. That was very scary. I thought sure I was having a heart attack."

"The symptoms are quite similar," Victoria said.

"I know you're trying to make me feel better," Clare said. "And thank you. I really enjoyed talking recipes this morning."

"I did too," Maggie said. "We need to do more of that."

Clare thanked them again as she exited the car in front of her house. They could see Samson waiting in the front window, scratching at the glass with his little paws.

Maggie felt sure his stump of a tail would be going like a metronome. Clare would be fine.

CHAPTER 29

Thursday, December 17th; 8 days before Christmas.

Dottie Taylor hurried into the Quilting Bee's room the next morning, interrupting the quilters soon after they got started. Maggie could see that Dottie was excited about something, and Maggie had a suspicion she knew what it was. The previous evening's news had been full of the story. The police had served a warrant on the house owned jointly by Dylan and Chad Markham, previously owned by their parents. And right next door to Dottie Taylor's home.

"Wait until you hear!" Dottie began.

"Were you there when the police searched the house?" Clare asked.

"Well, it all went down yesterday while we were here," Dottie admitted.

Maggie hid a smile at Dottie's use of vocabulary she must have learned from television crime shows. Maggie could also see how disappointed Dottie was to have missed so much of the excitement.

"When we got home, we heard a lot from the neighbors who'd been there all morning."

"I'm surprised the police told them anything," Maggie said.

"Oh, they didn't. People pieced things together from the questions they asked and what we learned later from the television news. They did have a police spokesperson speak around three, and of course I was home by then. I guess they wanted to give the TV news people something for the early news. That's when we heard they were investigating Dylan Markham's financial dealings."

"And here we thought that house was just for partying." Louise pulled a thread through the quilt top, gave it a quick tug, then snipped it close to the fabric. "Did Dylan really keep financial records there? It doesn't seem very smart if they were letting the house to people for meetings and parties."

"Not if his files were in the main house," Dottie said. "But there was a guest house, and they might not have allowed others in there."

"A guest house?" Clare paused in her stitching while she thought about that.

"Oh, yes. Chad and Dylan had it built shortly after they bought the house. No one in the neighborhood ever saw inside it, but it was a pretty good size. Used up a good chunk of the property. We figured it had a living room with kitchenette, one or two bedrooms and a bath. Isn't that how they're usually done?"

"A guest house," Clare repeated. "Locked file cabinets in a guest house! And in a house owned by a corporation that doesn't have his name in it. That sounds like something from a mystery novel!"

Maggie and Victoria exchanged a smile.

Dottie smiled, a smug smile that let them know she was quite happy the brothers had gotten their comeuppance. "That Dylan always did think he was smarter than anyone else. He probably thought no one would think to look in his parents' old house for anything important."

"Renting it out for parties may have been part of the cover for them," Maggie theorized. "Who would suspect there would be anything important kept in a house they rented out periodically? It was actually a pretty good idea."

"But wouldn't Chad have known?" Victoria asked.

"Maybe. Maybe not." Dottie thought about it. "As I told you before, they were never close, so there's no way to know how much they would share with one another. Dylan might have let Chad think the house was just for playing."

"Did you ever see Dylan there on his own?" Theresa asked.

"I was trying to think if I did — last night, after I heard what the police were looking for." Dottie's eyebrows drew together as she tried to work it out. "I could only recall one or two times when I saw him there alone, and I can't say that I ever saw him with anything that looked like files."

"Maybe those cardboard banker's boxes that people use to store papers?" Theresa suggested.

Dottie shook her head back and forth slowly. "I don't think so." Her eyes brightened. "But he probably had a briefcase. He always seemed to have one, so I might not even have noticed."

Edie nodded, agreeing that a briefcase would be an effective way to bring files onto the property.

"They still haven't officially stated how Dylan died." Louise frowned. "Perhaps it really was a suicide, though I still think he wasn't the type to kill himself."

"You think someone killed him?" Dottie's eyes widened. "Someone he cheated?"

"We discussed it when it happened," Theresa told her. "It seemed too much of a coincidence that he died so soon after Kathy's murder. If he didn't commit suicide, and Louise doesn't think his personality type would, then someone killed him."

"The problem is that there are so many possibilities in Dylan's case," Maggie said. "With his financial shenanigans, there are sure to be a lot of people who hated him. But why would one of those go to the bother of making it look like suicide? It seems to me that someone who had lost all his money would just walk up and shoot him."

"Good point." Louise snipped a thread and put the scissors aside. "It would be much like a crime of passion."

Several of the other quilters nodded their agreement.

"But if it wasn't suicide, a lot of us still like Chad for it," Clare said.

Dottie's eyes widened. "Chad? Whyever would you suspect him? I mean, I know that charitable young professional image is mostly just that — image, I mean. But why kill Kathy and, especially, Matt?"

"The idea has always been that Matt saw someone shoot his mother and that's why he was killed." Louise provided the standard reasoning everyone was using as a working hypothesis.

Edie was pleased to explain the rest. "Murders are usually about money, love, power, or revenge. It seems like it could be any of these with the two brothers. We learned from you about their rivalry growing up. Norma told us about Chad and Kathy working together and how they argued a lot. Sometimes that can reflect a kind of frustrated love. And Chad introduced Dylan to Kathy, so if there was some kind of unrequited love there, it could have reached a breaking point. But it seems to me money is the biggest motivator when it comes to murder, and I think it's likely that Chad would ask his brother's advice about investing his money. After all, they were brothers, and it was Dylan's business. On the surface, Dylan appeared to be a very successful businessman, so why not? But we learned early on that Dylan's financial dealings were suspect. So I figure Dylan took and lost a lot of Chad's hard-earned money. And that could certainly lead to murder." Edie stopped, satisfied with her explanation.

Dottie stared. "Wow," she finally murmured.

"What do you think?" Clare asked. "Does that sound like a possibility?"

"You know . . . it does." Dottie suddenly seemed to remember something. "The police did ask everyone when they'd last seen Chad Markham. And they also asked if we knew where he might be."

"You mean they don't know where he is?" Edie's voice crept up an octave at least.

"*And* they're *looking* for him!" Dottie seemed quite pleased with this new info she was able to share.

"Oh!" Clare eyes danced. "He may have run off. If he did, that makes him suspect number one, don't you think?"

"But suspect number one for killing Dylan, or Kathy?" Anna asked.

"Either," Clare said. "Or both," she added, more convinced. "It *must* be both. Oh, this will finally get Rusty off the hook. What a great Christmas gift that would be for Gen and Rick."

"And for Rusty," Victoria added.

CHAPTER 30

Friday, December 18th; 7 days before Christmas.

For the second morning in a row, Dottie entered the Quilting Bee room before heading to her own group.

"Did you hear?" She didn't wait for an invitation, but pulled a chair up near the quilting frame and sat down.

Clare was nodding so vigorously, she couldn't see to stitch. "Gerald and I always turn on the morning show while we have breakfast, and there was a breaking news update."

Despite this verification that Clare at least knew about it, Dottie had to say it all. "They arrested Chad Markham at the Dallas airport. He was heading for Costa Rica. He said he was going to do volunteer work with one of those charitable doctor groups, but he was just trying to get out of the country. They arrested him for murder.

317

Killed his own brother! It's like Cain and Abel all over again."

Maggie almost smiled at the drama, but it was a sad truth.

Victoria did not smile. "Remember he's innocent until proven guilty. We don't know that he did kill his brother. The state will have to prove that beyond a reasonable doubt."

"It will be interesting to hear what proof they have." Maggie tugged at her thread that was suddenly too short. The gentle pressure released the snarl, and the thread lengthened again. "The report I heard just said they suspected there were some tricky financial dealings between the two brothers and that a lot of money was lost."

"That must be why they waited so long to say that Dylan was murdered and it was only *made* to look like suicide," Clare said. "They must have been collecting evidence against his brother."

"What did Gerald think of his arrest?" Victoria asked.

"Oh, he said it didn't surprise him at all. He said he never liked him. Men!" Clare shook her head at the vagaries of men.

"That goes to show that the TSA is good for something," Edie said. "The searches might be an inconvenience, but in a case like this, they can track down someone quickly before they can leave the country."

"That's true." Dottie rose, but didn't head for the door. "It was sure a lot of excitement for our neighborhood. But we're all glad it's over. The neighbor on the other side of the Markham house is hopeful that the house will be put up for sale and a nice family will purchase it. None of us will miss the kind of clientele that came with those corporate parties."

"It might be a while before the house can be sold. I imagine it will probably be tied up in court cases for a while." Maggie reached for the spool of thread.

"Are there any other relatives who might inherit?" Theresa asked.

"It doesn't matter." Edie spoke before Dottie had a chance to reply. "Chad isn't dead, so he still owns it. Though he might put it up for sale if he goes to prison."

"It may have to be sold to cover debts," Maggie said. "After all, they know the house was tied to Dylan and his financial dealings. They did say the police found a lot of his papers there. I believe I also heard that the federal authorities are involved. That house is going to be tied up in legal matters for years to come."

Dottie frowned. "I hadn't thought of that.

I don't think I'll mention it around the neighborhood just yet. Might as well let people have a nice Christmas, thinking the house will be on the market soon."

And with that she left for the sewing room.

"Now that they have Chad in custody, maybe they'll learn more about the Romelli murders." Clare's tone was more hopeful than certain. "Don't you think they'll have to ask him about it, seeing as how Dylan was Kathy's fiancé?"

"Maybe." Maggie hesitated to agree wholeheartedly. "I'm more interested in hearing what everyone is bringing to the gift exchange potluck tomorrow. Have you all made a final decision? There were so many good ideas mentioned the other day."

Chapter 31

Saturday, December 19th; 6 days before Christmas.

The mood was lively that Saturday as the Senior Guild gathered for a potluck lunch and the Secret Santa gift exchange. Maggie and Victoria arrived together as usual, wrapped packages under their arms, and food bowls in their hands. Maggie was delighted to see a smiling Bridget setting a pie on the dessert table. Even during Senior Guild breaks, she'd been so sad. They had rarely seen her smile since her personal tragedy.

A ho-ho-ho-ing Leo Eckhold, dressed in his Santa best, greeted them near the door, jingling his sleigh bells. Several large laundry baskets squatted on the floor beside him, many already overflowing with gaily wrapped packages. Maggie and Victoria acknowledged "Santa" with smiles and Christmas greetings and deposited their own packages among the others. Then they continued on toward the food tables. Thinking there would be plenty of rich dishes available, both Maggie and Victoria had made salads as their contributions. Victoria had a pretty ceramic bowl filled with tuna-and-pasta salad. Maggie had a teak salad bowl overflowing with baby spinach, strawberries, and pecans. Sharlene, her own string of sleigh bells strung across her midsection like a long purse strap, jingled her way over to thank them, then rushed off to do the same to others dropping off food.

The large social hall was so thick with people, Maggie wondered if they would be able to find the rest of their Quilting Bee friends.

To Maggie's surprise, one of the first to greet her was Julian Chasen himself. They had talked so much about him recently, but barely caught a glimpse of him around the church. And now here he was. He wished Maggie a merry Christmas and even gripped her shoulders loosely in his version of a hug.

"Why, Julian. Merry Christmas to you too." As they separated and Maggie introduced Victoria, she looked him up and down. "Are you well, Julian? You've lost a lot of weight. Not ill, I hope."

Julian dismissed her concern with a wave of his hand. "You know the saying. You can never be too rich or too thin."

"I don't know about that." Maggie frowned. "How is Jude?"

It was Julian's turn to frown. "He's managing. I feel bad, but I can't afford the bail, so he has to stay in jail for now."

Maggie tried to look both sad and understanding. "I hear he was trying to help you out."

Julian's eyes filled with tears and he blinked rapidly. "Yes. He's a good boy. His mother is furious, of course."

Maggie would have liked to hear more, but they were separated before she had a chance. Julian was pulled away by another woodworker wanting to introduce him to his wife. And Vinnie and Louise approached Maggie and Victoria, asking if they had found a table yet.

"We'd better get one before it becomes impossible to find seats together," Victoria said.

But as soon as they cleared the jam of people around the food tables, they spotted Clare and Gerald waving them toward a table halfway down the room. Theresa and Carl were standing beside them, and Anna and Edie were already seated at the far end of the table. Clare stood and waved again, and Maggie turned to see Louise and Vinnie heading toward them.

"Why, Edie," Maggie said as soon as they were all settled. "I thought you weren't doing the Secret Santa exchange."

"I'm not. But Anna needed a ride and I offered. And I did bring a slow cooker of cassoulet to share, so I won't be mooching." Edie's nose rose slightly into the air. Maggie thought someone might mistake that for a snobbish insult, but she knew Edie was doing it to cover her embarrassment. She'd denigrated the party, but she probably felt bad for doing so now that she could see how popular the idea had been. And heaven knew, with the past month they'd had, everyone in the Senior Guild could use some lighthearted fun. If only the murder of Kathy and Matt had been solved, everything would be perfect. But many of the Senior Guild members thought Dylan or Chad responsible and that it was only a matter of time before the truth came out.

Clare smiled at Edie. "Oh, I love your cassoulet, Edie. I hope I can get some before it's all gone." She turned toward Gerald to tell him about Edie's special dish — tasty baked beans cooked with sausage and the tenderest bits of ham.

There were many more hugs and greetings and merry-Christmases before Leo and Sharlene turned on a portable microphone and asked for attention.

"Merry Christmas to you all. And let's not forget the reason for the season."

Leo shook his bells as the crowd cheered.

Then Sharlene took over. "We asked Father Bob to join us for lunch, and he's going to say grace."

Heads around the room bowed, and many people made the sign of the cross. Afterward, there was a rush toward the food tables, so the Quilting Bee decided to wait a bit for their chance. Maggie told them how Julian had approached her with a merry-Christmas and a hug. "I was very surprised," she said. "I don't know him very well, just casually."

"But he does business with Hal, so he's probably networking," Louise said.

Victoria smiled. "Maggie looked him up and down and asked if he was well. You should have seen her."

"No!" Anna appeared shocked. "That was very brave of you, Maggie."

But Maggie dismissed it. "I wanted to see what he would say. And he just shrugged it off. It's not as if he's a hardened criminal, Anna. White-collar crooks like him aren't into violence."

"What about his son?" Theresa asked, lowering her voice. "It sounds like that could be a case of like father like son, don't you think?"

"But the son wasn't into white-collar crime," Louise said. "He was robbing innocent people. It's a little different from making their money disappear on paper, which is what his father did."

"Julian got tears in his eyes when he told me what a good boy Jude is." Maggie tried not to show just what she thought of that, but one side of her mouth did twitch upward. "And he said his wife is furious."

"Wouldn't you be?" Theresa said. "I heard she left him as soon as the whole thing broke."

"It's a trial separation." Victoria chimed in. "She left, but they talk, and she says she doesn't want a divorce. She just needs some time apart while all of the investigation business goes on. I have a friend who is close to her, and she's been staying with her until the whole thing blows over. I didn't have the heart to tell my friend that she may be there for months yet."

"Maybe years," Edie offered.

"I still can't believe Jude Chasen was the brains behind that whole fraternity thing."

Clare shook her head. "To think it was someone from right here in St. Rose parish."

"Well, technically, he was living in Tempe, so he wasn't really part of the parish." Edie liked to be precise.

Clare merely waved her hand at her impatiently. "Oh, pooh. He grew up here. It's so sad to realize that he turned out so poorly. I guess he didn't learn anything in his church school lessons."

"Morals are more often learned at home." Edie looked suggestively toward Julian, who was just approaching the food table. "I wonder if they'll ever get around to arresting him."

"It surprises me that he still has so many friends here at the church," Theresa said. "Doesn't everyone know about the Ponzi scheme and the investigations?"

"Of course they know." Edie was brusque. "But he tried to keep the people at church happy, because they were his friends. So they can afford to be more forgiving." Edie rose from her chair. "Shall we join the line?"

CHAPTER 32

Sunday, December 20th; 5 days before Christmas.

The various Browne families were filled with Christmas spirit as they assembled for their last brunch before the holiday. The children were excited to be out of school, and even more excited about the possible presents under the Christmas trees. The families planned visits to see some of the decorated neighborhoods and the zoo lights extravaganza, which added to their excitement.

Maggie was taking her only granddaughter to a matinee of *The Nutcracker Suite* that afternoon and Megan could barely contain her enthusiasm. So the children ate and ran off to play, unable to sit still for long. Which gave the adults plenty of time to talk about adult topics. Like the arrest of Chad Markham.

"So the doctor wasn't involved in his

brother's financial schemes?" Hal asked.

"Only as an investor," Michael said.

"Imagine taking your brother on as an investor when you know you're taking advantage of your clients." Sara shook her head in disapproval. "Dylan was a real user."

"That's why Louise was so sure he didn't kill himself," Maggie said. "From all we heard about him, he was proud, arrogant, and egotistical. That kind of person just doesn't kill himself. He would always figure that he was smarter than everyone else and that he would get himself out of whatever trouble he was accused of."

"His secretary, or administrative assistant," Michael corrected himself, "says he got a lot of angry e-mails. Even a few death threats. She didn't see them herself, but she says he used to joke about it."

"I guess the police have all his computers and records." Hal picked up his coffee cup and took a sip, testing the temperature.

"The Feds have everything," Michael told them. "They were there when we raided the so-called party house, and there were a lot of incriminating records there. It looks like he took tens of thousands of dollars from his brother, and he wasn't giving him much of a return. He kept putting him off, saying the investment market wasn't hot, but that it was turning. Chad says it was when he heard about the attorney general looking into Dylan's dealings that he finally confronted his brother."

"But he didn't just shoot him in a rage," Frank said. "He had to plan beforehand to make it look like suicide, didn't he?"

Michael nodded. "Definitely first-degree murder. He did a pretty good job of setting it up too. It really did look like a suicide, and it took some good investigating to uncover the truth. Like a lot of arrogant people, he got a little too fancy. He wrote a short note, copying his brother's handwriting. But it wasn't good enough. That was the initial tip-off."

"Forensics saves the day," Frank said with a laugh.

"Their handwriting was similar enough to fool a lay person, but not similar enough for an expert."

"Was it really a house for partying — the kind of partying Ma implied when she first told us about it?" Merrie looked wide-eyed at her brother-in-law.

Michael grinned back at her. "Oh, yeah. Dylan took all his best clients there. He kept meticulous records of his entertainment budget. Gourmet catered parties, string quartets and jazz combos, champagne and good wines. And high-class call girls. Only the best for him and his clients. And Chad took a lot of doctor friends along to meet Dylan and hear his sales pitch. He probably felt it made him look bad when they started to complain about the lack of return on their money."

Maggie finished her coffee and put down her empty cup. "Has Chad said anything about Kathy's murder? Does he know if Dylan killed her?"

Michael merely shook his head. "I hate coincidences too, but there doesn't seem to be a connection. And the detectives have been looking. It's such a cliché, but the truth is, everyone loved Kathy Romelli. Everyone who knew her agrees that she was a sweet, gentle person who would give you the shirt off her back. The only negative I've heard is that she was a little too trusting."

"Naïve," Maggie said with a nod.

"Yes. So that pretty much leaves Dylan and Rusty as suspects." Michael glanced at his mother. "I know you won't believe Rusty did it, but there are those who do."

The others looked toward Maggie. "I can't believe it of him. Perhaps if it had only been Kathy who was killed. But Rusty was crazy about his son — and Kathy too, for that matter." Maggie shook her head. "Nothing will ever convince me that Rusty killed his son."

Sara refilled Maggie's coffee cup and any others that were empty, then returned to her seat. She exchanged troubled looks with her sisters-in-law. Maggie wasn't usually so adamant in her views. Even when Clare had sworn that Kenny Upland was an innocent victim, Maggie had held back her own opinion, waiting for more proof. How would their mother-in-law feel if Michael was correct and Rusty was arrested for the two murders?

"Maybe this will be one of those cases that goes cold, then gets picked up again years later and solved." Sara winked over at Maggie. "You know, like in those *Forensic Files* programs you like so much."

"I hope it doesn't take *that* long to solve the case," Michael muttered.

But Maggie sighed. "I'd really hoped those packages Bella saw at Kathy's front door would be the key to solving who killed her. There was a real possibility that the thief was there right at the important moment to see who did it." Maggie turned in her seat so she could face Michael. "But you say there was no trace of the packages among the things recovered at the fraternity?"

"We found some packing boxes, but nothing tied to Kathy. I don't know if there's any way to know exactly what was in those packages, since Kathy is dead, and she probably ordered them." Michael looked as frustrated as Maggie did.

"Oh, come on, Michael, there has to be a way." Hal liked to play big brother, but Maggie wasn't sure he had an angle to pursue. But it seemed that he did. "What about UPS tracking? And if they came from Amazon, that would be even easier to track. I'm assuming you have Kathy's computer." Hal turned to his mother. "Did Bella say if the boxes had a smile on the side?"

"No, she didn't, but she did seem to think it was some kind of computer equipment. I wouldn't be surprised to learn she'd ordered the things online. You'll have to tell Detective Warner, Michael. Maybe he should speak to Bella again."

Michael frowned. "That tracking angle is a good one. I can't believe I didn't think of it. *Someone* in the computer department must have, though. I'll definitely mention it to Detective Warner when I tell him what you said, Ma."

As usual, his brothers had to rib him for not coming up with that angle. Maggie had to smile at her boys still acting like the children they once were.

"Have you learned anything more about the thefts?" Maggie asked Michael. "A lot of people at church were called in to identify things, and they're very excited to think they'll get items back before Christmas. Was it really Jude Chasen running it all? I heard that he's a computer whiz, and majored in accounting or something like it."

"It looks like Jude was the records man. He's not admitting to actually taking things himself, but I'm not sure I believe him."

"Julian told me yesterday that Jude was trying to help him out by getting some money for restitution." Maggie crumbled a bit of the leftover muffin on her plate. "He even got teary eyed when he said it."

"Hmm. That doesn't square with thinking at the cop shop," Michael said. "Some of the fraternity boys say someone outside the fraternity was really in charge. Detective Warner suspects that would be Julian, but don't mention that to anyone outside the family. He's trying to build a case."

"He may have to get in line." Hal gave a short laugh. "In financial circles, word is that Julian is going to be arrested soon on fraud charges for that Ponzi scheme."

"Theresa was surprised to see Julian at the party yesterday, and everyone so friendly. She thought there would be resentment since a lot of people had invested with him." Maggie picked up the last of her muffin, held it up in front of her briefly, then put it back on her plate.

"He was smarter than Dylan there," Michael said. "While Dylan went right ahead and stole from his brother along with everyone else, Julian returned profits to his church friends. So for the most part, they're willing to give him the benefit of the doubt."

"Good grief."

Maggie had to agree with Merrie there. She felt lucky that she had Hal to handle her investments. Otherwise, she might well have been sucked into Julian's schemes. She'd heard wonderful things from other Senior Guild members about high interest and swift returns. That alone should have warned them all, but people were always looking for an easy way to make money. Especially senior citizens on fixed incomes.

"Did you ever find out how the boys were breaking into the parked cars without leaving any trace?" Frank was more interested in that aspect of the case than in who was in charge.

"Now there is a connection with Julian there. But it's not enough to arrest him, because Jude could have contacted him on

335

his own. Julian has a locksmith friend who seems to have consulted with the boys on a new type of electronic lock pick. It would be a useful item if you locked yourself out of your car, but not so good in a thief's hands."

"Did you ever manage to find out who approached Clare's car that day and scared her so much? She didn't mention seeing any kind of electronic device." Maggie sipped from her cooling coffee. "Was it someone from the fraternity, trying to take her packages?"

"I thought you said none of the fraternity guys had guns?" April raised her eyebrows at Michael. "Wouldn't that make the charges tougher?"

"It would," Michael replied. "None of them had a *real* gun. But it turned out one kid had a toy gun that looked like the real thing. He thought he was pretty cool for carrying it around with him while he was breaking into cars. That day with Clare, he was high from smoking weed, didn't even see her in the car. He just saw all the bags in the backseat and thought he'd hit it big. Bags from expensive stores, he said. He was really surprised when the car backed up and took off. It *will* be tougher for him, even though the gun wasn't real."

"Are they all cooperating then?" Maggie asked.

"They are. They're all middle-class kids, and most have never been in trouble before. They really did think they were just having a little fun, making some extra money for Christmas." Michael shook his head in disbelief. "It's amazing how these guys can talk themselves into believing this stuff. One of them actually said that they were only taking things from expensive cars, where the people could afford to buy another of whatever it was they lost."

"That's terrible." Sara bit down on her bottom lip. "Where does that kind of attitude come from?"

"I hope Edie never hears about that." Maggie shuddered in horror. "We'd never hear the end of it. We'd all have to bring in news articles about young people doing good deeds to counteract her fears and accusations."

"I guess they all have lawyers?" Hal's voice was matter-of-fact.

"Oh, yes. The parents all came right over with lawyers in tow. But I think that's why they're all talking. The lawyers told them it would go easier if they did. Most of them may get away with just a few years of parole and some public service."

"Not Jude, I suspect."

"No, not Jude. Or the idiot with the toy gun. Jude was in charge of the books, and his brothers all finger him for coming up with the idea. So far he hasn't implicated Julian, if he is involved. He's said the least of any of them."

"If only Chad had been able to clear up the Romelli murders, it would be a peaceful Christmas." Maggie sighed. "It would have been perfect if he'd said that Dylan confessed to it at some point."

Maggie suddenly looked up at Michael. "Come to think of it, after Dylan's death, we all said that if he committed suicide with the same gun that killed Kathy, then all three murders were solved. But nothing's been said about the gun, or guns. *Was* it the same gun?"

"No," Michael said. "Dylan was killed with a handgun that Chad admitted purchasing at a local gun show. We think Kathy was killed with her own gun, but it's never been found."

"Like those darned packages," Maggie muttered.

"That's enough murder for a Sunday," April said.

"Megan," she called. "It's time to get ready for the show. Come on inside and I'll help you and Grandma clean up."

The three disappeared inside, broad grins on all three faces.

CHAPTER 33

Monday, December 21st; 4 days before Christmas.

The Quilting Bee came in as usual that Monday morning before Christmas. They had completed the quilting on the redwork quilt the previous Friday, and they wanted to do the binding and get a new quilt top into the frame so that they could start fresh on a new quilt in the New Year. Most of the Senior Guild members had taken time off from their craft work; still, many of them were present on the church campus helping to get ready for the Christmas celebration.

With church members having their stolen property returned, things were more upbeat. Father Bob seemed to have picked up on it, as Mannheim Steamroller was playing on the audio system. Maggie was grateful for the lighter mood as the quilters talked about the food at Saturday's party and the gift exchange.

"Such lovely things people made." Clare was happy because Bridget had loved her lap quilt and raved about it to everyone who would listen. Plus, she'd received a wooden footrest for her gift. "I just love my footrest. I think it will be great for using while I quilt."

"Bridget really loved your lap quilt," Maggie told Clare. "She was actually smiling for most of the party. I think she had a really good time."

"You did a nice job on the machine quilting," Edie said.

Clare preened. Since Edie was a marvelous machine quilter, her compliment meant a lot to Clare, who was a mere beginner.

"I love my pillow," Victoria told Maggie. "I still can't believe you pulled my name."

"And then managed to keep it a secret!" Theresa found this more amazing than the coincidence of pulling her best friend's name.

Maggie laughed. "I couldn't believe it either. I guess all the speculation about Kathy, Dylan, and the thefts helped keep us all distracted. We barely talked about the gift exchange at all, except when Clare asked for opinions about her quilt."

"Or to talk about what food to take," Clare added.

As Edie and Louise worked on the binding, Maggie pulled several quilt tops from the closet. "We have to decide on what top to quilt next."

"What do we have in there?" Anna asked. "I remember bringing in a scrap Spider Web."

"Yes, that's here," Maggie replied, sorting through the short stack. "There's also a Bear's Paw, a Carolina Lily, Drunkard's Path. Oh, and here's that lovely Tree of Life that Edie brought in. I suggest we stitch that one."

Maggie opened up the quilt top and spread it out on the table. Edie had pieced four trees with mixed scraps of green fabric. The four large quilt blocks were surrounded by appliquéd vines. It was a beautiful top, and would be a joy to quilt.

Everyone admired the top, and they quickly agreed that it would be a perfect way to begin the year.

"I saw you drive in this morning, Clare," Edie commented. She sat at the portable sewing machine, stitching the final side of the binding into place.

"Did you!" Louise grinned at Clare. "That's wonderful."

"I was a little nervous when I stopped in the parking lot, but there were people I knew getting in and out of their cars, so I was okay."

"That's terrific, Clare." Maggie had pulled out the ironing board and was waiting for the iron to heat up. "You'll be just fine from now on. Each time you drive, it will be a little easier."

Clare nodded absently as she helped Edie spread the redwork quilt on an empty table. Each of them took a scissors and began to trim off the excess backing and fabric.

"Rusty's truck was in the lot again when I came in." Clare kept her head down as she spoke. "I peeked into the church and there he was, all hunched over and praying."

"He's working things through," Louise said. "I'm sure it's a good thing."

Clare sighed. "I hope so."

Chapter 34

Monday, December 28th; 3 days after Christmas.

Bridget entered the Quilting Bee's room on silent, crepe-soled shoes. The Quilting Bee women sat around the quilt frame as usual, scissors, spools, grabbers, and needle threaders scattered over the quilt top. None of them heard the newcomer enter.

"I knew I'd find you all in here. Do you ladies ever take a day off? You know the rest of the Senior Guild won't be back until after the New Year."

Maggie laughed. "We really love quilting, so it's no sacrifice to come in. And after years of stitching, I have more quilts than I'll ever need for myself and my family. So this is a nice way to continue doing what I enjoy without cluttering up my home."

"With finished quilts, at least." Victoria laughed.

At Bridget's puzzled look, Louise elaborated. "Quilting in itself involves quite a bit of clutter. Lots of fabric, patterns, books . . . So all Maggie is saying is that there won't be a lot of finished quilts no one is using sitting in her closets."

Bridget smiled politely. Maggie's brows drew together as she examined the newcomer's face. Bridget had come to speak to them, that much was obvious. And she seemed to be worrying over something as well.

"We finished up the redwork quilt before Christmas, and got this one in the frame." Louise gestured to the Tree of Life quilt spread out before them. "We couldn't wait to get started, so decided to come in this morning. And this way we can tell one another about our Christmas celebrations."

There were nods all around from the other Quilting Bee members.

"And with Christmas on a Friday, we had all weekend to shop the after-Christmas sales," Clare added.

"If we were so inclined." Victoria smiled. They all knew that Victoria wasn't much of a shopper.

Clare took a closer look at Bridget, then rose from her seat and stepped forward. "Bridget, you've been crying."

"I came to tell you about my Christmas.

My *dreadful* Christmas."

"Oh, dear, Bridget, it couldn't have been that bad," Louise told her, passing her a tissue.

"Oh, but it could," Bridget assured her. "I knew I'd probably find all of you here, stitching away and talking about your own festivities. I'm sure you all had lovely family dinners and celebrations." Her voice caught on a sob as she ended the sentence. "I hate to ruin your day with this, but I just had to talk to someone. And I couldn't think of anyone else who would be better to discuss this with. You've all been so good to me this past month, so you really deserve to hear the rest of it."

Bridget crumpled the soggy tissue and took another from her purse, using it to dab at her eyes. The one Louise had just given her was already beyond such niceties.

"Have the police found the murderer?" Edie sat straight and tall in her chair, waiting for an answer, her needle held motionless in her right hand.

But Bridget turned to face Clare. "Have you heard from Gen and Rick?"

"No, I haven't. Why, what's happened?" With a sudden intake of breath, Clare grasped Bridget's arm. "Have they arrested Rusty?"

Bridget swallowed and wiped her eyes. "Odd you should ask that. Do you suspect him of killing Kathy and Matt?" Bridget glanced at the women around the frame.

"We've talked about it," Maggie admitted. "More as a devil's advocate exercise. Their murder has been a true puzzle. We'd all hoped everything would be resolved before Christmas, but Michael told me it's a real dilemma, that everyone they've talked to loved Kathy." Maggie met Bridget's eyes across the expanse of quilt. "You should be proud to have raised such a beloved child, Bridget. He told me it's highly unusual to find so few people who might wish the victim dead. Michael said they're back to looking at Rusty and Dylan as the main suspects just because there's no one else."

"Come and sit down." Victoria gestured toward the seat Clare had vacated and another empty chair that she pulled forward.

Good idea, Maggie thought. Bridget looked like a soft breeze would knock her over.

"Chad is my prime suspect," Clare told Bridget once they were seated with the others. "But the police don't seem to consider him a serious suspect for Kathy's murder."

"They seem sure he killed Dylan, though," Edie said.

"There's a good motive there, with all the money he invested with his brother." Theresa raised her eyebrows. " 'Invested' being merely a word in this context, of course."

"I still think Chad might have been in love with Kathy too," Clare insisted.

Bridget looked at Clare in obvious surprise. "Oh, I don't think so. They fought all the time at work. Kathy said she sometimes thought he took the opposite view of a patient's condition just to disagree with her."

"But in romance novels, the men always quarrel with the women they love." Clare nodded as though this was proof of her theory. "And then they suddenly realize it's because they're so madly in love."

Edie laughed. "There you go. That's probably enough to disprove it right there. Clare, those are just fictional stories and much more unrealistic than the murder mysteries we all love."

"We're getting off track here," Maggie said. "Bridget came in because she had something to tell us. Didn't you, Bridget?"

Bridget began to tear up again. "I didn't think I could possibly cry any more," she said, swiping at her seeping eyes. "But I just can't seem to stop."

With a deep sigh, she took a new tissue

from her purse and faced the quilters, who were calmly — if impatiently, on the part of Clare and Edie — waiting to hear what she had to say.

"I joined Rusty and his parents for Christmas dinner," she began. "Just the four of us. Gen had asked the girls to come on Christmas Eve to celebrate, as she knew Rusty's mood would dampen everyone else's and it wasn't fair to the grandchildren."

"That was nice of her," Clare said.

Maggie blinked, unsure if Clare meant it was nice of Gen to have her daughters' families on Christmas Eve, or nice of her to invite Bridget on Christmas Day. Bridget took it for the latter.

"It was very nice of them to invite me, since I knew none of us were in the mood to be festive. So why not make the attempt to celebrate together?" Bridget shrugged. "Still, Gen had a lovely dinner on the table. I was glad to accept the invitation. I thought being alone would have been more than I could handle, with all those feel-good stories on television." She took a deep breath and released it in jerky pants. "It turned out it was Rusty who couldn't handle it."

"What do you mean?" Clare stopped

stitching to look curiously at Bridget. "Did he break down again, like he did at the graveside?"

"It's . . ." Bridget hiccupped — or perhaps it was a sob, Maggie thought. Bridget was extremely upset about something; that much was obvious.

"Remember that day I came in, telling you Rusty was crying in the church?"

Everyone nodded. It was hard to forget seeing a grown man in so much emotional pain.

"I saw him in there another time too," Clare told her. "Several times. We think he was praying, maybe asking God to help him cope."

"Well, during Christmas dinner, Rusty broke down. He'd just been pushing the food around on his plate, but after a while he couldn't even pretend anymore. He said Matt should have been there, and Kathy too. Then he broke down completely." Bridget swallowed hard, unaware that she was repeating herself, but still telling them little of import.

"Then what happened?" Edie was tired of the slow recitation. She wanted Bridget to get to the point. "Did Rusty confess to something? Something to do with the murder?"

But Maggie could see how difficult this was for Bridget. Whatever she had to share, she really didn't want to have to say it.

"Did Rusty confess to killing Kathy and Matt?" Victoria asked. Her calm, quiet voice helped Bridget focus.

"No, not quite." Bridget pulled air into her lungs with a shaky sob. "It's so painful. What that man must have endured!"

"Just say it slowly," Victoria urged. "You'll feel better once you finally get it out."

Edie rolled her eyes — like a teenage girl, Maggie thought. Shame on her. Couldn't she see how Bridget was suffering? Maggie just hoped Victoria was correct and that telling them would help her cope.

"Remember how the police couldn't find Rusty the day of the murders? They weren't able to tell him about the deaths until very late that night. He said he was just driving around, thinking about getting his family back together. I was shocked that he hadn't heard about it on the radio, but he said he usually listens to CDs and that's what he had on that night."

"That's the reason the police have been so suspicious." Maggie pulled her thread through the fabric, then paused in her stitching. "Not only because Rusty is the ex-husband, but because driving around was such a bad alibi. He couldn't say where he'd been driving, didn't have any receipts from stops, didn't see anyone he knew."

"But then it's usually the innocent people who have the worst alibis," Edie said. "It's the guilty ones that set things up and try to make it look like they were elsewhere."

Bridget glanced at Edie but barely seemed to register what she was saying. "It's worse than just a bad alibi. It turns out Rusty couldn't remember much of anything about that day. He only remembers that he dropped Matt off, talked to Kathy about meeting with a marriage counselor — and that was it. He said the next thing he knew, it was almost midnight and he was driving past the art museum downtown. That's when he went home and found the police there waiting to tell him about the murders."

"Do you think he saw the murders and just blocked it out?" Louise asked. "Temporary amnesia or something?"

"Or something." Bridget sighed. "Over that Christmas dinner that Rusty barely touched, he told us how he couldn't remember most of that day — the latter part of it. But then he started to have strange dreams in which he was seeing Kathy and Matt dying."

"Oh, my." Anna gasped and Clare abandoned her stitching to dab at her eyes with a tissue.

"He said the dreams were so real, he began to think he had been there." Bridget looked down into her lap where she was tugging the most recent tissue into soggy shreds. "It was after the dreams began that he started coming to the church to pray. He said he talked to Father Bob too, but they weren't able to discover the truth. But at least he did talk to Father about his increasing tendency to contemplate suicide. I'm sure it was due to Father's influence that we don't have a third body to bury."

Clare leaned over to rub Bridget's back. There's something about this kind of sad news that makes human contact seem vital, Maggie thought. She thought she saw Bridget's shoulders relax somewhat at Clare's touch.

"It wasn't until Gen and Rick and I started making phone calls on Saturday that things began to come together. So we think we know what happened now."

Bridget offered their theory quickly, all on one breath, ending on a rheumy sob. Maggie wasn't sure she heard her correctly. But from the looks on the faces of her friends, Bridget *must* have said what Maggie thought she heard.

"Matt killed Kathy, and Rusty killed Matt."

"What?"

"No!"

Maggie didn't exclaim. But she too could barely believe it. How could Rusty kill his beloved son? But then, as Bridget went on with the explanation, it began to make a sick kind of sense.

"Rusty had Matt that last afternoon. It was when he brought him home that Kathy told him she wanted to try again with their marriage. Rusty said he was over the moon. That was really all he remembered before he began to have those dreams."

All stitching had stopped as the women listened intently.

"I called Dr. Gregory, who I remembered from my court years. He's a psychologist and used to testify as an expert witness. He always struck me as very knowledgeable. And when I saw him outside the courtroom, he was always very nice." Pausing in her recitation, Bridget fumbled in her purse for another tissue. "Anyway, I asked him to talk to Rusty, and he said it sounded like dissociative fugue, a kind of amnesia that can be brought on by traumatic events. And I guess there's nothing more traumatic than seeing your wife killed by your only child."

"But Matt . . ."

Maggie thought Clare meant to ask how Matt could have done it. Or perhaps, how Rusty could have killed Matt. But Clare wasn't able to get out more than those two words. Luckily for their unfeigned curiosity, Bridget *was* able to continue.

"Rusty said his memory began tweaking when he got a thank-you note from that television station that's doing the big food and toy drive. It was a short, handwritten note thanking him for his donation, but especially for donating so much of his time on Wednesday, December second. He didn't remember helping with the toy drive *or* the food drive, but then he recalled some packages on Kathy's stoop. He said that was the first time he remembered something from that blank space in his mind. He remembered that Kathy asked him to bring in the boxes and hide them in her office because they were gifts for Matt. But then he thought he remembered putting them in his car and taking them downtown to donate."

"It sounds like he knew Matt wouldn't be needing them." Louise started another line of stitching, but continued to listen intently to what Bridget had to say.

"That was the beginning of his nightmare. He said that night he dreamed he saw Matt die. In his dream, Matt is running down the hall, goes through the patio doors, and then he's shot and falls. Rusty said he thought it meant he had shot him, but how could he kill his own son?"

"Oh, Bridget." Clare put her arm around her friend's shoulders, hoping some human contact would offer a bit of comfort.

"Has he spent the past few weeks thinking that he killed his wife and son?" Victoria's question came in such a soft voice, Maggie just barely heard the words. But Bridget heard them and hung her head.

"That's why he's been coming to the church and praying. He thought he might have. That's when he said he thought about suicide, especially after that whole thing about Dylan, where they thought he committed suicide for so long. But then, after talking to Father, Rusty said he realized that killing himself was an even greater sin than murder, so he's been trying to work things out in his mind. Only his mind has been a jumbled mess with a lot of missing pieces."

"But why does he think Matt killed Kathy?" Maggie felt that someone had to ask the question, so she went ahead and did so. If he couldn't remember that afternoon, how could he know that?

"It was another dream. That one came

later, he said. It's only now that he's been talking to Dr. Gregory that he thinks he remembers what happened."

"What?" Clare was so anxious, she blurted out the question.

"While he went to get the packages from the front door, Kathy headed for the master bedroom. Rusty said she didn't like Matt puttering around in her bedroom, and she thought she heard him in there. Rusty said he knew she had a handgun in the bedroom, but he didn't even think about some kind of accident, when it happened." The tears came again. "Rusty said he was still at the door when he heard a sound that could have been a gunshot. He ran into the bedroom — saw Kathy on the floor and Matt standing over her in a daze. He thinks Kathy found Matt handling her gun and tried to take it away from him. And it went off."

"Oh, Bridget!"

Maggie was glad Clare sat right beside Bridget. Clare was good in these situations that called for a bit of mothering. She put her arm back around Bridget now, squeezing her close.

Tears continued to stream down Bridget's cheeks. "Rusty said Matt was incoherent — in shock, most likely. Then he ran from the room. Rusty says he doesn't remember how he got the gun — it was just there in his hand. And then he was running after Matt and then Matt was on the ground."

"And then he took those boxes to the toy drive?" Edie sounded skeptical, but Maggie knew it was just her usual manner of processing information.

"Rusty says he just didn't remember anything past Kathy telling him about the reconciliation. Dr. Gregory says that's what happens with this fugue-state thing. It's very rare, but he said Kathy's death is exactly the type of incident that could set it off. He's had Rusty in the hospital since Saturday, and he's been working with him."

"How awful. I'm not surprised that he couldn't remember any of it." Theresa picked up her needle and inserted it into the fabric sandwich. "Will he have to go to jail?"

"The lawyer Rick consulted said he'll have to turn himself in and then they'll see. But he's already talked to the county attorney and he thinks they'll treat him well."

"It's so unusual, it's going to be a media sensation." Edie was only speaking the truth, but Maggie wished she hadn't. Bridget's shoulders slumped, and she seemed to lose stature.

"At least Rusty is more at peace than he

has been since it happened. He says he finally realized what his subconscious decided for him that day — that he sent his son to heaven so that he wouldn't have to live with the knowledge that he'd killed his own mother."

There was a moment of complete silence at this. Maggie wasn't sure she'd ever seen the Quilting Bee members speechless. But they were now. Such terrible, tragic logic. Not logical at all, really. But then, murder rarely was.

"Has he turned himself in yet?"

Maggie was glad Victoria asked the question before Edie did. Edie could be kind and sympathetic, but her speaking voice was too often brusque and businesslike.

Bridget seemed to have an endless supply of tissues in her handbag, and she reached for another one. "As I said, his lawyer has talked to the county attorney. So has Dr. Gregory. They think they'll be able to get him released on his own recognizance because he really is not a danger to anyone else. And Dr. Gregory wants to keep him in the hospital for now anyway. He'll be turning himself in some time this week." Bridget mopped at her face with another damp tissue, and reached into her purse for another. "I still can't wrap my mind around the whole thing."

"It all seemed so complicated, and in the end it was a tragic accident gone wrong." Louise released a heavy sigh, her hand resting idle on the quilt top.

"What will happen to Rusty?" Clare looked ready to join Bridget in her quiet sobbing.

"I don't know. None of us do. Rick is hoping they'll be able to work out something with community service, but that might be too optimistic. Rusty wants to go to jail, now that he knows what happened. He thinks he deserves it. He also thinks he could help some of the inmates, maybe teach some classes on plumbing." Bridget shook her head, swallowing another sob. "Anyone who sees him telling his story will know how heartbroken he is. They'll have to know that it all happened in some kind of fugue state . . ."

"Make sure you have an excellent lawyer," Edie said. "Someone who can arrange a plea deal with the county attorney and not use this to make a big name for himself. It will be difficult enough to control the story, once word gets out."

"We do have a good lawyer." Bridget sighed. "In fact, Rick asked me for some names right away and said he got on the phone first thing Saturday morning. It wasn't the best time to be looking for a lawyer — not only a weekend, but the weekend after Christmas." She sighed again. "I was extremely lucky to find Dr. Gregory in town, and have him agree to examine Rusty."

"At least you know what happened now," Anna said.

"We've been wondering about those boxes." Edie shook her head. "The ones Rusty donated to the toy drive. We kept thinking that perhaps the delivery man, or even a thief, might have seen the killer. Or something that might lead to finding the killer. The police had said they didn't find them in the house."

"They did ask us about them," Bridget said. "That must have been after you learned about the delivery. But I certainly didn't know about them, and I wasn't even sure what was inside them. Rusty said the same, then."

Bridget shook her head, sadness radiating off her slumped figure. "This fugue-state thing is pretty awful. Gen and Rick are hoping the police or the judge will take it into consideration when it's time for sentencing."

There was little more to say, but the

women offered platitudes and prayers, and Maggie thought they brought comfort to Bridget. They'd all been so sure of Rusty's innocence.

By the time Bridget left, she had enough damp tissues on her lap to fill their small wastebasket.

"I don't think I've ever read about a fugue state in a mystery novel," Clare said.

Edie tugged at her thread. "I'm sure there will be a few after this."

Unfortunately, Maggie had to agree.

CHAPTER 35

Friday, New Year's Day.

The Browne family met for brunch on New Year's Day, inviting all of the Quilting Bee members to join them. Hal set up extra folding tables beneath the large mesquite tree, while the children remained at their usual smaller table on the patio. With the Browne family and all of the quilters and their husbands, it made for a large group. And there was a definite party atmosphere as they filled their plates and found seats at the tables.

Sara began the conversation with the topic that was uppermost in all minds.

"I'm glad that all that business from December was cleared up before the start of the New Year. So much better to begin with a clean slate."

"Exactly how we felt about starting a new quilt," Maggie said. "The Tree of Life. It's a good pattern for this time of year, and to celebrate the ending of all this business."

"Not that we knew it was all ended when we chose it," Edie said.

"It's just terrible about Rusty." Hal was still slightly shell-shocked at his friend's confession. "How could he do it?"

"He didn't even realize he did it," Louise told him. "He was in such a state of shock and horror after seeing Kathy lying dead at Matt's feet, and then the gun in Matt's hand . . . Well, he went into a fugue state and killed his beloved son, thinking he was saving him from a lifetime of grief."

"Instead, he inflicted that grief on himself." Maggie sighed, feeling infinitely sad.

"I saw him in the church several times, all hunched over in a pew, crying and praying. I just tear up every time I think about it." Clare dabbed at her eyes with a tissue, and Gerald put his arm around her shoulders, pulling her against his side. Maggie smiled to see them. Such a loving gesture for a couple who'd been together for many decades.

"The media has been kind," Victoria said.

Merrie laughed. "What a sensation they've made of it! It's also been a godsend for the television people, as this is usually a slow news period."

"What do you mean?" Frank asked. "You

don't like year-in-review programs?"

There were laughs from several parts of the group.

"The local stations must be calling every psychiatrist in town for news spots." Sara's mouth curved into a moue that reminded Maggie of a certain medal-winning gymnast. "Whoever had heard of a fugue state?"

"The national news picked it up, and I even saw a segment on CNN," Edie commented, pouring a little extra syrup on her pancakes.

Merrie had joined in the earlier laughter and was still smiling. "I'll bet a lot of those so-called experts had to look up fugue state."

"Maybe it will be the next thing on the TV detective shows," Clare suggested. "Have you ever noticed that something new will show up on one of them, then, within a month or so, two more shows will hinge on the same plot device?"

"Synchronicity," Bobby said.

"It happens with books too," Louise said. "One new mystery will have a particularly interesting plot device and another book with the exact same one will come out in the same month. Or the month after."

That threw the women into a discussion of books with similar plots, and they were soon debating when the various stories had been released. The younger people watched, smiles on their faces. None of them were quite as into mysteries, so they had nothing to contribute.

"I wish I had the time to read the way they do," April said with a sigh. Working as a vet assistant in her husband's office, plus dealing with an eight-year-old daughter and taking care of housework took up all of her time.

"You can do it when you retire," Sara assured her. "I'm sure they didn't read so much when they were working and raising children."

The quilters were drawn back into the general conversation when Hal asked Michael, "What do you think will happen to Rusty?"

"Hard to say." Michael poked his fork into a small triangle of pancake and pushed it into his mouth.

"I hope Rusty can make some kind of deal where he doesn't have to serve time." Clare still got tears in her eyes whenever the subject of Rusty came up.

"He killed a child, Clare," Edie reminded her.

"Bridget says he wants to pay the price for what he did," Maggie said. "She told us he offered to teach plumbing skills to the other inmates while he's in prison."

"Boy, that's who I'd like to invite into my home to fix the leak in the toilet — an ex-con plumber." Merrie shuddered, and the others laughed. All except Edie, who agreed with Merrie, right down to the small shudder.

"It's an unusual case, and the media attention has brought in some big names to help Rusty. There's no telling how it will turn out." Michael dipped a fresh croissant, brought by Edie, into his coffee and transferred it into his mouth without a drip.

"Gen told me he got a call from some of those reporters on CNN who do the crime shows. But she said he isn't interested in being on television shows." Clare picked up a piece of toast slathered with cactus jelly, but didn't bite into it. "Gen said he's so depressed, she's grateful to Father Bob for talking him out of suicide."

"That would have saved the taxpayers a lot of money," Vinnie said, only to be shushed by Louise.

"But think of all those poor reporters, pining for a great end-of-the-year story."

Everyone laughed at Theresa's comment. Maggie thought it a good thing that they were able to laugh about the tragedy. It meant they were moving on. The Tree of Life quilt top was a good choice for their next quilting project, the one they would work on for the next few weeks. It would mean they were all getting on with their lives.

"I hope we never have another month like this past one," Louise said. There were a few soft amens. "I've never thought of Scottsdale as being particularly crime ridden, but somehow several different crimes all ended up directly affecting St. Rose parishioners."

"Oh, there is plenty of crime in Scottsdale," Edie began, but she was shushed by the others.

"Not now, Edie," Maggie finally said. "It's January first in a bright new year. Let's not get into crime rates and the formation of gangs, okay?"

Edie reluctantly agreed, but Maggie felt sure Edie thought she'd made her point with her initial objection. No matter. It was a gorgeous winter day, the sun shone bright and warm, the air was clear, and the birds singing.

"I'm sure there are a lot of bogus investment schemes floating around in the city of Scottsdale," Hal said. "There's a lot of money here, and people are looking for good investments. The banks are offering virtually zero interest, so everyone is looking elsewhere. It leaves them ripe for people like Julian and Dylan. No matter how often you say 'if it's too good to be true, it probably isn't,' people continue to put money into wild schemes that promise big returns."

"Only one of those schemes was really tied to St. Rose," Louise reminded them. "Julian, with his Ponzi scheme, was the one who got the St. Rose people involved. We just knew about Dylan through his relationship with Kathy."

The conversation about the recent crimes came to an abrupt halt when the sound of sleigh bells drifted into the yard — to the surprise of all except Maggie and Hal, who had arranged something special for the grandchildren. Heads went up and turned, ears trying to locate the origin of the sound; the children started toward the gate, their excitement evident.

"Ho, ho, ho."

Leo Eckhold strolled into the yard, gaily dressed in red Bermuda shorts and a red floral Hawaiian shirt. His white beard shone in the bright sunlight. Sharlene entered behind him, wearing a red muumuu and shaking her sleigh bells. Maggie smiled when she heard Edie stifle a groan.

With squeals of delight, the children ran toward them.

"Mrs. Santa and I are on our way to Hawai'i for a vacation," Leo told them. "We need one after all our hard work in December. But I heard from my good friend Maggie that there would be some extra good girls and boys here today."

"There's only *one* girl," Megan said, bouncing on her toes before Leo.

"We had some extra cookies," Sharlene said, offering Megan a large tin decorated with a jolly snowman. "You share those with your cousins, okay?"

"Hey, what about her uncles?" Hal asked.

Everyone laughed.

"I found a few things at the bottom of my sack," Leo said, reaching into the red sack that Maggie had not noticed hanging over his shoulder. "Wouldn't want these things to go to waste when children like you might like to play with them." He pulled out a large box gaily wrapped in red and green, which he handed to Jason. "Now you all be careful with that. Have fun, but remember to be safe."

Surprised at the warning, Jason tore the paper off the box, then beamed at his brother. "A bow!"

"Not with arrows, I hope," Sara said, peering over his shoulder to see the box. "Oh, thank goodness. Foam darts."

"Still," their father said, "keep them away from people, especially from faces."

The two boys nodded their agreement and ran off to open the package.

Leo meanwhile found another, smaller box in his sack that he handed to Megan. "I know you'll enjoy the bow too, but this is something you can play with little Harry." He glanced at the two-year-old who was hanging back near his mom, a little afraid of the strangers in the brightly colored clothes.

Megan quickly uncovered a yard game composed of a board and several bean bags. "Come on, Harry, I'll show you how to play. This will be fun."

Leo and Sharlene looked after them, smiles on both faces.

"They're great-looking kids, Maggie," Leo said. "You're a lucky lady. Especially having them all right here near you."

Maggie looked at her friends, several of whom had grandchildren living in other states. "Yes, I thank God every day for my wonderful family."

"Before we get too maudlin," Hal said, "come on over and have something to drink. Sara, are there any more mimosas?"

"Yes." Sara raised a pitcher showing just enough for another two glasses. "There are plenty of desserts too," she offered.

"This is great," Leo said, accepting a glass of orange juice and champagne.

"I hope you all had a nice Christmas." Sharlene looked around at the women she knew so well from the Senior Guild.

"It's been difficult," Clare said.

"But it's all over now." Louise poured herself a new cup of coffee and lifted the pot in an open offer of refills. Only Maggie raised her cup for more.

"There's a 'For Sale' sign in front of Kathy's place," Leo told Maggie as she sipped from her warmed cup. "I hope it sells quickly."

"It would be great to have another young family in there," Sharlene agreed. "It will help all of us in the neighborhood forget."

"Won't it be hard to sell a house where two murders took place?" Anna asked. "Two high-profile ones, as it turns out."

"Oh, I think that might attract some buyers," Clare said.

"There's just no accounting for taste." Edie offered her opinion before taking a sip of coffee. She grimaced as she realized it was cold, and gestured to Louise to pass the carafe to her.

"That house in Mesa sold, and there was tremendous publicity about the murder in the shower, and then the trial. Remember? It was on *Nancy Grace* and everything," Clare informed them.

"I'm sure most of us don't watch *Nancy Grace,*" Edie said, her tone dry.

"Maybe they tore out the shower and redid the master bath," Merrie suggested with a smile, drawing another round of laughter.

"The buyers would want to redo the master bedroom anyway, don't you think?" Sharlene looked thoughtful. "At least change the carpeting. Most people want to make a place their own, after all."

"Do you think there was a blood stain on the master bedroom carpet?" Clare looked over to Michael, fascinated by this new idea.

But Michael pretended not to hear the question, preferring not to go there. Instead he turned away from the women chatting, reaching for a bowl of trifle Victoria had brought for their brunch. Maggie heard his playful comment, even though he was not facing her. "I think I'll have more of this. It counts as a serving of fruit, right?"

Meanwhile, Leo took his wife's arm. "Before you ladies start talking redecorating, Sharlene and I have to go. Our plane to

Hawai'i doesn't leave until tomorrow morning, but we have a lot to do beforehand."

Everyone gathered again to say good-bye, and Maggie tore the children away from their new games to say thank you and happy New Year to the departing guests.

As they settled into their seats around the tables once again, they inevitably turned back to recent events.

"Did you see Julian at mass on Christmas? He was with Jude, which really surprised me," Theresa said. "I thought Jude would be in jail."

"He's out on bail," Michael said, around a mouthful of cream, cake, and strawberries.

"I wonder where they got the money for that." Edie's lips drew into a thin line as she contemplated. "Do you suppose Jude used his ill-gotten gains for the bail bond?"

"Could he do that?" Anna asked.

No one seemed to know, but the consensus was that his funds would have been frozen — leaving them wondering about the source of the money.

"Julian has lots of friends who might have helped him out," Maggie said. "Being the holidays and all."

"I was just shocked to hear what Julian's son was doing." Clare stirred some cream into her coffee, her face a puzzle at what a nice young man had started.

"Why?" Edie asked. "In reality, his father is a thief too."

"But white-collar crimes seem *different*," Clare insisted. "It's not going out and stealing property from locked cars parked in front of someone's house."

"People are too lax in their thinking about white-collar crimes," Michael said. "Julian hurt just as many people with his Ponzi scheme as Jude did with his gang of thieves."

Edie looked over at Maggie and smiled. Michael had used the word "gang" in regard to the fraternity boys — the word Edie favored. However, the Quilting Bee had argued against such a designation.

"There were a lot of good feelings about the police at church on Sunday, from people who lost things from their cars." Theresa nibbled on a sugar cookie shaped like a reindeer. There was a little cinnamon candy stuck on its nose. "They were all so happy to have gotten their things back so quickly."

"Even with everything settled, it was a terrible Christmas for a lot of people." Multiple heads nodded at Victoria's statement. "So many people lost money in fraudulent schemes. Then so many more lost goods in the holiday thefts. Many of them did get their things back, but there was a lot of stress beforehand. And some of the things were sold and not recoverable."

Merrie shook her head. "All those supposedly clean-cut fraternity boys — such a shock for their parents."

"At least Yolanda's grandson was not involved." Maggie had been happy to hear that Joe had been completely exonerated. It was a small bit of good news in a hectic pre-Christmas week.

"But poor Bridget lost everything." Clare's words were spoken in a soft voice, but everyone heard them.

"Kathy was very naïve," Edie said. "Perhaps if she had had more worldly experience, she wouldn't have fallen for Dylan's lines."

"She should have had more faith in her husband, photos or no." Sara punctuated her statement with a loving look toward Hal.

"Yeah, Dylan was really something. Julian was small potatoes compared to him. Julian was actually paying people back, which is why so many of the church people weren't too angry with him. Granted, he was using the new money coming in to pay the initial investors, but at least they didn't lose money." Hal refilled his coffee, stirring in a packet of sweetener as he continued. "Julian really seemed to believe that he would be able to keep his scheme going as long as he could find businessmen with deep pockets to invest. He planned to keep feeding profits back to his friends in the initial investment groups and slim down the profits to the later investors. What he didn't count on was the greed factor among those deep-pocket investors. As soon as their payback was less than expected, they wanted their money back."

"Dylan had something else entirely." It was Michael's turn to expound on the two shysters. "His wasn't a pyramid scheme. Dylan's ploy was to get businessmen involved in what he called great opportunities. He'd take their money, return as small an amount as possible in interest — then keep fending them off with project delays of various sorts. Or he'd say an important loan fell through, so he'd have to find more money elsewhere. Sometimes he'd even get more money from an investor with that one. He'd been juggling businesses for years, and it was all ready to implode. If his brother hadn't killed him, the truth would have come out, and fairly soon."

"I expect the information from Bridget's friend helped that along," Maggie said.

"It did. Once the attorney general's office

got involved, his business practices didn't hold up at all. That property wasn't the only one he'd managed to put in his name illegally. Lots of people who've done business with him are coming forward, hoping to get some money back."

"*Will* they get their money back?" Edie asked.

"Doubtful," Michael said. "There are scores of investors and not much money. Dylan lived high — *very* high. He apparently began as a legitimate real-estate developer, back when the market was so good it was virtually impossible to do anything wrong. He was making millions at one point, and it must have given him a taste for the good life. Once the real-estate market tanked, he didn't want to give all that up. That's when the fraud began."

"That house they showed on the television news, the one where the body was found," Gerald said. "That easily cost him a few million."

"And you should see the inside," Michael said. "Furnished by an expensive decorator, I'm sure. The best of everything. You wouldn't believe the kitchen, Ma."

"Why did it take so long for his death to be labeled murder?" Clare asked.

"We had to be sure it *wasn't* suicide," Michael responded. "Chad did a darned good job of setting the scene. And with the attorney general's investigation started and all those upset investors turning up, suicide was a real possibility."

"And, with all this going on, you didn't even have to get after Ma not to get involved." Hal grinned at his younger brother.

"Heck, I asked for her help." Michael grinned back.

"He did." Clare too grinned, her eyes filled with joy. She was still tickled that he and Detective Warner had wanted the quilting women's input.

As conversations broke up into smaller groups, Kimi tapped her spoon against a glass and Michael stood. Everyone looked up, surprise evident on all faces. It was rare to have something unexpected occur at one of their brunches, and they'd already had the visit from Mr. and Mrs. Santa, a surprise to most of them.

"Before we all go, I have an announcement to make," Michael said.

Maggie's breath caught in her throat. Had he proposed to Kimi over Christmas after all? And kept his own mother in the dark for a week? Her heart began to beat a little faster.

"I took the detective's exam earlier this

year." Michael looked down, then back up again. "Make that last year." His brothers laughed at his gaffe, one they knew they would all be making in the coming weeks. "In any case, I passed the exam and will be starting work as a detective in a few weeks."

There was applause, and his brothers whooped. Maggie's heart returned to its regular beat. How nice that he had received a promotion. Not quite as exciting as a marriage, but excellent news. Perhaps the next step would be asking Kimi to be his bride.

Maggie stood, raising her cup. "A toast!"

Sara popped up out of her seat. "No, no, not with orange juice and coffee. This is special. We don't have any more champagne, but Hal's boss gave us some nice wine for Christmas. Come on, hon, let's open a couple of bottles to toast your brother's new job."

Everyone chattered about the promotion while their hosts were gone. Maggie just stared across the tables at Michael, a proud smile on her lips. As soon as the wine was opened and poured, the glasses distributed around the tables, and the children provided with apple juice, Maggie stood once more.

"To my fine youngest son, Michael Browne! Congratulations!"

ABOUT THE AUTHOR

Annette Mahon has always wanted to write novels. A voracious reader from her youth, her interest in books and literature fueled her career choice. Mahon has a master's degree in library science, has worked in public and university libraries, and even spent a year in a Veteran's Administration hospital library. In Fort Wayne, IN, she starred in a library cable television show, *The Children's Room.*

When not writing, Mahon works on her quilts. She is addicted to appliqué work, especially Hawaiian quilting.

A native of Hilo, Hawai'i, Annette now lives in Arizona.

Readers may contact Annette at annette@annettemahon.com, or visit her online at www.annettemahon.com and/or www.facebook.com/author.annettemahon. Check out Pinterest.com/annettemahon/ for photos that illustrate her various books.